SCATTERWOOD

Scatterwood is Piers Alexander's second novel. His debut, *The Bitter Trade*, won TLC's Pen Factor, a Global Ebook Award and the Historical Novel Society's Editor's Choice (Indie Review). Both *The Bitter Trade* and *Scatterwood* were selected by WHSmith for their Fresh Talent list. Piers is also a serial media entrepreneur, and he lives in London with the singer-songwriter and author Rebecca Promitzer.

This paperback was edited and first serialised by The Pigeonhole, an exciting new publishing company that sends out episodes just like a TV series.

PRAISE FOR *THE BITTER TRADE*

"A fantastic debut novel" – Robert Elms, BBC Radio London

"The ambitious, cheeky Calumny Spinks is a great guide through the sensory overload of 17th-century London, in an adventure that combines unexpected insights with just the right amount of rollicking ribaldry. I hope it's the opener to a series" – Christopher Fowler, author of the Bryant and May novels

"An excellent debut novel by a talented author. Piers Alexander will be a writer to watch" – The Historical Novel Society

"This is an epic adventure, full of pungent period detail, a Dickensian cast of vibrant characters, plus a complex and brilliantly conceived plot which makes your head spin. 17th-century London comes fully to life, with all its triumphs and inequalities, colour, texture and structure. One of those worlds you absorb so wholly, you itch to return. The language deserves a special mention. This is a beautifully written story, a master class in voice, character and description. So many lines stopped me in my tracks to just admire the craftsmanship of this prose" – JJ Marsh, Bookmuse

"This debut novel is a gripping evocation of late seventeenth-century London, rich in persuasive dialect and period detail and with a bold protagonist. An unusual thriller that just keeps you wanting to know more about the many facets of this story. You'll never view your coffee in quite the same way again" – Daniel Pembrey, bestselling author of *The Candidate*

"I just finished The Bitter Trade by Piers Alexander – perhaps the best book I've read this year. Rollicking historical fiction set in 17th-century London. It's brilliant. Read it!" – David Gaughran, bestselling author of *Mercenary* and *A Storm Hits Valparaiso*

"A very exciting and superbly researched novel" – Mel Ulm, The Reading Life

"The author creates a rich, evocative impression of life in the city of London through the eyes of his colourful cast. The ever-twisting plot, beginning in an Essex backwater before reaching the fetid stench of London, is full of lust, crime, corruption and downright malevolence ... Although indelibly grubby, the metropolitan stage forms the perfect counterpoint to this wonderfully spun novel that is lucid, lurid and fleet-of-foot ... An addictive read that assaulted my sense. *The Bitter Trade* is very highly recommended" – Tim Beresford, Miniature Wargames and Battlegames

Winner of the MWBG Award for Excellence.

SCATTERWOOD

Being the Violent History of
CALUMNY SPINKS,
The Notorious White-skinned Maroon

PIERS ALEXANDER

Tenderfoot

First published in 2017 by Tenderfoot

www.piersalexander.com

Copyright © EPA Bearne, 2017

The moral right of the author has been asserted.

A CIP catalogue record for this book is available from the British Library

ISBN 978-0-9928645-5-2

Cover design by David Eldridge of Two Associates
www.twoassociates.co.uk

Typeset by Jonathan Baker of Seagull Design
www.seagulls.net

Printed and bound by Clays Ltd, Bungay, Suffolk NR35 1ED
www.clays.co.uk

For my parents, Anne and Chris

Dedicated to the Maroons of Jamaica, past and present

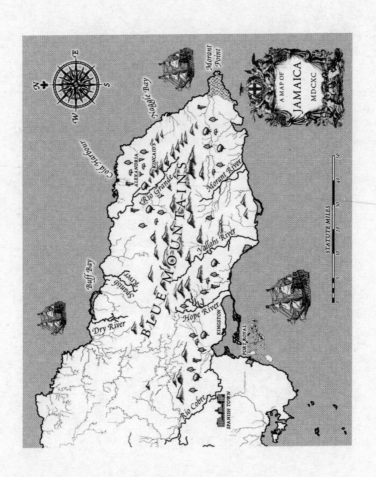

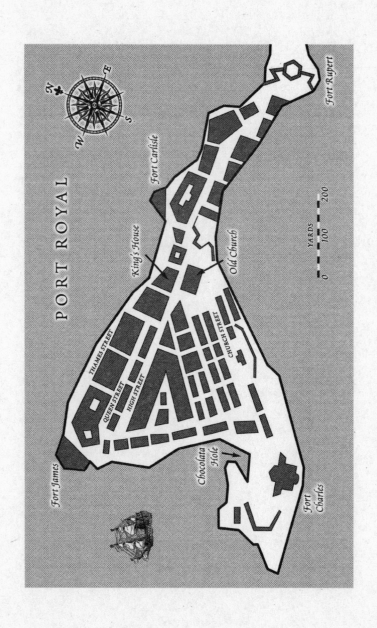

PORT ROYAL

Fort James

Chocolata Hole

Fort Charles

Queen Street
Thames Street
High Street

Church Street

King's House

Old Church

Fort Carlisle

Fort Rupert

YARDS
0   100   200

I am Calumny Spinks.

I have struggled against the powerful, but struck down only friends.

I have stolen without profit from the innocent.

And now they have branded and bonded me, and shipped me off to Hell.

1692: King William III's rule is new and fragile, with constant rumours of plots against his life. War with Louis XIV of France continues, and invasion is expected any day.

The Caribbean colonies are desperately short of men, swallowing up slaves in their thousands from Africa.

Working alongside them are white indentured servants, who have traded poverty or conviction for years of hard labour and the promise of a few acres of land.

The *Esperance*

Twenty-fourth and twenty-fifth days of March

Seven years' servitude. In all that time, to be another man's possession. To speak humbly, work like a mule, and never once breathe the warm wheatfield scent of my woman's hair.

I twisted the ivory thimble. The tiny carved battlements left dents on my fingertip.

As soon as I'd signed the deed of indenture, my new masters had bound me to a dangerous purpose. Damn their educated eyes; I'd have my liberty soon enough.

I had been confined to the lowest deck for ten miserable, unsleeping weeks. The hammocks, slung three high and three abreast on either side of the slippery gangway, were so tightly packed that one man's sickness would spray his neighbours as well as the poor fellow lying below.

This was worse than the Hell I'd once believed in. The sea pounded at the timbers without relent, day and night; there was scarcely a moment when there was no whimpering, puking or praying. We only knew if it was day or night when we were hustled up the ladders for our daily hour on deck.

Our quarters were so full that men took turns to sleep on hammocks. The fellows who were too weak to fight for them were left to lie on the foul floor. After the first storm, we found their bodies huddled against the bulkheads, some unmoving.

I learned how to pass the time by sleeping, how to lie down for half a day. How to hold my piss, how to ignore my hunger, how to swing with the violent movement of the ship; how to spend every moment among strangers without learning to care for them.

There was little else to do but think on my troubles, and curse myself for making them.

Another storm was building.

I had no prayers to speak. I put the thimble back in my pocket for safety, brushing the little picture that nestled there: of Emilia de Corvis' plantation, nestling among glowering blue mountains. I had kept it for three years, dreaming of coming to the New World, but not like this. Not as a chattel.

The ship's belly struck the waves with a cannon-fire roar. My hammock reared, and began to swing so hard that my shoulders bumped the beam above. The bodies of my neighbours thudded onto wood as they fell from their beds, and the air grew vile with seasick sputters.

Further down the deck, the mules began to screech and kick their stalls.

Shadows danced madly. An oil lamp swung off its hook and burst on the deck, flaring into a blaze that was quickly suffocated by a sailor. The man below me began to jabber, kicking up as if he feared I would fall and crush him.

The lanterns were snuffed out for safety, and men held onto each other in the wet darkness. One of the eldest cried out for his mother, his voice weakening as the storm grew fiercer.

We carried his body up on deck the next day. The ship's store of sailcloth had been used up on the eight men who'd died before him, so his stiff carcass was not given a shroud. We dropped it overboard without even a prayer. He floated for a brief moment, then was snatched under in a black swirl.

The ship's crew were well-armed, since many of us indentured were thieves and criminals who'd signed a bond to escape gaol or the noose. Some had been deceived by smooth-tongued recruiting agents for the colonies; others claimed to have been taken by "spirits", men who would kidnap for coin.

Fully half our number were raw-skinned Irish farm lads. These fellows were all volunteers who'd had enough of tilling a landlord's field, and thought seven years a small price to pay for land of their own.

Richard Collingwood was standing in front of the cabin under the main deck, watching me. He ran his thick fingers through his hair and looked up. The air was softer now, carrying flights of seabirds from the islands that smudged the horizon. We were in the Caribbean.

"You," he called, beckoning me over. I went slowly through the throng of indentured men and followed him inside.

Closing the door, Collingwood's shadow hulked about the room. He seemed to press up against the rafters and suck the daylight from the cabin windows; but my spirits lifted to see my only friend, Ty Pettit, sitting in a heavy wheelback chair, his ebony wool waistcoat buttoned despite the heat. Before him was a sheaf of papers, topmost a map showing a tangle of streets. Ty was drawing arrows on the map, fireworks bursting from four huge buildings into the smaller houses.

Collingwood grunted and pushed me towards the middle of the cabin.

"Ty – thank God," I said. "Mister Collingwood, may I speak to Master Pettit alone?"

"You may not," replied Collingwood. Ty brushed the raven's wing of hair from his pale forehead. His hands and shoulders were too big for his frame.

"I am bound to a mission, sir," I said at last, "of which I know nothing. I for one do not believe that ignorance is the path to success – I hope that Master Pettit might tell me what I will need to do."

Collingwood stared at Ty, who took a heavy object from under the papers and slowly stood up. I held out my hand.

"Master Secretary," he said coldly, advancing. Collingwood seized my arms and held them tightly behind me. Before I could speak, Ty swung his fist. It glistened for an instant, and then a cold weight struck me just below the eye. My head snapped back. Ty hit me again. Gold filled my sight.

CHAPTER ONE

The Proposal

Third day of January

The gold bar rubbed against my thigh with each step. Each morning I bound it around my leg and went off with my traitor's prize. I'd kept it hidden there for so long that my skin had become leathery from the friction.

I was cold, and God-damned hungry. As I trudged through Holborn's narrow streets, my breath made little jags of mist in the January air. The smell of cooking pierced the city's usual reek: mutton-fat, roasted chestnuts, rich pastries. My guts rumbled.

Eight coffeehouses I'd visited that day, and only one order. My last call was to John Hollow's coffeehouse, newly bought by a crippled ship's captain. That fellow had wasted plenty of time and coin on throwing out the smoke-stained oak panelling, and it had only just opened again.

The coffeehouse had been painted the green of winter moss. A coatless gentleman of perhaps thirty or so was watching a boy nail up a brass plate. A ship was etched on the plate: it foundered in a storm, its back broken by a jagged shore.

I made for the door, but the gentleman barred my way. Fine greying hair peeped out from under his silver periwig;

his strutting legs and puffed shoulders put me in mind of a stork. His small dark eyes were ill at ease with each other. One peered at me above his spectacles, while the other drooped down to the list of names he was clutching.

"Of Liverpool, sir? Mister Jarrod?" he asked me, glancing at my hair, which was often taken for an Irishman's. "You were due here a week since."

"I am not of the Liverpool, sir," I replied. I was ankle-deep in snow.

On hearing my Essex accent, he put away his list and took off his spectacles, saying briskly, "This house is not open to the general commons this evening."

"Indeed, I would be glad to leave the commons behind me. I shall thank you to wait here on the outside while I pay visit to Captain Aloysius Beck," I said, copying his dry tones; I had a gift for mimicry which had gained me much, but also cost me greatly.

I put my hand on the door, but he did not move out of my way. Well, I'd dealt with stronger men than he.

"Captain Beck's establishment," he whispered, violently seizing my wrist, "is strictly preserved and solemnly restricted to gentlemen of capital, and owners and captains of English ships alone."

I lifted his fingers one by one. One by one, he snapped them back in place.

"Mister Calumny Spinks, sir. Gentleman of capital, official supplier to Mistress Hollow ..."

"Ah. A tradesman."

We stared at each other. He let go of my wrist and folded his arms, still barring my way. He was near as tall as I, with a tight strength in his clenched lips and jutting throat.

"Good day, Spinks," he said. The wind was bitter, and he was trying as best he could to hide his shivers.

"You will do me the courtesy of presenting this coffee to Captain Beck. It is the finest bean in Christendom, and comes from our private estates in the outremer," I blustered. "Try it for yourself, if you have the taste."

He took the bag of beans and reluctantly sniffed it. God damn him, it was the best coffee in the world, the only to be grown in the rich soil of Jamaica – and it was nearly the last of my stock.

"We purchased a rather similar coffee this very morning," he said. "Fine sugar is what we need here. Do you have any?" He saw the look on my face and smiled malignantly. "I thought perhaps not. Good day, then."

Before I could open my mouth to protest, the stork had returned to his damned 'establishment'. The servant-boy finished nailing up the plate, gave me a brisk nod and followed his master inside.

My feet ached. I wanted to go home, but I'd promised to visit Ty at the College Secular; he'd been back from a long voyage for a fortnight already.

A single petal of snow caressed my cheek, melting into a tear. I sighed, thinking of Violet, and set off through the icy slush.

As dusk fell, it became hard going. Men thronged under the overhanging houses. After years of war, victory in Ireland had filled London back up with fighting-men, with victuallers and diggers and carpenters.

The gold pressed relentlessly against my leg as I hurried past the Clerkenwell, into the clattering hum of the printers' alley. Londoners were hungry for news of war, of the new king's laws and licences, of how they could profit from the changing world.

For us, it had been a barren winter. I'd made barely enough coin to feed Violet and Simona, and my creditors would not lend me any more to buy new stock. And I could not sell that Christ-cursed ingot.

The College had hired a gatekeeper, a quiet fellow who'd known my father well. I gave a hard look at the two long-barrelled pistols he now wore.

"There's a French fleet in the Channel, which is good business for printers and looters," he said curtly. "What's your business, Calumny Spinks?"

"Ty Pettit?" I asked. Three years before, I might have put on a French accent to mock him; but cold and penury had sapped my humour.

"In the Provost's antechamber, most likely," he replied, letting me pass.

The Provost's rooms were on the highest floor. The winding steps had once sagged with age but were now bolstered with granite flags, neatly dovetailed into the old sandstone. The windowless staircase had the fresh yellow smell of paint: money had been spent here since the Glorious Revolution.

At the top of the stairs, I paused. I was soaked with muddy slush, and the front of my waistcoat was torn. I closed my coat over it, took a deep breath and opened the door.

The Provost's antechamber sat atop the whole breadth of the College. In the daytime, the light from both sides seemed to lift the low sky-blue ceiling. Its walls were clad with varnished oak panels, adorned with curling vines. There were three writing-desks along the right-hand side, where the windows looked out towards Holborn. I could tell which of them was Ty's: a wooden serpent sat atop a pile of his papers. His father had whittled it.

The antechamber was empty, but voices came from the Provost's private room at the other end. I approached its gilt-framed doors, which were flanked by a small pair of carved marble men on pedestals.

I knocked.

"Enter," chimed a calm voice: Doctor Justinian Platon Northmoor, Provost of the College Secular.

The Provost was sitting behind his desk with his lips pursed. His broad placid face was framed by a youthful wig of dark brown curls – his own hair was white and wild – and he wore the purple robes of his College.

His private chamber was small but elegant. Its walls were lined with books, their leather spines worn with age. Many of titles had flaked away, leaving a line of fine golden dust, glimmering in the oil-light. From the panelled ceiling hung delicate copper loops, each holding brass balls of different sizes. At their centre was a large glass sphere.

Sitting opposite the Provost with an open book in his lap, his eyes grey with tiredness, was Tyburn Tree Pettit. A lock of jet-black hair hung lankly over his sallow forehead. He sat upright, but his bony knees drooped to one side.

When he saw my face, the corner of his mouth twitched, but he waited for the older man to speak first.

"Calumny Spinks," said the Provost serenely. Though my father had taken me to meet him but once, he did not seem surprised to see me entering his private chamber.

"Sir – forgive me, but Master Pettit here had asked to see me."

"Then you are most welcome, though I had not expected you," he replied, half-rising. "Tyburn, you did not tell me that—"

Ty shook his head quickly. He looked weary, and far older than his years.

"Ah," said the Provost, adjusting his wig as he got fully to his feet. "Well … you are most welcome to use my chamber for your colloquy."

He came slowly round the desk. Ty did not rise, which seemed insolent to me. The candlelight seemed to lose itself in the matte folds of his coat.

I stepped out of the doorway to allow the Provost to leave. He paused and gazed at me.

"Your … trade, Calumny?"

"The price is meagre these days, sir; but I still have good stocks in my warehouse. I thank you for your condescension."

He nodded curtly, briefly held my wrist, and then was gone.

I laughed quietly and opened my arms for an embrace. "Ty, are you the master here now? Is he drunk, to lend you his own chamber like this?"

Ty stayed seated, looking at the book in his lap: he'd been writing little groups of numbers on a paper wedged inside it. He snapped the book shut and put it on the desk.

"I'd never thought to see you read a Bible," I teased him, "least of all in the College Secular."

He coughed. He had never liked his work to be mocked.

"You don't sleep at your mother's house, even after so many months away?" I asked.

"She does not understand that the College *needs* my work," he replied, picking at his breeches. "The College says …"

He spoke of his precious College like it was his own dead father, and not a talking-house for gentlemen of science and philosophy.

After a good long wait, I realised that he would not be telling me what the College said. Well, I could understand his mistrust: I had barely spoken to him these past three years. It had grown harder and harder to laugh with Ty.

The gold I carried had been meant for his father, a reward for supporting our new Dutch king. I'd taken it for myself, thinking to begin a life in the New World; but Violet had been with child, and I'd stayed, unwilling to sell it yet unable to give it to Ty. He would never forgive me if he found out.

"You asked to see me?" I asked.

"I sent word through my mother a fortnight ago," he replied, "and again last week. After such a long absence, I had little thought you of all people would keep me waiting. The College is barely two miles from Silk Street, after all."

"Ty, I would have come sooner if commerce were better ..."

Reluctant to take the Provost's chair, I leaned against the door and told him how hard the trade had become, how little was left of my coin and stocks, and how the debts were mounting.

"Why do you not go home and tell Violet?" he asked with a little grimace. "She is deserving of any man's trust."

"She knows," I said. "She thinks we should take indenture. But I would rather earn passage to America through my trade than ever bond myself to a master again."

Sleet spattered against the windows.

Ty slowly straightened up in his seat, taking a little writing-quiver and a scrap of paper from his pocket. He wrote a few words and symbols with a sharpened charcoal.

"This is not a mathematical problem, Ty!" I chided him lightly. He did not smile, but put down the charcoal. His left hand twitched to pick it up again.

"You will not get to America by selling coffee, Cal. That trade is dead. As for indenture—"

I cut him off. "Why did you ask to see me?"

"Well, the College did request me to do so. Now, Cal ..."

I stared at him. I knew that voice: it is used when one man has something the other desperately needs.

"Well?"

"Well, the College Secular ... My employer ... The College is obtaining a charter for a colony in America where it may make its *own* laws. Where people of different religions may live together. Violet and Simona are *Catholics*, Cal."

"And?"

Ty latticed his fingers and pushed them against his lips.

"*And?*" I insisted.

"And all that must be done ... to *obtain* that charter from the Crown, is to carry out a mission of *scientific* and *human* investigation. It is the work I have been carrying out in the Caribbean, Cal – and I thought that you ... that we ..."

It was not like him to be so shy: Ty usually voiced his thoughts full-formed. Suddenly hot, I unbuttoned my coat. Muddy slush dropped from my torn waistcoat.

"I should cross half the world for the *College*? And while I'm gone, what would become of Violet and Simona – and my trade? Jesus Satan, Ty, d'you have no feeling for my life?"

"But Cal – you could all live in this colony—"

"A mission of *scientific investigation*? In exchange for a royal charter? Are you moony?"

I was nearly shouting.

Ty batted the air with his arms.

"Be quiet, Cal!" he hissed. "I did not believe you would want to come. But the Provost insisted that you should be asked, and the College is not to be denied lightly. All we must do is carry out a mission in the Caribbean, and help the College to get a charter for its colony in America."

I pressed a knuckle into the middle of my forehead.

"The College's charter. The Provost's demands. *Your* ambition. No more, Ty! I have been through Hell for other people's desires. And I do not understand why the College needs me."

"Because it concerns Lord Montalbion," breathed Ty, "and Emilia de Corvis."

I shook my head in disbelief. "I came to you for help, Ty, not to be used by your damned College. Why should I care about Montalbion?"

"You saw him hang Mister de Corvis, your own master," he said, staring up at the glass sphere. "And take Emilia. And …"

He did not have to say what came next. We both knew that devil had ordered the death of Ty's father. I rose to my feet.

"So you think I should abandon my family in order to revenge myself?" I asked quietly.

"Cal—"

I quit the room. The Provost was standing not three feet from the door, pretending to examine one of the diagrams on Ty's desk. He gave me a bland nod, as if he had not been listening to our argument. I was too angry to bow back.

Violet held the needle up to the light of the warm tallow candle. She was halfway through a basket of mendings for gentlewomen. The work brought little by way of coin, but she treated her workbox like a treasure chest; and it gave me peace of an evening, to watch her frown over her craft.

"Did Ty have any word for me?" asked Abigail from the hearth, carefully ladling stew into bowls. It was she who'd asked me to see Ty at the College: his mother, practically my own for that matter.

"He is the only man I know who could spend a year in the Caribbean and still have no colour in his cheeks,"

I replied lightly, stroking Simona's wispy hair. It would have been an unkindness to say how much he'd aged.

Simona was curled up in my lap, as if I were her father by blood, and not a man who'd been brought up to hate Catholics.

Abigail put a bowl down in front of me. The child opened her eyes, startlingly blue under her dense black brows. She looked gravely at the food. I gave her my spoon, and she fished a piece of potato out of the stew.

"Blow on it," said Violet. Simona disobeyed her and swallowed it. She stuck out her scalded tongue and panted.

Abigail tugged the bowl out of Simona's reach. "That's for your father."

"Ah, let the girl have it," snapped Violet, noisily putting her workbox away. Under the table, I reached my foot out and put it on hers. I still had my dirty boots on, and she made a face, but she knew what I meant. Without Abigail's kindness, we would hardly have eaten at all.

Abigail put a bowl in front of Violet, who put a hand on her arm and thanked her prettily. The older woman grunted and went back to the hearth.

We ate for a while in silence. I chopped up the bigger pieces of potato and turnip for Simona. She made a pantomime of blowing on each mouthful, spraying the juices onto the table until Violet made her stop.

Against the back wall, dust gathering in its crannies, was the old silk-loom. My father had been dead two years, and I could not throw it away. Each sighting of the old frame conjured him in the corner of my eye, hunched over his weaving, telling me how we would live a righteous life in the New World.

"Violet says you intend to go to America?" asked Abigail, heavily.

"When we have the coin," I said. "The price of coffee is low for now."

"It's low for always, Cal," said Violet. "But come here and see, love – there was a recruiting agent for Carolina in Spitalfields today. Look what he gave me."

She spread a roll of paper on the table. Finishing her small bowl of stew, Abigail took her eyeglasses out of her petticoat pocket, and came back to the table to look at it with me.

I read the pamphlet silently.

There was a knock at the door. Abigail, who was closest, turned and opened it. With a little whoop, she whirled Ty inside, hugging him until I thought his slender bones would crack.

"Well, Ty – by the blessed Virgin …" began Violet. I shook my head violently. We lived in the midst of Huguenot Spitalfields, and had agreed that no popish words would be spoken in our home. She shrugged and went to extract Ty from his mother's embrace, giving him a warm kiss on each cheek in the French fashion.

I remained seated. Simona, still on my lap, lifted her bowl and drank off the remains, staring at Ty over the rim. He had left when she was barely two years old.

Violet brushed dust off the weaving stool and brought it for Ty to sit on.

"Here," she said, "it's warmest near the fire."

Though she had hardly eaten half of it, Abigail filled up her own bowl to the brim and gave it to her son. He stared at it until she nudged him, then reluctantly took a half-spoonful, blew on it, and let the contents drop back into the bowl.

"I suppose they fed you well at that College, did they?" she asked.

He shrugged.

"Hear this, Ty," said Violet brightly, holding the pamphlet to the candlelight. "Is it not wonderful? '*CAROLINA: A Godly COLONY, dedicated to the greater Good of Man and His Majesty's Glory. Where Persons of all Faiths may live in Peace and benefit from the great ABUN-DANCE of the Lands.*'"

"Does that mean that you and Cal could be married there?" asked Abigail, sharply. Simona looked up. Violet frowned: Simona did not rightly know that there was no church in England that would marry a Catholic to a right-thinking man. She went on reading.

"'*The Lords Proprietors of CAROLINA do invite all Right-Thinking Persons who have Labour to offer, to take Indenture: a Marvellous Contract whereby TEN ACRES of Land are to be gifted after a Mere Seven Years of Service in the Balmy Airs and Gentle Earth of this most Beauteous Portion of AMERICA ...*'"

At seventeen, I had dreamed of going to the New World married to a rich man's daughter. Now, at twenty, my best hope of crossing the ocean was to take seven years' servitude.

"'*Furthermore, and in Contradistinction to the Dubious Practices of our Caribbean colonies, Whole Families may be transported together to this new Paradise ...*'"

"What is ''sported'?" asked Simona, putting a grubby finger on the pamphlet.

"It means that the families will be taken by ship," said Abigail, gently lifting Simona's hand and wiping the stew juices off the paper.

"You said that all ships are filthy and deadly," said Simona. "You said the Coll'ge stole your son and put him on a ship to Hell."

Ty met my eyes over the table. His mouth twitched.

"Which they did, Simona," he said. "But as you can see, I am back here in Heaven with all you angels."

"Are *you* Abigail's son?" she asked, eyes wide.

Violet shushed her.

"How go your studies, Ty?" she said.

Ty fiddled with his spoon.

"I am engaged in practical work. Overseas."

"A man must have *coin* to study," said Abigail.

I put my hands in my lap. The gold was warm against my thigh. If Garric had lived to receive it, he would have used it to pay for Ty's education.

Ignoring his mother, Ty addressed himself to Violet.

"And so – do you intend to take the indenture?"

She looked at me. "We have not … Cal does not want to."

"He is perhaps right," said Ty. "I have not been to Carolina, but the Caribbean indentures can be harsh indeed. Though, if you do not have the money …"

Violet gave me a look. I rose to my feet and lifted Simona over the table, dropping her in her mother's lap.

"Well," I said, "I must go upstairs and reckon my accounts, if we are ever to go to America. Bless you for that stew, Abigail."

Laying a hand on Simona's crown, I kissed Violet on the lips. Ty rose and tried to embrace me. I broke away, lit a taper from the candle, and went up to the little attic room.

I kept my box of ledgers in the eaves. At the bottom was a sheaf of coffee licences, and wedged among them a small, vivid painting I had not looked at for three years.

A white house in a nest of ivy-green bushes, built on the slopes of tall jagged mountains, with a purplish sky glowering behind it all; I had been thinking of this picture since Ty spoke Emilia de Corvis' name. My old master's daughter, who'd painted the coffee plantation she'd been raised on.

I was still looking at the picture when I heard Abigail and Ty leaving. I folded it quickly inside my waistcoat; Emilia had been my lover before Violet, and I'd never shown her the picture.

I was staring at a ledger by the time Violet came upstairs.

"How was the trade today?" she asked wearily.

"One order. For two shillings. And the new man at John Hollow's will have none of it. *Sugar*, they want."

"Come here," said Violet, sitting on the bed. Her strong curved brows were knitted together; she gave me a look that opened me up.

"We still have stock," I said.

She patted the pallet next to her. I went reluctantly over.

"Cal, I've no wish to be bonded either," she said. "We'll take the indenture when we have to, and not before. Now blow that taper out and give me a kiss before sleep."

I took off my waistcoat in the dark.

Emilia's painting crackled faintly inside it.

CHAPTER TWO

The Lion Rampant

Eighth and ninth days of January

"The French are coming! The French are coming!"

The boy twitched his broadside in front of my face.

"Penny for the news, sir – French fleet in the Channel! Invasion!"

I had been hitching Cucullan to the cart when the loud-voiced lad came through, hawking fear and rousing Silk Street. After five fruitless days of hawking my coffee across London, I was ready to strike somebody.

Abigail appeared in her doorway, frowning. She knew what this news might mean: after all, every Huguenot family on this street had fled the French king's terrors. She came out into the roadway and gave the lad a copper coin.

"Now go on, before you frighten these good people," she said, but the lad flashed his gappy teeth and darted off to sell another of his sheets to Mistress Jeanquartier.

"God-damned printers," I said to Abigail. She normally smiled at my little blasphemies, but she was intent on the broadside.

"They have discovered a plot against the King," she said heavily. "A great fleet has been seen in the Channel. It says that there has been a riot at the docks – against Catholics ..."

My warehouse was close by the docks. The looting might have started already.

"Cal, you must stay here with Simona and her mother!" shouted Abigail, but I was already in the driving seat, jerking the old horse out of his doze.

Cucullan knew the way to the warehouse, but I made him go faster than usual, too fast for a carthorse long past his prime, urging him through the thickening crowds of sailors, porters and merchant's apprentices. The air buzzed with rumour. Smoke rose above Wapping.

The warehouses were burning.

I drove Cucullan harder, but we were moving against the flow.

The chimes had long since struck three when we reached my warehouse, tucked away at the end of a row. The fires had not reached it yet.

I took out lantern, flint and tinder from the box under my seat. Hands trembling from the chill sea-wind, I had to strike a dozen times before the light caught. Cucullan waited as I jumped down and went to open the smoke-house lock – but it had been forced, broken, and dropped in the muddy roadway.

Fear writhed in my belly.

The warehouse had once been home to two hundred sacks of green, unroasted coffee from the de Corvis plantation, which had dwindled to twenty since my master's death three years before. The desk by the doorway usually held neat ledgers of orders and payments. Now the shelves lay empty, and the desk had been smashed by whoever had stolen my stock. Crushed coffee beans were scattered across the straw-covered floor.

I raised the lantern and ran to the back of the warehouse, scouring the shelves, but the last sacks had gone. All I had was the coin in my pocket, the horse and the cart.

And the gold, digging its cold edges into my flesh.

Cucullan whinnied, and I ran back out. Two men were trying to drag him away, but he dug his hooves in.

"Thieves!" I yelled, though there was no one else in sight. "Call the Watch!"

I flung the lantern at the nearest of them. It caught him on the arm. He cried out and fled, taking the other thief with him.

"To Hell with you, papist!" he yelled. "We'll rid London of all you traitors!"

"I'm no papist, damn you!" I shouted after them. London floated on a swamp of hatred for Romans. In plague, in fire and in wartime, it flooded the streets.

I should never have left Violet and the girl.

The air in Silk Street shimmered with rage. A handful of children, their day's work done, were parading at the end of the roadway. They dragged a straw Pope by a noose, poking it with sticks, spitting and hooting. Grim-faced Huguenot weavers and their goodwives were watching. The effigy seemed to be on its feet, staggering backwards through the filthy meltwater. As I drew closer, I realised that it had been tied to a child's back.

It was Simona.

"Satan! Satan!" chanted the Huguenot children, tossing her favourite three-cornered hat into the slush. She spat and scratched, but they would not let her go.

I dropped the reins and leapt down, yelling at the weaver-boy who was pulling Simona's hair to keep her from biting him. Furious, I unhooked my belt as I ran, and before they could flee I dealt them some hard blows across the thighs. I untied Simona, ignoring the uproar from the watching weavers.

Her face was scratched and her knuckles bruised. Though she was not quite three years old, she refused to cry.

The boys I'd hit ran to their mothers.

"Antichrist! Irish vagrant!" shouted a goodwife from across the street. Lifting the child, I pointed back at her, finger trembling. I could not believe in my heart that they'd turn on me: one of their own, half-Huguenot; and if we had lost the sanctuary of Silk Street, where could I take a Catholic woman and her bastard?

The street fell silent.

I strode back to the cart and lifted Simona into the driving seat. As I put her down, she crossed herself. At the sight of her papist gesture, the children whistled, and then the roadway began to fill with hooting, jeering weavers and their goodwives. I climbed up and slapped the reins on the horse's back, ignoring their taunts, making for my house at the other end of the street.

Men half-heartedly pulled at Cucullan's bridle, but we drove on. An egg smashed on my shoulder. I pulled Simona closer and looked straight ahead, pretending that the street was clear, willing the horse to trot faster through the mob. A hundred paces away, I could see two women wrestling in the doorway of my house: Abigail Pettit, pushing my Violet back inside.

But we were still too far away. Two weavers, men who'd welcomed me to Silk Street after my mother's death, threw their weight on the horse's harness, dragging him to a halt. The boys I'd hit began to throw handfuls of snowmelt, and I felt the cart tilt as grown men climbed on the back of it. I wrapped myself around Simona and waited for the blows to fall.

Then Abigail came running down the street, pushing and punching her way through the mob. She was a widow, the daughter of a guildmaster, and her presence stopped the attack. Anger drained from the air, and the men who'd climbed on the cart jumped back down. Abigail waited for the way to clear, then led Cucullan slowly up Silk Street and into the alley next to our house.

"The child crossed itself," said one of the men. Abigail spat in the mud; though whether at Simona's popishness or his words, I could not tell.

I lifted Simona down from the cart and carried her to where Violet sat, pale-faced. Shaking, Simona buried her face in her mother's lap.

"You should have stayed here, Cal, like I told you," said Abigail in a hard voice. Then she splashed across the street to her workshop, scattering the last weavers in the roadway.

I tugged at Violet's arm. She stayed sitting on the steps, tightening her grip around Simona's body.

"Inside!" I insisted, dragging Violet to her feet and bundling the pair of them through the door. I threw the bolts.

I lit the fire while Violet tended to Simona. She made a nest of blankets in front of the hearth and curled up around the girl, who did not stop trembling for a good long while.

I knelt and stroked Simona's head. She made a small noise and twisted into her mother's clothes. Her face had been cleaned, but there were still flakes of street-grit in her hairline.

We sat in the warmth of the fire, looking at each other. Once Simona fell asleep, I told Violet what had happened at the warehouse.

Many a woman might have cursed a man for falling into penury, and letting her daughter be beaten in the roadway; but Violet had been a Catholic in England for most of her life. She was brisk, ready to fight or fly, and I loved her for it.

"How long can we live, for now?" she asked.

I took a deep breath. "If Abigail will still feed us, perhaps a week. But without those stocks, I have no trade, and no capital either."

"Then it's time."

Violet reached forward and tugged at the drawstring to my breeches.

"We have this," she said, carefully unbinding the gold bar.

That Christ-cursed bullion.

"It's Ty's," I said.

"Then give it to him."

I sighed. She knew that I could not.

"Cal, you know what will happen if we stay in Spital-fields."

I did. My own mother had been drowned for being foreign, for being of a different faith. First the children throw stones; then your house is burned; then the mob takes you.

It began to rain. The patter on the windows took me back, to five days before.

"The Provost," I said slowly. "He would know what to do with the gold."

Seeing the worry in my face, Violet pulled me towards her. I wrapped my arms around her and Simona, and told her what had been said at the College.

"Have faith, Cal," she said. "He will help you, for your father's sake."

I waited till it was fully dark and Silk Street had fallen quiet.

Violet and Simona were still sleeping in front of the hearth. I slowly took my arm back from around them and put another log on the embers.

"Take the thimble for luck," whispered Violet.

I hesitated. She gave me a sharp nod, as she always did when I was being stubborn. I went to her workbox and took it out.

A tiny hollow castle fashioned from ivory: her only gift from a long-dead father, who'd bargained for it from a Norweyan seaman. I slipped the thimble into my pocket.

As I trudged down Silk Street into a rainy headwind, a dim spash of colour caught my eye: a little three-cornered hat, trodden into the muck. I snatched it up, squeezing the velvet brim until it was as warm as my own blood.

"Tyburn Pettit is not at the College today," said the Provost.

"I have come to see you, sir. Ty said ... There may be a place for me, he said; for my family. In the New World ... if I aid the College."

The Provost pointed to the chair opposite him. I sat down, my wet breeches bunching coldly.

"Did he elucidate, Calumny Spinks?"

I put my hand in my overcoat pocket and touched a fingertip to the ingot's slippery surface.

"Ah ... You do not comprehend. Forgive me. I remember now that you were intemperate the last time you visited the College. Tyburn can hardly have had time to ... Well. He spoke of a mission in the Caribbean and a colony in America, did he not?"

I nodded. The Provost rose to his feet. His wig brushed one of the balls hanging from the ceiling. It banged against its neighbour, making the entire arrangement sway. The glass sphere in the middle began to circle, sending a shaft of reflected candlelight on a wild chase across the bookshelves.

"It is more than a colony, young man; we intend to create a Republic Secular in the great emptiness of America. A place of toleration, law and peace, governed by men of reason – property-holding men. Your good father fought for such a Republic, Calumny Spinks."

"And he failed," I said impatiently. "London was right-murderous today, and on a mere rumour of invasion."

"Not a rumour," he said, stilling the glass sphere. "If it were not for the Channel's capricious weather, Louis' fleet would have landed in England this week. Which makes the College's work all the more urgent. We have tried twice before, you know. Cromwell promised us a Republic, so we aided him in the war against the King. Likewise, we worked for William's Revolution, only to see him seek absolute rule. If we get a charter for our colony, we can finally begin our true work."

"Such a colony would require great funds," I said quietly.

"Indeed," he replied, putting his knuckles on the desk and leaning towards me. The Provost was not a fighting man, but when he spoke of the Republic, the force of his intention robbed my breath.

He waited.

I turned to make sure the door was shut, took the gold out of my pocket and put it gently on the table.

The Provost traced the lion rampant that was stamped into the bar.

"This is Garric Pettit's ingot, is it not? His reward for raising the guilds in support of our new king, William?"

I let go of the ingot and put my hands together in my lap.

"I did wonder if you had it," he said. "To hold on three years ... And you have been poor, Mister Spinks, do not deny it. But why do you bring me this now?"

I did not want to tell him about the warehouse.

"Sir – if I give you this treasure – will you vouchsafe passage for my family? A place in your new colony in America?"

"Well – that is a curious proposal …" The Provost picked up the gold and gave it back to me. "Do not bring this into the College again. Tell me, how have you kept it safe?"

"On my person."

He frowned.

"I suppose I could hide it in Violet's workbox, sir – she is never without it."

"Good. Make it so. I must consider this with care. I will send for you tomorrow – and do not speak to Tyburn or his mother about your visit. That would go ill for you."

They came at dawn.

Expecting a messenger from the College, I answered the knock. There was a flash of red uniform, then a strong arm against my throat, pushing me inside.

I called out, but it was Sunday morning, and Silk Street was empty. There were four of them. One drove me into the corner by the loom, holding a bayonet to my throat, while another ran upstairs. The others closed the door and began to ransack the room, digging through the nest of blankets by the fire.

Violet's voice rang out from above, a biting stream of Gaelic. The soldier shouted at her, and Simona began to cry.

One of the redcoats, squat and quick, began to shuffle through Violet's piles of mendings. He threw her thread and needle-pouch aside with the careless violence of a man who has never practised a craft. The other tried to pull the loom away from the wall, but it was so tightly bolted that he cracked the frame and then gave up.

Violet appeared at the top of the stairs, arms pinned by the soldier. As she came down, she tried to wriggle out of his grip so she could lunge at the man who had handled her mending-tools; but her captor held on, wrestling her towards the hearth. Her eyes were black with rage, her bare forearm bruised with fingermarks.

"I am Calumny Spinks," I protested. "Counsellor to the College Secular. I say you are to quit and desist—"

The squat fellow left off his searching and touched the star that hung on an orange band around his neck.

"I am Colonel de Groot, and I say that you are no counsellor but a pauper who raises a bastard and fornicates with a Catholic thief," he said calmly. He was swarthy for a Dutchman, wiry black curls oiled tight to his forehead. Simona, sitting at the top of the stairs, buried her face in her hands and cried louder.

De Groot found Violet's workbox. I tried to slip past the man who had cornered me, but he blocked my way and pressed the bayonet into my breast, not quite hard enough to draw blood.

"Do not harm that man; he has committed no crime," said the Dutchman. "But his whore ..."

Smiling faintly, he reached into the workbox and took out the ingot. The gold lion glowed wetly as he held it up to the light from the doorway.

"This belongs to the treasury of Holland, would you not say, Mister Spinks?"

"It is mine," I said.

"And yet it is in your whore's possession. Is she your wife? No? Then you may not protect her by right of coverture. Crouch, take the girl."

The man who'd broken the loom went upstairs. Simona ran into our little room. He reappeared with her, moments later.

"Let her go," said Violet, "I beg—"

Without looking away from me, Colonel de Groot shook his head. "Pray that the magistrate transports mother and child together …"

He dropped the workbox on the floor. A pale crack appeared in the weathered wood.

Violet stood limply. The morning light showed the worry-lines on her tanned cheeks, and the rough skin on her neck where she scratched at herself. She looked nearer thirty than twenty: her eyes still deep and beautiful, but their colour faded.

"It is mine," I said again, ducking away from the blade at my chest so that I could block the doorway. "I took the—"

A blinding pain in my head, and then blackness.

CHAPTER THREE

The Seven Year Bond

Ninth day of January

Iron-shod words marched into my left ear.

"That is not the College's concern," said the Provost.

I began to open my eyes. Light was the tip of an auger. It began to drill. I closed them again.

"Yet the College is *concerned* to obtain its territory in the New World, is it not?" demanded Colonel de Groot.

I coughed up a salted slug of bile.

"Peace now," said the Provost. "He wakes."

Queasily, keeping my neck straight to stop the world from rocking, I opened my eyes into slits. I was propped up in a chair, hands folded in my lap. Three men sat facing me, their faces limned by oil-light. Darkness swung drunkenly behind them.

On the narrow table between us were an inkpot, a quill and Ty's gold.

I forced my eyelids to open wider. Light glinted on hundreds of pieces of steel: polished breastplates and gorgets hanging from hooks, gleaming stacks of egg-domed helmets, neat pyramids of cannon-shot, all squeezed between rack upon rack of pikes.

The Provost sat in the middle. The lantern made a startled halo of his white hair. On his right sat Colonel de Groot; on his left was a heavyset fellow, his grey hair parted neatly down the middle. Bushy whiskers flanked a boyish face. The eyes, too close together for such a big head, gazed just beyond my left shoulder, as if he did not see me.

"Where am I?" I asked. The words came out thin and wretched. My guts clenched. I leaned forward and puked between my knees. They watched in long silence as I threw up again, waiting till I was empty. I cleaned my lips and fell back into the chair, one hand to the pulsing bruise on my skull. Someone had struck me hard. My throat burned.

"The Tower," replied de Groot. "Stealing from the treasury is a crime against the Crown."

"Three years you held the treasure, Master Spinks," said the Provost softly. "Never sold it, never bettered your lot, never spoke a word. Yet I did always suspect that you held Master Pettit's gold."

"Suspect" be damned: he'd known it, and I had been fool enough to give him proof. He himself must have told de Groot about Violet's religion, and Simona's bastardy.

"So you say," I said. "It was you who gave me to this Dutchman. Is it you who accuses me? Is this a court of law?"

"Come, Northmoor," said the Dutchman rudely, "this damned *kerel* will not serve. Let him be executed!"

"Go to Hell, cheese-head," I said.

"Colonel de Groot," the third man said swiftly, "you would do well to hear our Provost out."

"Your clerk is truly insolent," said de Groot.

"This is Richard Collingwood, Master Secretary to the College, and our plenipotentiary in the Caribbean," the Provost replied. "Execution is a heavy sentence, Colonel de Groot. Let this man be transported instead. And his woman and child too, of course."

De Groot stared at the gold.

"Perhaps this man could serve the Crown," said Collingwood.

"Nonsense," said de Groot.

"Sir, the French are close to invasion. Our king's life is being plotted against. And now I have brought you intelligence of a planned rebellion in the West Indies. This man could discover proof of Montalbion's treason. Would that not merit a pardon for himself and his family?"

De Groot banged the side of his hand on the table. "This 'intelligence' must be wrong – I do not understand why Montalbion would help to bring King William to the throne, only to betray him. My concern is with the French—"

"Montalbion has accumulated a great fortune in the colonies," said Collingwood. "The College has discovered that his purpose is to fund an invasion and take the throne himself, as the natural son of King Charles the Second."

"I am bound for Jamaica myself," said the Dutchman, "and I assure you that I am a match for any Montalbion."

The Provost's papery cheeks wrinkled.

"I am no lawyer," he murmured, "but I believe you would find it hard to arrest an earl, who is Governor of the Company of the Caribbean, without hard evidence of treason. Such an act would undoubtedly increase the risks to His Majesty's person."

I am no scholar, I thought, *but I can tell when a man is about to risk another's life for his own gain.*

"What do you propose?" asked de Groot reluctantly.

"Indenture of seven years, to be redeemed by proof of Montalbion's treason," said Collingwood coldly. "His woman and child to be held here at the Tower until that obligation is discharged. If it is not, they are to be transported – and I shall ensure they are sent to separate colonies."

He took out a paper from inside his coat, unrolled it, and pressed it flat on the table in front of the Provost. De Groot leaned across to read it.

"Perhaps this will do – but will this *kerel* sign it?"

The Provost lightly moved de Groot's hand off the document and turned it round for me.

My head swam. I read it three times.

"It does not say what I am to do – only that I will be released if Mister Collingwood here is *satisfied.* I cannot risk Violet and Simona against such empty terms."

Collingwood stared at the rafters. He did not look as if he had been much satisfied by anything in his life.

"Mister Spinks," said the Provost, "you stole, and you betrayed your friend. We cannot advance you trust without having collateral of our own. Miss Fintry and the girl will stay here, in the Tower."

I should have thrown that gold in the river three years before. I did not sign.

"Come, man," insisted the Provost. "Your warehouse is empty. How will your family fare if you are in debtors' prison?"

I had not told him about the warehouse. I stared at him, and understood how well he had laid the trap for me.

"Sign, or be tried for your crime," said de Groot to me directly.

"There must be a codicil to this contract, Colonel," said the Provost. "On completion of the mission, this College shall be granted a charter over certain lands in Carolina, the dimensions and particulars of which have been submitted to His Majesty on several occasions. It shall be a new Athens, a place of scientific endeavour, of free—"

Collingwood cleared his throat loudly. The room shifted dizzily.

De Groot puffed loudly, but tapped the table in agreement. The Provost pushed the inkpot and quill towards me.

All I had to do was give up my freedom, cross the great ocean, and face down the most powerful man in the Caribbean.

I made my mark on the deed of indenture.

CHAPTER FOUR

Port Royal

Twenty-sixth and twenty-seventh days of March

Jamaica, rising stormily out of the night-horizon.

Mountains in shades of winter grey, floating on a blazing strip of light: the Sodom of the Caribbean; sleepless, home of the damned.

Dawn overtook us, pulled away the shadows, lit the slender causeway that joined the town to the mainland.

"Port Royal," breathed a sailor next to me.

The air shimmered. Hundreds of buildings were crammed onto a low hill at the end of the causeway, tiny against the distant mountains' forested bulk. As we rounded the headland, we passed under the guns of four forts.

The indentured had been permitted on deck. We crowded the starboard rail, and were barged and cursed by the crew, who were hard put to work the sails in an inconstant wind.

A stony old Navy officer in a sailboat made the *Esperance* heave to: the Clerk of the Naval Office, come to inspect the ship's goods. Though we were all impatient to reach land, he was not to be hurried. He went through the ship's papers, then inspected the hold while a lesser clerk counted how many indentured men were aboard: we were nine fewer than when we'd left Ireland.

Ty appeared at the far end of the ship. He caught my eye for the briefest moment. I turned away.

"I hope you find a kinder master in Jamaica," said the fellow next to me: Bonfoy, a stunted thief from Hackney. "You're twice as ugly with those bruises."

I touched my face and winced. Ty had struck me with the heavy gold ingot, blackening both my eyes, before Collingwood had returned me to the lower deck.

Bonfoy drifted away from the rail. I grabbed his thinning hair and yanked. He shrugged, grinned and gave me back my thimble.

By the time we sailed into port, the sun was high above us. My skin, dry and salty, began to burn. After being cooped up in the dark for more than ten weeks, the light seared my skull. The harbour was strewn with rotten, stinking waste. If I had known how to swim, I might have jumped into the dirty waters just to feel cool for a moment; instead, I threw up over the side to relieve my aching head.

Despite the heat and the stench, none of the indentured asked to go below decks. Instead we watched Port Royal's leavings drift slowly out to sea: cabbage waste, turds, mouldering rat carcasses and shattered casks.

Wedged between the forts was a clumsy higgle-piggle of streets, houses leaning this way and that. Smoke thickened the air: fires had burned all night, as if no man cared to save fuel. From one side of town came drumming, a fearsome heathen pounding; and from the other, two gangs of men sang two different drinking songs, raising their voices higher and higher in competition until it was but one raw yell without music or meaning.

The harbour bristled with ships and sailboats, skiffs and barges, ferrying passengers and cargo to the quaysides. The *Esperance* nosed through the busy waters, sailors and indentured alike bunched at the rail. We gaped at the noise and bustle, the dozens of tongues and accents. It was not the world I'd imagined, all those nights I'd spent staring at Emilia de Corvis' painting.

"Tawnies," said a crewman next to me, pointing at a boat that had been hacked out of a log. "Indians from one of the other islands."

Six clay-skinned men were paddling through the bay. A mound of crabs twitched and shivered in the bow of their dugout.

Another small boat thumped against the *Esperance*'s side. Three blackamoor women stood up in it, showing us handfuls of bright-coloured fruit. The sailor standing next to me spat in the sea and backed away from the railing, but I smiled at them, shaking my head to show I had no coin.

The eldest of them, her cheeks slashed with ink-stained scars, bared her gappy teeth and sang up to me:

New-come buckra
He get sick
He tak fever
He be die ...

The other two screeched with laughter and joined in, louder and louder: "*He be die, new-come buckra, new-come buckra he be die* ..."

The sailor came back to my side and flung a bucket of slops, close enough to splash the women. The eldest clacked her teeth at me, but they sat back down and rowed away. An angry white man shouted at them from the shore: their master, no doubt.

"I'd not mind them," said the sailor, tapping his button nose. "Not everyone dies of the fever ..."

He grinned without smiling, held up five fingers, and let two of them fall into his palm. He meant that only three in five newcomers to Jamaica survived. I shrugged and turned my back on him. Why would God take me, when he could punish me so much more on this earth?

We moored next to a slave ship, the *Bristol Charm*, whose scuppers ran black with filth. It reeked of death. Dozens of naked blackamoors, their ankles chained, made a shuffling dance across its deck and down the gangplank. The *Charm*'s sailors looked on silently, muskets at the ready; but the slaves were limp and weak, their skin marked with sores.

I'd signed my name to seven years of bondage, of being a white-skinned slave, and I still did not know what I would be required to do to escape it. I held the ship's rail tightly and looked at the quay. Narrow-eyed men were standing in a huddle, watching how each slave moved: traders and gangmasters. One of them drew my eye, a powerfully built man holding a coiled whip. A tattoo writhed down his neck and into his jerkin.

A slender, clerkish fellow, his silver hair neatly combed into an upside-down bowl, stood close by, making marks on a slim ledger.

Feeling my gaze, he glanced up, cast a calm look at me, and returned to his work. His features were striking: jet-black brows, a sharp nose, pressed lips, and a chin that jutted with authority. There was a calm wit in his gaze, taking in every man on our deck.

"Play your part," said Richard Collingwood, who had come quietly up behind me. "That man is Michael Hicks: he has loans outstanding from half the captains in Port Royal. Look away."

"Then give me my orders," I muttered, obeying.

He cuffed me across the back of the head.

"Do not think of running," he said loudly, "or it'll be worse than a beating next time."

An idle crowd seeped out of the waterfront taverns. Startling orange and black feathers jaunted in broad-brimmed hats. Pistol-stuffed baldrics sagged over pot bellies. Whores in velvet dresses leaned on their companions, poking and stroking inside untucked shirts as they whispered of delights to come; men wearing the bright sashes and spurs of soldiery staggered along behind, scratching their infested groins. It was clear this mob had been drinking all night: their tongues lolling and eyes half-cut.

A gentleman in a neat suit of pale broadcloth came out of the harbourmaster's little hut at the other end of the quay.

"Back, you whoreson ghouls!" he called out, the sun flaring on his half-drawn sword as he strode towards the mob. "We'll have order in this port – no man is to touch the goods."

He halted at the foot of our gangplank, and waited for the crowd of drinkers and doxies to obey him. As they eddied past the blackamoors, some of them winked and whistled at the sullen slaves.

"This is no man's dock to own, Ordene," said the slender, clerkish fellow mildly.

A woman cried out. One of the Port Royal cockies was grasping at a slave-woman's bare flesh, his arm tight around her neck to hold her still. She wriggled free and stumbled to the quay's edge, making to drown herself with the weight of her chains.

The tattooed gangmaster took three steps after the fleeing slave and flicked his whip. The lash wrapped around the woman's calves, pulling her feet out from under her. She landed on the quay-stones with the sound of cleaver on joint, and lay unmoving. Another African called out a word and tried to go to her, but the gangmaster warned him off with a pointing finger.

"Thank you, Master Kiet," said Ordene, the gentleman who'd called for order earlier. "The rest of you – quit this place. Or Lord Montalbion will hear of this affray."

The mob complained, but drifted slowly away from the wharf. The sound of Montalbion's name made my cheek twitch.

"Now there's a vicious bastard," said the sailor who'd thrown slops at the boat-women. "I went to sea to get away from men like him."

We watched the man with the whip walk slowly along the line of blackamoors, pointing some of them out to another man. This second fellow dipped his fingers into a small pot so he could daub the chosen slaves with a stripe of limewash.

"That is Kenver Kiet, is it? Lord Montalbion's overseer?" Collingwood asked.

The sailor looked at my bruised face.

"Not a man to be sold to if you've a mind of your own," he said, ignoring Collingwood. "Kiet likes to break a strong spirit."

He spat, then turned to go to his work.

"His master's rich, so I've heard," said Collingwood, resting a heavy hand on his shoulder.

"Montalbion has a king's ransom from raiding New Spain, if that's what you mean," replied the sailor, wresting himself away. "He follows the good old ways – not like those drunkards down there, who haven't set foot on a ship for years. As for me, my time is my own; I'll not answer more of your questions."

He left. The gangmasters had lined the blackamoors up once more. One of them dragged the fallen woman to her feet to stand on the landside. They'd not take the chance of her leaping again.

"Sir Fergus Ordene," said Collingwood, after the blackamoors had left and the *Esperance*'s indentured men had been sent below decks, "has sailed with Montalbion these past two years. He is a Catholic and a Jacobite. If treason is planned, he will be part of it."

"How do you know so, Mister Collingwood?"

He looked at me. Sweat trickled down the folds in his neck, staining his collar. "By spending a hard year in Barbados and Jamaica, Calumny Spinks. Every ship and every captain that sails her, every shipwreck in the last twenty years: we have a list."

"You mean, you and Ty? Was that his business for the College?"

"Perhaps," he said. "But it is not your business."

The wharf ran alongside a wide thoroughfare. At either end of the road was a fort, with sturdy walls and cannon facing the bay.

"Your business," said Collingwood, "if I can secure it, will be to serve Fergus Ordene, and from within his household to discover evidence – and I do mean *written* evidence – of Montalbion's plot to invade England. In the meantime, though, you will have to remain on board the *Esperance*. I cannot have you running about Port Royal; I believe you fully capable of abandoning your woman and her bastard."

I touched my throat.

"Sir – what if you are unable to sell me to Ordene?"

"Then you will remain bound to the College. For seven years, if need be."

I did not like this idea of serving Ordene; Montalbion had but to see my face, and it would be over.

"Is there no other way I can serve Colonel de Groot's purpose? Ty – I mean, Master Pettit – surely told you that I have some skill with voices and accents. I could go into the port – you could follow me for surety, sir

– and perhaps find some other proof of Montalbion's rebellion?"

Collingwood took out a kerchief and wiped his neck. Tiny flakes of skin fell from his whiskery chops. The muggy air was hard to breathe.

"Mister Collingwood, I do beg you to grant me the chance to free my family."

He put his hands on the rail, watching the ship's first mate haggle with a line of porters who were touting for work. "For now, we shall forget about Ordene and his master. If you wish to earn my trust, I would have you try a smaller task. We need divers; and if you are to spy effectively for the College, we must make it known that you are a difficult, rebellious sort that I would happily part company with."

"Divers, sir?"

Collingwood sighed. "It is hard to believe that you are so lacking in wit. You know the College is in need of funds; you also know that I have a very long list of wrecks, both salvaged and unsalvaged; therefore, we will need divers."

"Very good," I said. "I shall simply wander the port, find you the best divers, and discover who is disloyal to the Crown."

The first mate had chosen his porters, and was coming up the gangplank. Collingwood waited for him to pass us.

"There is nothing simple in this life," he whispered heatedly, "until the fighting begins. All else is messy, and mingled, and uncertain. No, you are not to *wander*. You are to play the Irishman; you are to complain against the

Crown and your own transportation, proposing that you will run from your indenture; you are to idle and drink with the ships' crews and freedmen until you have made a list of who is for the King, and who for Montalbion. You'll sleep on the ship with the other indentured men – and I shall have my eyes on you by day and by night."

The porters were coming on board to begin unloading.

"Quit your idling, Calumny Spinks," said Collingwood loudly. "Come – find me some divers for Master Pettit's mission."

I followed the Secretary down the steep gangplank to the wharf, riding the ship's rise and fall. The back of his neck was blotched from the heat.

I had not touched solid ground since I left England, and was so used to the buck and roll of sailing that I almost lost my balance. Collingwood snorted in annoyance, then stopped a gaunt porter.

"See here – we need men who can dive under the sea. For a *scientific* task," he said, awkwardly.

The porter shrugged. His shoulders made sharp peaks under his sweat-stained shirt. "Not for me," he said.

"Then where can we find them?" demanded Collingwood, blocking the man's way. Again, he shrugged.

"Master Secretary," I said humbly, finding the Irish accent as I spoke, "this fellow will not get paid for his work if we detain him. I pray you let him pass."

Collingwood frowned but stepped aside.

The porter gave me a nod. "Go down Thames Street to the wharf by Fort Carlisle, and ask for Francis Coyle," he said.

The Secretary tilted his head from side to side until his spine crackled, then led the way down Thames Street, the broadway that ran along the harbourside. It was near as wide as the Strand in London, and even harder to travel along. Porters crossed our path, carrying their loads from wharf to warehouse and back again. They had to fight their way through a cram of carts carrying dyes, nuts, ale and skins: everything that vanity and greed could desire.

My head still ached from Ty's blows, and I began to feel sick. Doxies smoking clay pipes sweated under their leaden face-paint. Instead of calling out, they simply hitched their skirts and left their venuses to twitch and tease in the shimmering heat until they caught their custom. After the long, lonely weeks of the voyage, the sight and smell of the women, used and hollow though they were, stirred my urges.

Rum-hawkers, eyes dull from sipping on their own wares, darted out from piss-ridden alleys to proffer their tuppenny pints. Each man seemed to care only for his own work and pleasures; there was no friendly chit-chat, only the flash of coin.

Collingwood ignored it all, shouldering his way through the crowds.

When we got to Fort Carlisle, puffing and dizzy, I asked a nearby porter to point Francis Coyle out to us.

He was leaning up against a stanchion on the dock facing the fort, his brock-browed eyes in deep shadow. The men he was conversing with had weathered, still faces and faded clothes; they had the air of men who had waited long years for good fortune. Collingwood pushed me forward, then went to stand in the shade of the fort.

I did not ask them straight away if they wanted work. I told them I was newly arrived in Jamaica, and that my master Collingwood was looking for divers. I gave my voice the faintest of Irish flavours, trying to put Coyle at his ease. He demanded to know why I had taken the indenture. When I said that I had been in debt, he stood straight, folded his arms and stared at me.

"I've not heard of a fellow being transported for being poor," he said.

"Not even when he beats his creditors half to death, Francis Coyle?" I demanded, and after a long moment he smiled. The others shook their heads and chuckled; there's little pleases the Irish more than to hear of an Englishman's suffering.

Coyle put the cracked toe of his boot in a dog's ribs and nudged it out of his way. It jumped to its feet and darted at another hound, snapping and snarling.

"Why does your man" – he jerked his head at Collingwood – "need divers? And why's he lack the stomach to ask us straight?"

"He's Master Secretary of a great College in London. Ah, he's not a bad one, but he hasn't the habit of speaking to a tradesman."

Coyle raised his voice and said directly to Collingwood, "Where in these God-forsaken seas d'you hope to find fresh treasures, Master Secretary, sir?"

A small crowd had begun to gather: porters, sailors, warehouse-keepers.

"The question is not *where*, Master Coyle," replied Collingwood, staying where he was. "But *in what*; and you'll have to come to the *Esperance* to see what I mean by that. We pay one-sixth of what we raise, and we need only two divers to begin with."

Coyle frowned and scratched his grizzled cheek.

"A quarter is the rate," said one of the other Irishmen.

"Not when the Crown takes half the trove," said Collingwood loudly.

"That's not the law!" shouted an onlooker.

"It certainly is *now*, since our salvage licences say so," replied the Secretary. "Come here, Calumny. Master Coyle, if you wish to discuss my offer, you should follow us to our ship."

Coyle hesitated. Then he shrugged, and came along with us.

"Half the trove!" hissed one of the other divers as we left. "Wait till Fergus Ordene hears of this …"

His words were swallowed in the rumble and banter of the crowd. Watching the sweat seeping through the back of Collingwood's waistcoat, I asked the Irishman how he'd come to be in Jamaica.

Francis Coyle had been a play-actor. Twenty-five years before, the Dutch had sailed right up the Thames and burned several Navy ships, and Francis had performed a play that made a mockery of the King's defeat. He was sentenced to ten years on a sugar plantation. In his last season, a new owner's overseer had sliced off his right forefinger for insolence.

At the end of it, he was due to take his acres, but the land office gave him a plot deep in the Cockpit Country, where heathen runaways shot poison arrows, and the earth was tangled with deep roots.

So in a year there, Francis grew little, ate nought and slept less; in the end he had to abandon his land and come to Port Royal to sign up as a privateer. But the ships of marque barely sailed in those days; he ran out of coin, and had to make do with portering. From time to time, he found work as a diver.

"There's been many a wreck on these shores," he said, "but few of them bore much of value, and those that are shallow enough for diving have been stripped bare already. I doubt your master will have more luck than the last fool I sailed with."

"Then why'd you come with us?"

"Food, rum, and a month or two away from Port Royal."

We gave each other a quick grin, and walked on for a while without speaking. Every so often Francis would give a wave to a warehouse foreman, and in return he would get a grim shake of the head. There was no work for him there.

"Was it hard living, on the plantation?" I blurted out at last. "I've heard—"

"How long's your indenture? Five years?"

We had fallen far behind. Collingwood turned and stared at me angrily, and we quickened our pace.

"Seven," I said.

"Bear it," he said, and showed me his mutilated, indigo-stained right hand. "Perhaps you think you might run, but Jamaica is not the place to try it. If you try to board a ship, they'll sell you back to your master for whipping, or cutting, or worse; and if you run to the hills, there are wild hogs, and poisoned fruits, and escaped blacka-moors. And those devils are the worst: they eat the flesh of white men."

"Hogs may be caught and eaten," I said fiercely. "If I run, I'll live."

I strode on to catch up with Collingwood. Francis gave a little low whistle behind me. For a breath, I was pleased: I'd played the part of a rebellious servant well.

We boarded the *Esperance*. The porters had paused their work to allow the horses and mules to be brought out. The beasts were skittish: excited by the fresh air and the smell of land, but afraid to leave their quarters. Four of the ship's crew were struggling to drag them up a long sloping gangway to the upper deck.

Ty was waiting for us. Despite the heat, he was dressed in a fine black coat, breeches and silk stockings. Though he had never been foppish, on this occasion he wore ribbons at the knees, and had tied a cream silk scarf around his neck instead of his usual black lace collar. He nodded at Collingwood.

"Good day," he said to Francis.

"This is Francis Coyle, sir, a diver," I said, and gave a little bow.

Ty approached, both hands held out. Francis lifted a hand, as if he would shake Ty's, but that was not my friend's intention. Instead, he clasped Francis' arms, pressing the muscles and bones from forearm to shoulder; and then took a length of string from his pocket and threw it around the diver's chest, measuring its extent with a charcoal mark.

"Breathe deep, fellow, as if you were about to plunge," he said.

Francis snorted.

"Master Pettit is a natural philosopher, and a man of method," said Collingwood sharply. "We shall not engage you without first examining your physical strengths."

Francis stuck his tongue in his lower lip, considering.

"Half a crown in advance," he demanded.

Collingwood hesitated, then dug a coin out of his pocket and handed it over gracelessly.

Francis glanced at me, and took a deep breath.

"Raise your arms … I thank you," said Ty, as if it had not occurred to him to ask permission of the Irishman.

He let the string pay out until he had taken the greater measurement. "Forty-six," he muttered to himself, "of approximately half a fourteen-inch-radius sphere, less the mass of the upper organs …"

"Come and watch," said Collingwood, leading the way to the upper deck. "Not you, Calumny Spinks. Get down and help with the crew, or there's another beating for you."

"*Bear it*," whispered Francis as he passed me.

Once the mules were unloaded, I helped the *Esperance*'s crew set up a great scaffold on the main deck. We opened the double hatch at the stern of the ship, and the first mate lowered a thirty-pound iron hook from a block and tackle. I was ordered down to the lower deck with three other men. Holding our breaths against the smell, we made our way towards the patch of light. The hook cast a swinging shadow on a sailcloth-shrouded dome, twice as tall as a man.

The first mate shouted an order, and we untied the many heavy ropes that bound the object in place. After a hot, wordless half-hour, we were able to tug the canvas away, unveiling a huge cast-iron bell. One of the men clambered up onto it barefoot. He caught the hook and slipped it into a four-inch eye, then leapt gracefully down to the cargo deck next to me.

The crew above whooped; the mate snapped a word or two, and then their faces disappeared. The hawser tightened and the great bell lifted on one side – but the other was still weighed down by the bunched sailcloth. More shouts from above, and then it dropped to the deck, nearly crushing my feet.

Collingwood's big head appeared above us.

"Lift!" he bellowed. "And if it drops again, I'll beat the man responsible."

The men on the main deck heaved away. We held the bell's rim as it rose, keeping it trim and steady, but were ready to leap back at any instant.

Once it was out of our reach, we went back through the mule stalls and shinned up the ladders to the main deck. We were in time to watch the crew swing the scaffold in a quarter-circle and lower the bell to the deck. Embossed with a symbol and several capital letters, it was slick from the damp air of the hold.

Ty came down from the upper deck. I could tell that he could barely restrain himself from running to touch the device; I stood back, the way a servant must when his master is at the heart of matters.

He put his long slender fingers on the symbol, which was a great eye set within a triangle, and excitedly beckoned to Francis Coyle.

"See, Master Coyle: this great bell is my Nereid Device. Of great mass to conquer submarine currents; of great strength to protect against the reefs; designed for these very waters. We shall make a demonstration of its practical utility, you and I."

Francis came down the stairway very slowly, rubbing his upper lip. Below, a curious crowd had gathered on the wharf. I had heard of these diving bells, but I doubted one had been seen in these waters before.

I edged closer to read the writing below the embossed eye: *FEC. T.T. PETTIT MDCXCI.*

"And where shall we make this demonstration, sir?" asked Francis.

"Naggle Bay," said Ty. "It is well known that the *Vale of Health* went down there with a fortune in Spanish silver not two years ago—"

"You're mad," said Francis, rudely touching Ty's temple, "and what's worse, you've the money to inflict your madness on the good divers of this port."

Collingwood pushed the Irishman violently away. Without thinking, I stepped between them both, bracing myself for a blow from the Master Secretary.

"No, Richard," murmured Ty. "Let the man speak."

Francis, his fists clenched, raised his voice. "Naggle Bay has murderous currents; she'll drag your ship onto her rocks, even on a calm day. Even if you manage to anchor safely, there's an undertow that has broken many a diver's body on the sharp rocks down deep. Not a single man got off the *Vale of Health* that night. Keep your silver, masters."

Ty's hands flew forwards.

"But, Master Coyle – we know about the currents – the Nereid Device has sufficient inertia to overcome them—"

But Francis was already loping down the gangplank to his waiting comrades. They conferred for a moment. Francis laughed once, bitterly, and then they were away down Thames Street.

The crew had been silent since the talk of their ship being dragged onto the rocks. They looked at each other uncomfortably.

Collingwood clapped his hands. "Cover the Device, men. And pay no heed to the Irishman: the finest minds at our College have given us mathematical certainty of recovering that treasure. There'll be shares for the entire crew when we raise it!"

It was enough to rouse a confused cheer from the sailors. One or two of them even helped us to hoist the heavy canvas cover out of the hold and shroud the bell again.

Collingwood kept me on board the *Esperance*, helping to drag the remaining mules out of the hold.

Towards dusk, a Navy ship, the *Swan*, rounded the point and sailed slowly into harbour. She berthed in the lee of Fort James, a hundred paces or so from us. Within an hour, she had disgorged a large company of redcoated soldiers, led by Colonel de Groot.

His arrival was an unnecessary reminder that I was to be sold at that Thursday's market, and had but a few days left to find the evidence we needed.

As I worked, I watched his company march around the headland towards Fort Charles, the greatest of Port Royal's defences.

Once she was unloaded, the *Swan* was grounded by a stony ramp. Many of her crew disembarked, to begin the gruelling task of careening her onto one side.

I slept poorly that night.

There was no breeze, and the sweat-sheen on my skin had become a flood. In the end, I stripped off my shirt and lay, eyes wide, in the damp hammock.

The Secretary woke me well before dawn. I followed him quietly up on deck.

His eyes sagged. "We will need that diver to change his mind," he said, "and quickly, before he spreads the word. Find him; convince him that the Device is sound; drink with him."

He handed me ten shillings. The silver was warm in my palm. I nodded.

"It's true that you are a fine mimic," he said. "I'd have taken you for an Irishman myself. Master Pettit says … That is, the little girl you're raising is Irish, too?"

"She is, I suppose."

"Do right by me, Calumny Spinks, and I'll see that she's safe. Now get you gone. I'll be watching you – and be sure that you take that drink in the Spanish Dogg."

It was that blessed quiet hour when the drunk are asleep, and the ambitious make their plans. I walked a little way down Thames Street, then turned inland to Lime Street. Going left along Queen Street, I passed merchants' houses with their shutters pinned back, revealing lavish displays of porcelain plate. I'd heard that there was no fear of thievery in Port Royal, because no man dared to receive stolen goods in such a violent town. Yet there was much wealth: four-storey houses, many with cellars dug into the sandy earth; tiled roofs, sash windows, and shops as fine as any in Westminster.

It was curiously English. The clothes, the houses, the stink of shit and corruption were all familiar; but the spices and warmth were utterly strange. I realised then that I might never see London again.

In the stillness, I could hear Collingwood's heavy tread, forty paces back.

I put a hand in my pocket. The folded painting was soft in the heat, and inside its crumple was the ivory thimble. Somewhere in the clouded mountains was Mister de Corvis' plantation. I felt a sudden urge to protect the painting from Ordene and Montalbion. I needed to find a safe place for it.

I went back down to Thames Street and found myself in front of a tall, half-timbered building. Its gate was guarded by two bluecoated soldiers on the ground, and four musketeers on the high wall above.

Collingwood caught me up. He bundled me away, cursing me loudly for a poor servant.

"That is the King's House, you fool," he hissed, "Montalbion's quarters when he is in Port Royal. You cannot be seen staring at it. Now away with you, and get me that diver."

He turned and went back to the ship.

I looked at the gate's guards for a moment longer: so the bluecoats were Montalbion's soldiers. I thought about de Groot's men in Fort Charles; a battle was coming. I doubted I had much time to earn Violet and Simona's freedom.

Francis Coyle and his friends were slumped against a warehouse near Fort Carlisle. A bold, blackbirdish doxy was crouching at Francis' side, poking his chest. He groaned and grumbled, but his companions jeered him awake.

"What d'you have left of that half-crown from yesterday?" she demanded.

"Ah, go away with you, Hoopy," grumbled Francis. One of his friends, a mischievous whippet of a man, beckoned me to join them.

"Hand it over, you fool," said the whore calmly.

"All gone," he muttered, and rubbed his face.

She knelt, dug his purse out of his shirt and looked at the contents.

"Two shillings ha'penny," she said. "I'll mark it in the book for you. And you'll thank me for my trouble."

"Thank her kindly!" ordered the man who'd waved me over. Francis snarled, and the others burst out laughing. Hoopy gave them all a mock-curtsey and quit the wharf.

"A word, Francis," I said loudly.

He came with me willingly enough, keen to get away from the jeers. A tongue-lolling yellow hound, with one brown eye and one of frosty blue, followed us, sniffing at my calves.

"D'you owe that Hoopy a debt, then?" I asked him.

He shook his head. "She looks after my savings, is all. She has a strong door and a locked box, which is more than I have to my name. If I keep it, I drink it."

"You'd trust a whore with your coin? Is she your woman?"

"No, but I'd trust her before any man on this island," replied Francis.

Hoopy Yaxley, he said, was the daughter of a Quaker minister who'd been burned at the stake in Barbados. He'd given secret Christian ministry to slaves, and the plantation owners had hanged him and cut out the slaves' tongues so they could not spread the word of God to their fellows. Orphaned at twelve years old, Hoopy had become the whore of every planter and privateer from Bridgetown to St Lucia. As soon as she'd stolen enough coin for the passage, she took ship for Port Royal.

"And she'd take care of a drunk Irishman's savings," I said. "Perhaps she would ... No, I couldn't ask it of her."

"What, man?" asked Francis. "Tell me."

"Let's drink," I said, and showed him the ten shillings. He folded my fingers back over the coins in case his friends could see them.

"That's barely enough for the two of us," he said. "Come on – if you need me to ask Hoopy a favour, we must catch her before the custom arrives."

"A fine idea," I said. "Then we must talk. I'm for a drink or two at the Spanish Dogg, if you are."

The dog trotted along two paces behind us, snorting and farting. There was no sign of Richard Collingwood.

As we walked, Francis pointed out the *Swan*, all the way up Thames Street, sailors clinging to her crusted sides. Standing on the narrow strip of shore were two fire-gangs, carefully holding burning faggots against the weeds and shells that coated the keel.

"Breaming is the Devil's own work," said Francis. "They'll be at it for weeks."

"And whose ship is that?" I asked, pointing out a vessel in the harbour. It had been badly mauled: the hull had been shattered in three places above the waterline.

"The *Blessed James*," he said shortly. "Fergus Ordene's ship. Back from raiding the Spanish with Montalbion; they were so badly set about that they had to leave early."

"You don't care for him?"

Francis shrugged. "He's no Irishman. Lands he has in Mayo, no doubt, but his grandda will have stolen those when he served that demon Cromwell. Sir Fergus be damned: the fellow's a pirate, like every other captain here."

We walked on to Lime Street in silence. I could not hear Montalbion's name without thinking of Ty's father Garric, coughing out his life on the glass-strewn Strand.

Hoopy opened the door to Francis' soft knock. She gave him a hard look: she could not have expected to see him again so soon.

"I pay no bounty if you bring me custom, Francis, and don't be asking for any."

"This is Cal," said Francis. "A fellow that asks your help."
She did not move aside to let us in.

"Miss Yaxley," I said, "I'm to be sold on Thursday. Will you not keep something for me?"

Without waiting for her answer, I took out the folded paper and the thimble, and offered her five of my shillings. Francis sighed: I'd halved our drinking fund.

"I cannot say that I will be here for long. With twenty pounds more, I've enough to sail back to Barbados and get what's mine." She held her hands at her sides, unwilling to take on my burden.

"I cannot say that I will *serve* for long," I answered softly, "for I've a woman and a child to fetch from England."

I'd little hope I would see my treasures again, but I'd trust a whore over a merchant any day.

"Well, give it here, then," she said abruptly, taking the money, paper and thimble out of my hands. "You can pay me to get these things back if you live; but if you're more than a year, then I'll be keeping them…"

"It's yours, Miss Yaxley," I said, giving her a little bow. "I'll remember your kindness."

"Away with you," she said. "Master Coyle's hairy face is scaring away the custom."

Francis scratched his beard and laughed.

CHAPTER FIVE

Branded

Twenty-seventh day of March

The Spanish Dogg had once been a meetinghouse. The pews had been hacked down into benches; the balcony that ran round three sides was now lined with bare-breasted whores; and drink-worshippers stood three deep at the counter, an altar to rum and ale and blackened hog-ribs. It was louder than the closing hour of a fish market, and foul with pipe-smoke and tallow fumes. Three blackamoors chanted a mournful song from a corner, providing the rhythm for red-eyed men to ignore as they danced their whores clumsily across the open floor.

I could scarcely imagine why Collingwood had told me to come here; but I had more than a little Devil in my soul, and I resolved to enjoy the Dogg while time yet remained.

Though it was still before noon, drinkers roosted on every corner-table and railing, puff-breasted, their heads twitching whenever a woman passed. All eyes fell on me as we entered the tavern. I had not yet washed off the grime of two months in that fetid hold, and I stank of indentured servitude.

"Irish! Irish! Hoo-hoo-hoo!" called out a halfwit who was squatting in a puddle of another man's piss.

"No bondsmen here," growled the pisser, who was stood behind the idiot, tinkling down his back.

"God save the King!" I said quickly, touching my forehead.

"God save the *true* King – and perdition to the Hollander!" shouted Sir Fergus Ordene. I'd not seen him through the crowd at first. He was sitting in a high-backed chair with a slave-girl perched on each knee. His men, clad in the blue uniforms I'd seen at the King's House, echoed him. They waved their limp-feathered hats, but their cries were cut short as a shower fell on them from the balcony above. Michael Hicks, the moneylender I'd seen at the harbour, was standing at the balustrade holding two upturned tankards.

"Fergus, if there is any more talk of monarchy – or religion – or anything which disturbs the natural drinking of my guests," he said, shaking the last dregs out of the tankards, "then your entire crew shall be excluded from the Dogg."

Ordene's men roared their disapproval. Hicks gave the tankards to a harlot, and held up his hands.

"In the meantime, I'm sure *Sir* Fergus would buy every man in this place a mug of rum by way of apology. His purse has insufficient room for what he won in New Spain."

Another roar, this time of approval. All eyes turned to Ordene, who waved a hand airily without taking his face out of a slave-girl's bosom.

Francis had taken advantage of the commotion to push through to the counter. Beaming, he brought two mugs of rum over. Before we could drink, he was clapped heavily on the back by a heat-flushed gentleman in an enormous wig of the old fashion; and then we were surrounded by a braggart handful of planters, fat with wine and New England salted pork and their own sugar. The air was suddenly sweet with perfume, but soured by foul meaty farts and the dampness of riding boots. Their costumes were more frilled, frogged and tasselled than a Mussulman prince's.

"If you're down to accepting free drinks from Jacobites, Coyle, I can offer you better employment than you're getting," said the red-faced fellow.

"I doubt it, Mister Flowers," said Francis, trying to take a sip. A young planter nudged his elbow, braying with delight as half the free rum spilled.

"How dare you? Not only do I have a plantation of a thousand acres, I am a *colonel* of militia—" protested Flowers loudly.

"Who has never so much as poked a Spaniard in the eye," said Ordene, who'd risen from his seat. "But I'll give you a fight, sir, if you've a wish to prove your military powers. No man here has ever seen a planter best a real Port Royal man."

Flowers took a deep breath, puffed his cheeks and cast a wide-eyed glance at Michael Hicks on the balcony.

"I would happily oblige, sir, if Mister Hicks did not have such strict ordinances in this place …"

Ordene's men jeered, and Francis pulled me away.

"Ten more years, Coyle, and ten more acres!" mocked Flowers as we retreated.

Francis showed me the stump of his lost finger. "That's the *omadhaun* who sold me out after nine years, God rot him; if he'd kept me on, I'd still have a whole hand."

"On reflection," said Flowers to Ordene, "I'll not be spoken to thusly by a traitor—"

Chairs shrieked as Ordene's men scrambled to their feet. It is but a short step from crying treason to trading blows. Francis and I sidled behind the tavern-keeper's counter.

I could see this was not the first such fight at the Spanish Dogg. There were such courtesies as you only witness when men trade blows for sport: no blades were used, and no fellow was beset by more than two others. In the case of Sir Fergus Ordene, there were always four or five men waiting in line to hit him, ignoring the blows that flew around them. Though it would have been best for them to be less honourable, for Ordene was a snarling gargoyle in the fight, kicking and biting and gouging with his heavy rings – and his men were happy to break the rules and bear down on any fellow who looked like he could best their leader.

Two burly porters carrying clubs came down from the balcony, followed by the neat, commanding figure of Michael Hicks.

"Pray silence," he said. A few men desisted, but still the shouting and punching went on. Hicks nodded to his porters.

Shouting, "Pray *silence*!" they waded into the fight, dealing blows left and right until the rage went out of the room. Men spat out broken teeth, picked up half-spilled flagons, set their chairs back up.

"I thank you," said Hicks, his Liverpudlian accent clear and throaty in the stillness. He took a chair plumb in the middle of the room. "Now, I'll have some wine."

The serving-man brought over a bottle of Porto wine and poured three fingers for Hicks. He sipped at it, watching the planters brush themselves down; then he beckoned to Ordene and Flowers. They joined him at the table.

Murmuring began again, until Hicks cleared his throat and tapped his finger on the open ledger before him. No king has as much power as a moneylender.

"To business, gentlemen. The early risers among us will have noted that close to two hundred men disembarked from the Swan this morning. That's a doubling of Fort Charles' garrison. I have invited the new commander, one Colonel de Groot, to eat with us here and explain himself, for I do not like the smell of it."

Francis and I had our drink at last, that burning, sweet-lunged, heathen brew they called rum. He swiftly ordered a second, and a third, and within the hour, four of my shillings were gone. We had barely exchanged two words until then: his thick brows were knitted, and he kept pressing his thumb-tip into the stump of his missing finger.

"He has the right of it, that *omadhaun*: if I rely on the portering work, it'll take me a hundred years to get out of Jamaica. Damn his eyes."

"But your savings – at Hoopy's?"

"Twenty-nine shillings," he said.

We watched a doxy at work on the balcony. She was caressing a fat planter's groin with one hand while she cut his purse with the other.

"Your man ..." began Francis. "The slender fellow. Master Pettit – is he mad, d'you think?"

"I never knew anyone who could reckon things so clear and so cold," I said, truthfully.

"But that iron bell – if you go inside it, you'll drown," he insisted.

I hesitated.

"Not so," I said at last. "I've seen them do it in the Thames, Francis, currents and all. A fellow goes in the engine, fetches from the river-bottom, comes out dry as dust."

"Ah ... Jesus ..."

The man looked miserable. I put an arm around his shoulders.

"Francis, if Ty Pettit says you can raise a treasure and take a sixth for yourself, then like as not you can. He has the mathematic in his veins, see? Now go to the *Esperance* and sign with him before he gives the job to another man."

He breathed out heavily, nodded, and slapped my knee.

"You'll stay, then?" he asked.

I grinned and showed him the last shilling.

"Ask Master Pettit for an advance on your wages," I said, "and then we can try some more of this rum."

To my surprise, Colonel de Groot had accepted Michael Hicks' invitation. He arrived as the bells struck for noon, accompanied by a hard-faced lieutenant and a pair of ordinary soldiers. Their scarlet uniforms were startling in the smoky dimness of the Dogg. Men backed off a little.

"Colonel," said Hicks, rising half out of his seat. "Do join us for a drink before we dine."

"I will not," said de Groot. He took off his tricorn and tucked it under his arm. His curls had been cropped, and he looked considerably more trim than he had in London. If he recognised me, standing in the shadows behind Hicks' table, he did not show it.

"Then be seated at least – we do have business to discuss."

"The business of the day," said de Groot, "is that I will require from you and your confederates a ledger of all trade conducted in this port since Lady Day last year, and a reconciliation of all goods warehoused, so that compliance with the Navigation Acts may be established. Secondly, we will be requisitioning considerable stores of food to victual the now-larger garrison in Fort Charles. Thirdly—"

"Your name, sir?" demanded Ordene, who had put his boots up on the table.

"I am Colonel de Groot, commander of Fort Charles and of His Majesty's forces on this island."

"I knew a de Groot who owned a sugar-works in Pernambuco once," said Flowers, spraying wine down his front. "He was a Jew, though. Hicks, you are proposing to victual a band of Christ-killers."

"Good day," said Ordene to the space above de Groot's head. "I wish you a safe voyage back to London. Or Jerusalem, if you prefer. Lord Montalbion's compliments to His Majesty."

De Groot slowly drew his sword. Ordene's bluecoats quit drinking, uncoupled from their whores, and slowly assembled behind their leader, whose feet remained on the table.

"Weapons away," said Hicks in his flat Liverpudlian accent, and waited until the bluecoats complied. De Groot remained armed. "Colonel – I will send a man to Fort Charles to collect your written requisition; I must warn you that prices are tremendously high owing to His Majesty's continuing conflict with France. In the meantime, you should know that there has never been a standing army in Port Royal; your men's safety depends upon their remaining within the forts."

De Groot uttered a Dutch profanity, purple with fury, and quit the tavern without sheathing his sword.

"It is unwise to taunt a man who commands so many soldiers, Colonel Flowers," said Hicks, wagging a finger at the planter, who had earlier boasted of leading his own militia.

"Lord Montalbion shall hear of this," said Ordene loudly. "Compliance with the Navigation Acts? That'll reduce every captain in Port Royal to penury!"

Excited, I spent my last shilling on a pint of rum. Ordene's words were close to treason – surely I was close to finding the evidence I needed to win my freedom.

"That's as may be," said the Liverpudlian. "What's more troubling is that—"

"Runaway!" came a shout from the door.

Richard Collingwood had entered the Spanish Dogg, a foul look on his usually placid face. His side-whiskers were scruffy, the skin of his face blotched and raw from scratching. He pointed a stubby forefinger at me.

"That man is the property of my College, damn it to Hell! Seize him!"

I'd had too much rum. Before I knew what I was doing, I was running for the stairs. One of Ordene's men tripped me, and by the time I got up, Collingwood had hold of my shirt.

"Master Secretary, I did as you asked—"

Collingwood struck my mouth, hard.

"I say you are a God-damned runaway and a cheat," he said; but he spoke quietly now, aware that the whole room was watching us.

"You are secretary to Master Pettit, the scholar who has a salvage licence, are you not?" asked Hicks.

"Richard Collingwood, at your service."

"And what portion of your trove must you pay to the Crown?"

"Half, sir," answered the Secretary, "which I believe is the new rate for all captured and salvaged foreign treasures in these seas."

"Outrage," snapped Ordene, getting to his feet. "Our letters of marque are valid—"

"—but were signed by the last King," interrupted Hicks.

"Nevertheless, Lord Montalbion shall hear of this; the Crown has never pressed good Port Royal men, nor has it ever demanded a moiety—"

"It is said in London," said Collingwood, who was gripping my neck tightly, "that Montalbion is to be recalled from his Company Governorship. Rumour, no doubt – forgive me for mentioning it."

It struck me as no accident that he had arrived so soon after de Groot: they intended to provoke Montalbion into open rebellion. *The sooner the better*, I thought.

Hicks closed his ledger. "Join me, Master Secretary, if you please," he snapped.

"I cannot, sir," said Collingwood. "This runaway must be dealt with swiftly, as you well know."

"Hear, hear!" bellowed Flowers.

"Your servant may sit with us, so you can watch him," Hicks said firmly.

Collingwood jerked his head to show that I should obey, and put a palmful of coins on the counter for the tavern-keeper. I was given a flask of gin and a tankard of ale, which seemed a rich reward for a runaway. I drank while Collingwood and the others talked, their voices muffled by the roar of laughter and speculation around them. Every so often Collingwood let his gaze sweep over me, his bushy side-whiskers twitching. Each time, he lifted his goblet a little, to show me that I might take some more.

Ordene was trying to impress Collingwood with his deeds. He talked proudly of how he'd raided New Spain with the earl's regiment. Their flotilla had attacked towns and villages up and down the coast, ransoming the gentry for silver plate and gold coin. Montalbion himself had captained the flagship and led an attack on the port of Nueva Sevilla.

"His Lordship may be the Governor of the Company of the Caribbean, but he is also the defender of Jamaica, an island which does not even have a Governor of its own right now," said Ordene.

Collingwood nodded gravely, shook hands with the three men and led me away. "More rum?" he asked.

I drank.

Dusk dropped, darkening the bottle-thick windows.

Rum, ale, rum. I laughed and drank and spoke half-words like a madman. Collingwood watched me, his puffy face pale between the whisker-bushes that flanked it. His hair was parted sharply down the middle, curling apart like waves around a boat's bow.

"We have done our duty, Master Secretary," I mumbled. "We know who is for Montalbion, and who is not; now we can finish our task. No need to sell me to Fergus Ordene."

"You have most certainly done well," he breathed. "Tomorrow your work here will be complete."

"You're a good man, Collingwood," I said.

His eyes clouded over. He twisted his signet ring. It was solid gold, and spoke of wealthier times gone by.

He took another drink and waved at a knot of Port Royallers, inviting them to our table.

The Secretary was free with his coin, and soon we had half a dozen others sitting with us. They wore the salt-stiff sleeveless coats and curved blades of privateers, but their hands were soft and their cheeks veined scarlet from drinking port. These men had not sailed in years.

"Fellow drinks like a Creole already," laughed one, putting a hand on my shoulder.

They talked, draining the dregs of the day. As for me, I lost my reason; I was so far in my cups that I puked under the table to make room for more booze. There was a blissful moment when I lay there, letting my head loll back until the room began to spin. Then Collingwood's gogged eyes appeared, not three inches from my own.

And so I was weak and drunk when Collingwood took me back to the *Esperance*, still holding a tankard from the Dogg.

We stumbled past the rutting thieves and whores on Thames Street. Rum had scorched my throat, and the stench of Port Royal's shit-strewn harbour plagued my tongue. All that kept me from falling was Collingwood's bulky arm.

Shirt-linen clung to my damp flesh as I staggered, trying to slow him down. We were nearly at the *Esperance*'s gangplank, and I had little desire to spend another night in the reeking, bobbing mess of the servants' deck.

"Drink," said Collingwood, whose eyes were as black and withdrawn as a terrier's. He forced my fingers around the pewter handle and pushed my elbow up until the sugar-spirit trickled fierily between my lips. I choked; and then I drank some more.

Collingwood guided me up the gangplank. There were no sailors on watch, only Ty, sitting at a small desk on the poop deck. Next to his left hand, a sheaf of papers was held down by a gold brick, carved with a symbol. It gleamed wetly.

Close to him was a brazier.

The gold drew me in. I slowly approached the desk, guts swirling. My fingers lifted towards the ingot, dry heat from the brazier plucking at the hairs on the back of my hand.

"Ty …"

Collingwood blew hard through snotty nostrils.

"I do not care that you took my father's gold, for he was already dead by then," said Ty coldly. "I do not care that you put your own profit ahead of my future."

The *Esperance* wallowed on the harbour-waves. I lifted my shoulders, let them fall, rolled with the ship.

"But I do care greatly for our mission, even if you do not."

I took a fretful breath.

"Master Secretary …" snapped Ty.

Collingwood pinned my elbows behind my back. Straight away he pressed his knees into the back of mine, forcing me downwards. I did not fight him, did not cry out as my bones struck oak. I let the side of my face press against the deck.

"You may have supposed that your tasks in Jamaica were nearly done, but they are not. How could we trust a thief to keep his word?" Ty said. His voice faded as he walked to the brazier, skirting where Collingwood and I were clinched on the floor. He seized a poker that had been thrust into the coals. The tip, furnace-red, was twisted into the shape of a portly man.

It was Ty who'd first taught me letters. He cleared his throat.

Collingwood turned me onto my back, and pinned me down again with his knees and one hand. He ripped at my shirt until the left shoulder was bare.

"This is not for vengeance," lied Ty, kneeling next to me with the brand held away from his face. "*This* is your contract: you must kill Lord Montalbion. Run, and you die. If you do not attempt it, Violet and Simona are to be transported to the opposite ends of America."

"I never promised to do murder!" I protested, but it was too late. Ty clamped his free hand around my arm, just above the elbow, to brace himself. I did not fight. That God-damned theft had been a maggot in my flesh for more than three years.

Ty pressed the poker against my flesh. For a fleeting moment there was no pain, and then the violation struck deep, the stench of seared flesh scarred the air, and I screamed until my breath ran out. Red heat pierced my skull, my arms, my chest.

The scalding iron wrote its violent "R". Ty withdrew the brand, pulling my flesh apart. Reaching, pleading to be taken away from the corruption and charring within, meat parted from sinew, skin ripped away in strips.

"Not vengeance," repeated Ty hollowly. He stood and thrust the poker back into the coals. "But you are marked a runaway now. The College needs this guarantee, do you not see it? Do your duty and you will be freed, and Violet too. But now, if you run away and are caught they'll hang you. Or worse."

Bile clogged my throat.

"Richard, the harbour-surgeon ..."

As Collingwood let me go, nothingness took me.

A dry thumb jabbing into my eye to lift the lid, a doughy blurred face, a heathen burble of Latin words. Behind the face, a crimson staring spark, fizzing through the salt-cloyed air.

"... still open. Infection ..."

Like a dream, the poker came back; strong arms pinned me down again; and though I knew that I had already been burned, that this was not real, still the glowing tip bore down until it seared my flesh again—

"... to seal it!" hissed the dough-face, raining spittle on my neck. "To seal it!"

This time I was awake, the pain a sword driven through my arm, the bone, through rib and muscle and heart, pinning me to the deck. I could not escape it. In the midst of the searing flesh came a memory of Violet, of sunlight catching the fine hairs on her arm. I breathed; and from where my ragged fingernails had dug into my palm, blood trickled like sun-warmed sap.

Pain woke me an hour or two after the harbour-surgeon had sealed the brand, a bradawl driving into my wounded shoulder. When I opened my eyes, Collingwood was kneeling next to me, his face pale in the oil-light. We were alone in Ty's cabin.

"You will be sold into Lord Montalbion's service," he whispered. "That means you *must* be bought by his overseer, Kenver Kiet. He's a man who will only buy if the goods are spoiled and cheap, which is why you have been branded a runaway. Tap the deck if you understand."

I let my tongue loll.

"Tap," insisted the Secretary, pressing his forefinger into my breastbone. My shoulder complained. I choked back bile and touched my knuckle to the headboard of Ty's bed.

"Good." Collingwood glanced at the closed door, then leaned in. "Montalbion is expected at his plantation within weeks. You have three months to kill him. The Navy ship *Mordaunt* will arrive by the end of June, which will give de Groot the firepower to arrest Montalbion and take him to London, where I doubt we will have evidence enough to convict him. Which will mean an end to all our hopes; so he must die. Three months: tap if you understand, Calumny Spinks."

I snatched a breath of foul air and screwed up my eyes, but there was no escaping the man. He folded my hand and rapped the headboard with it.

"Succeed, and you are free. Find us in Naggle Bay, and we will keep you safe. But if you run, your woman and child will be transported to the opposite ends of America from each other. As for you, you're branded now: this island hates a runaway. She deals swifter and more cruel justice than a London court. Do not run."

I rolled onto my good arm, turning my back to him. Drool fell from my mouth.

"And if I try, and fail?"

"They go free."

His knees creaked as he got up. We both listened to the

water caressing the ship's timbers. *Come down*, I thought
I heard it call.

I clenched my fist.

Tap. Tap.

CHAPTER SIX

Bills of Sale

Thirty-first day of March and the first three days of April

My guts writhed. The air was bitter with lye. Men marched across the floorboards above, one voice raised in pitiful argument. The sounds clattered into my bursting brain-pan. Two men striding heavily, another being dragged along behind.

It was Thursday, the day of the indenture sales.

I lifted myself up on my left elbow, dizzy and dry-mouthed. I had been in a fever for two days and nights, and was still greatly weakened after another day in bed.

I tried to sit up fully, but my wound shrieked.

Invisible claws sank themselves into my left shoulder, let go, sank deeper. I fell back onto my good side and retched. The movement tugged at my branded flesh. I spat out a ladleful of bile, and looked at the furious "R" that marked me a runaway for life.

"God. Damned. Maggot."

Even as I whispered that curse, I felt a flicker of relief that my secret was out. That I'd paid for what I'd done to Ty.

Not that I did not rage at him and Collingwood, those meal-faced cuckold fleas; not that I did not swear to myself that I'd cut out their balls, roast them and stitch them back in their wrinkly sacks.

Dawn dribbled through the careless gaps in the planking above. All the indentured servants were in their hammocks, curled up in solitary misery.

I sank into the confusion of pain. I could not tell if hours passed, or mere moments, until a single cannon barked, a signal that our ship had labouring men to sell.

"Bear it," said Francis Coyle. I opened a bleary eye: he was standing next to my hammock.

"You signed the papers, eh?" I asked. He shrugged.

"Life is bondage," he said, "so I thought I may as well have a chance at some coin while I'm here."

The hatch rattled open. A man poked his head through the opening.

"Wake!" he ordered. "You signed your bonds, now you must hexecute them."

Not a man stirred.

"If I mun ask any man thrice, you'll hall take the lash for him," said the head quietly, and withdrew.

Grudgingly, men got out of their hammocks, picked up their belongings and gathered at the hatchway, helping each other to climb up through the hole.

At first I did not get up.

"You'll have to go," said Francis, "or it'll be the worse for you. That's Edwin Foulkes you're dealing with there: a fellow who sold his own half-breed son."

He helped me out of the hammock and over to the hatch.

"I'll see you at the sales," he said, and vanished into the shadows.

Foulkes was halfway up the ladder to the top deck, watching. "No b'longins," he droned, "no blanket, no pallet, no hovercoat, no blade nor cudgel no matter how small. It be capital crime for an denchured man to carry such."

Little sharp-chinned Bonfoy clutched his grubby calico sack. Filled, I had little doubt, with other men's keepsakes.

"Sir ... I have no weapons in my sack..." he pleaded, his voice rising into a child's whine. Without a word, the trader tugged a foot-long handle from his belt and flicked out his arm. A slender shadow leapt across the shaft of light. Bonfoy cried out and dropped the sack, clutching his hand. Blood trickled between his fingers.

"Master Foulkes!" called another voice from the main deck. The trader did not respond at first. He pointed his whipstock at each of us in turn, waiting until we had met his gaze; and then he vanished into the daylight.

One by one, the indentured dropped their belongings back down to the lowest deck. A blanket, a Bible, a piece of whittling, a small hammer. Lastly, a woman's silken scarf floated after the little treasures, emerald with plump white stitching; and then it too was gone.

I had nothing to throw away: my own treasures were entrusted to a whore I barely knew.

Indentured men were sold at a makeshift market at the landward end of Port Royal. Foulkes led us into the narrow streets, dense with watery dawn fog.

Despite the town's wealth, the streets were poorer than farm-tracks. Cracks spidered their way down the plasterwork of house-fronts and across the roadways, wide enough apart for fallen pennies to wedge themselves in.

A soft voice murmured from behind me, "Built on sand."

Two yards ahead of us, Foulkes' shoulders lifted, his hand drifting to the whipstock.

I slowed and walked alongside the man who had spoken. I did not look him in the face, but felt his squat bulk next to me, the stiff way he led with his head and not his hips.

"The port …" he whispered, speaking under the beat of Foulkes' leather heels, "is built on sand. No foundations at all."

Like a child, I had believed that Collingwood simply planned to sell me to an ally of Montalbion's, so that I could spy on him. In God's name, why had I thought they would need a fool like me for such a task? No: they needed me to be an assassin. If I failed, the earl would believe I had tried to murder him for revenge; so no accusation could be made against the College or the Crown. And how was I supposed to hide from a man who knew me, who'd recognise my height and flaming hair from a quarter-mile away?

They had trussed me tight, damn them to Hell.

The market was bounded at one end by the town wall, and on its sides by banked scaffolds, each bearing three rows of benches. In between was a sandy square. The benches already bore a few sunburned men in worn-out shirtsleeves. Even from far off, I could see the red earth under their nails. Free men, but poor – and I doubted one among them could afford to buy an indentured servant.

They had come for the spectacle, to watch white men sink even lower than themselves.

Foulkes made us halt. A pickaninny boy dashed out from under a scaffold, bringing a coil of rope for the auctioneer.

"Since you men are called free, law's aginst you bearing chains," he said roughly. "But you'll take a hold of this-here rope, one knot for one man, see? And if by and by you let it go, I'll break the fingers that loosed their grip. The goodmen of this parish want to see you bound, bound by the promise you did sign in Hengland."

The pickaninny, his head little higher than my waist, pushed us into a ragged line. When he was done, we were two feet apart, each of us holding a knot on the rope. Dizzy, I struggled to keep my eyes open.

Foulkes was a fidgeter: he flattened his greasy grey hair, scratched the side of his nose, and tapped the whipstock on his boot. We shuffled after him onto the sand, our shadows shorter and sharper now. My scalp prickled.

He lined us up in the middle of the square, one man facing left and the next right, so that both sides of the market had men to look at. We were ordered to take off our shirts and give them to the slave-boy. Foulkes shrugged at the sight of my brand, but glanced curiously at the dozens of tiny scars on my chest. I was meat to him.

I'd got them by crawling on my belly across the Strand, breaking my flesh on shattered glass, too late to save Ty's father. A day later I had stolen the gold that was intended for him; and today I would pay for it with seven years. Or with my life.

Slowly, in the rising heat, moneyed men and overseers began to come to market, three or four at a time. Before taking their seats, they came to inspect us, the loose sand marking their buckled shoes.

The first to arrive were still dressed in last night's clothes. They filled the air with stale whores' perfume and liquored breath. The feathers on their flop-brimmed hats tickled our faces as they prodded our chests and lifted lips to test our teeth. I choked back my rage, staring at the bright sky until I could barely see.

One fellow threw Foulkes a half-full purse without a haggle, taking with him a delicate-looking boy. He squirmed as the hairy-handed drunkard caressed his neck.

"If you bring him back, I'll pay you but a sovereign on your five guineas," called Foulkes.

The buyer belched, thrust his tongue at Foulkes between two spread fingers, and dragged his new plaything away.

"Start the bidding for the redhead!" shouted one of the poorer fellows, pointing at me.

I snarled, standing straight to show that I was half a head taller than any man on the sand. Since my new name was Runaway, I would wear it with pride; I could not afford to be bought by any man but Kenver Kiet, Montalbion's overseer.

Foulkes went to wait on a little shaded platform, ignoring the bidders' demands for the auction to start. Still more men came, Francis Coyle among them. He climbed heavily to the top bench and sat among the freedmen.

Collingwood arrived and sat alone in the front row. I realised then that Ty would not be coming.

I turned my eyes to the slave-trader. His bloodless lips flickered as he counted the customers. *Thirty-seven*, I thought, for I'd done the same, and my counting had grown a great deal faster since I'd been a trader myself. Not least because I'd failed: nobody knows the value of a shilling better than a bankrupt.

The pickaninny ran around, blowing through a seashell: it made an alarmed honk. The auction was soon to begin, and Kenver Kiet had not come.

Now the fear began to settle on me. If Kiet bought me, I had a reason to live, a foolish dab of hope; but if I were sold to any other man, then I'd lost my family and sold my youth for the promise of ten acres.

I looked up at the freedmen around Francis, their faces caked with dust. One man's hat was so threadbare that his face was patched with sunlight. One of them had been branded, too, leaving a lumpy scar on his cheek where he had slashed at the "R". All of them had once stood on this same piece of sand, waiting to be sold.

That was my future, if I did not kill Montalbion: to scratch out a living on a parcel of soil, never having the coin to hire help or buy passage back to England.

The first man went up for auction. The pickaninny rapped his fist to make him drop the rope, and then led him around the square by the hand, stopping in front of each scaffold and turning him slowly to show his body. The fellow, a single-browed farm boy with a cauliflower ear, shook so much with fear that the little blackamoor's body waggled back and forth from the effort of holding him still.

"A good digger, gentlemen, like all of his race," called out Foulkes in a soft voice, as if it were his own opinion and not his way of selling the poor lad. "Wit enough to plant, yet haccustomed to the orders of his betters. A loyal Irishman!"

The gentlemen in the front rows laughed out loud, though some of the freedmen glowered at the slave-trader.

"I'll take twenty pound for this'n," offered Foulkes, as if he parted with a dear nephew.

"Forty dollar!" said a pug-faced old man, his leathery neck sagging over the stiff brocaded collar of his long coat. His accent was light and frilled.

"*Mister* Melander – the Spanish coin may not be traded in this market, whether you be Swede or no—"

"Give you five sovereigns, son," drawled a bilious Scot, putting aside the green stick he'd been chewing on.

"I maun take the fellow myself for five!" snapped Foulkes.

The former runaway among them laughed and called out, "For shame, gentlemen! Would you value your own flesh so poor?"

"Ten of your English pounds then," said the Scot, sitting up straight.

"Eleven, precise," countered Melander. Neither man looked at the other. Foulkes stepped down from his little platform, beckoning the farm boy towards him. The lad stumbled on the sand.

"Let's see that there *dobeck* bend to work afore these two empty their purses," came a new voice from the side of the scaffold. Tin-bright, it squeezed out between locked teeth. An island of dark brown hair sat alone atop his forehead, surrounded by a sun-stained moat of scalp. Though his words had been light, he frowned.

"See now, Master Kiet," began Foulkes, "rules be rules. This be not Cornwall but an *English* market. Gentlemen buyers may only *see* and *touch* the denchured men …"

Kenver Kiet raised his powerful shoulders, which was enough to silence the slave-trader.

"Seventy-one pound four shilling you got from Lord Montalbion last month, *Master* Foulkes. Hundred pound the month afore …"

His voice was high, slow and hard, like a hammer striking a copper gong. Foulkes bobbed his head and poked the Irish lad. "Do as Master Kiet orders, boy."

"Now then, *dobeck*," said Kiet, "lift up that *hobbin* there."

As the watchers laughed, he pointed at Bonfoy, who'd chosen indenture over the noose. The lad wrapped his arms around the stunted burglar's hips and lifted him clean in the air.

"Drop him!" ordered Kiet, clapping his hands sharply. Dropped, the little man landed on his belly. He gasped for breath.

"Boy will take an order," breathed the Scot. "Twelve pound to you, Master Foulkes."

"Ten pound and done," countered Kiet, tucking a hand into his baldric. His long-barrelled pistol swung with the movement. Foulkes nodded, pushing the Irish lad towards him. The Scotsman and Melander looked at each other, but neither protested. Kenver Kiet had won with a lower bid because Montalbion was feared in this town.

Foulkes glanced at Collingwood, who nodded.

"How about five more for this here big lad?" the trader asked Kiet, putting a hand on my arm.

"Weak and sick," said Kiet, who seemed distracted by seeing Francis in the stands. "How're your acres, Coyle?"

Francis stared sullenly back.

"A man only needs six fingers to dig, Coyle, and I left you nine," Kiet went on, as if he were talking of loaves of bread and not a man's hand. So Francis had been sold to Kiet by Flowers. My own fingers twitched. "Now follow me, *dobeck*. One of your kind is enough for me today."

As the Irishman came towards him, he counted out ten gold coins and handed them to the blackamoor boy. Foulkes began the bidding for Bonfoy quickly, to make the watchers forget the dark mood Kiet had brought on them.

"Eight pound only, first bid – eight pound I say …"

Kenver Kiet, pushing the farm boy before him, was nearly out of sight. Collingwood stared at me. No time to think – Foulkes now had his back to me, and if I did not capture the Cornishman's attention, all was lost. I barged the slave-trader over and ran up the end of the scaffolding, where fewer men were sitting. I aimed blows at them to clear my way, reached the top bench and looked down. It was full ten feet to the roadway below.

"Run the *other* way," hissed Francis Coyle. "Scale the wall!"

He stood up to ward off the crowd – though most of the watchers had simply lolled back in their seats to enjoy the sport.

I ignored him and leapt, rolling away from the scaffold.

I tried to get to my feet, but roared out loud as iron fingers dug themselves into my brand. Kenver Kiet twisted his arm to keep me down.

"See here, *mincher*: you're marked. There's no house nor tree nor stream on this island as will shelter a runaway. So do not fly."

I spat on the russet dust. Half of the crowd had spilled out of their seats to come and watch; breaths were drawn to see me defy the Cornishman. He looked up at the scaffolding.

"Seventy shilling for this one, Foulkes. Not a man other would give you a penny for him; run away twice now, he has, and that's a hanging he's earned."

The trader nodded, and Kiet brought his face close to mine. Blood seeped from my brand.

"I have named you 'Mincher', which is to say that you are a truant. If you flee me, the law gives me your life, your guts, your limbs; and that's the kind of man I like to buy for Lord Montalbion's plantation."

"Plantation?"

"Did you think you'd be doing soft labour in a Port Royal house? I'd not have a runaway so close to a ship home. No – you're for Alexandria, which is our lord's estate in Portland parish. And then you'll know what it is to labour like a Cornishman. I reckon I'll break you, Mincher."

There was little delay before we left. Kenver Kiet made his mark on my bill of sale while I waited with Osca, the Irish lad. His spirits had begun to rise once he saw that I was to come with him. For myself, I'd rather have been alone.

"There'll be food, so there will," he whispered to me. "Food and no work on the Sunday."

"Right you are," I said.

Kiet finished his dealings, touched his forehead mockingly at Coyle, and strode past us. I knew it was a trick to make us fall behind and earn a beating, so I tugged Osca along with me as the overseer made for a gate in the town wall, overshadowed by the bulk of Fort Rupert.

At the gate, four blackamoor slaves awaited us, squatting next to a pile of laden sacks. They wore iron cuffs on their ankles and wrists. The two pikemen who guarded the gate greeted Kiet with nods, raising their crossed weapons to let us pass.

A slender spit of land girdled the bay, long sunburned miles we had to cross before reaching the mainland. The path wound its way between patches of dull spiky plants; from time to time, we were shaded by trees with long arrowhead leaves and shrivelled fruits.

Twice, we had to ford sea-channels that split the causeway. The tide was low, but the current was strong enough to make me stumble.

Kiet, who was walking at the rear, laughed.

"Most men would take a sloop from Port Royal; but I'd rather save His Lordship's coin and let you walk the length of these here Palisadoes. Move lively, Mincher."

At first, my ankle wobbled painfully, twisted by the jump; but before we had reached the mainland I was walking well, my body joyful at the chance to stretch out and breathe the uncorrupted sea air. The sun warmed my branded shoulder. Osca trudged along next to me, his eyes lowered as if he already bore a yoke.

As we walked, I thought of what lay ahead. I could mimic any man alive, which might be enough to get me close to Montalbion's chamber; but I did not wish to think about what I might do after that.

A vast cloud of clotted-cream butterflies swept through us, swinging in the flighty breeze. A little while later, Kiet let the blackamoors sing softly, a slow melody that rose from their footbeats and fell back to earth. Though the music was mournful, the sense of it was not: it was a marching song that hymned the ground, praying for a swift journey and warm food at its end. We all settled into a patient march.

The slaves quit their singing when we left the land-spit. It was well past noon now, and the air was doughy. Osca and I were sweating more heavily, big sticky globs that clung to our faces and arms like a second skin.

Ahead of us, the mountains became clearer: steeply sloping, forested, ridge upon ridge far into the distance. To our left was the bay, and I could make out half a dozen boats pulled up on a beach, an hour or more's walk from us. In the other direction, the road followed the coast for a while before curving towards a pass.

Kiet had seen me looking at it.

"Will Lord Montalbion come to the plantation soon?" I asked him. "Only I have heard he is a great man—"

"He may not come to Alexandria at all, not that it's any business of yours," he replied. "Our task is to tend to

His Lordship's lands, not lick his boots. Now quit your babbling: there's a hard climb ahead."

We stopped for a meal of cold red beans, fruits that tasted of bark, and two boiled eggs apiece. The food sat heavily in my stomach.

Then we were off again.

Kiet led us through fields of long grass shadowed by purple-flowering trees. Magpies swooped past us, crying *Kreeeatt!*

The trail led into a forest. Ghostly fronds barred the light. Bulbous yellow fruit loomed and fell, bursting on the root-knotted earth.

Distant bird-shrieks and howls haunted the air. Once, a lizard as big as a dog scuttled across our path. Osca and I closed up on Kiet until he threatened us with his lash; but still we kept near to him. The path led upwards, and the air grew mercifully cooler.

After a second halt for water and rest, the forest began to open out so that we could see patches of sky. Wild laughter rang out ahead, and I saw children leaping through the high branches, shrieking and chattering. Kiet and the Africans scattered to the sides of the path, sheltering under the trees. The children swung closer to where Osca and I stood looking up in wonder.

The canopy high above us filled with the chatterers, black against the brightening sky, and fruit began to spatter on the path around us. One of the slaves called out, "*Daabi*! Move. You!"

Something foul struck me on the shoulder, and then a larger lump hit Osca on his upturned face. I bundled him off the path and into the lee of a twisted tree. Wiping ourselves, we watched as a torrent of shit spattered the ground.

"Monkeys!" laughed Kiet, enjoying our disgrace. The African who had warned us smiled. Osca sniffed, his pride hurt. To tell true, the apes' fruity leavings were not so bad as a man's or a dog's. Though I did not try to persuade Osca of that as he wiped his face on his shirt.

At last, the monkeys swung away, and we took to the path again.

"Those there demons have been shot at by too many a white man," grunted Kiet. "They know how to deal with the God-damned English now."

"Master Kiet, are you not English yourself?" I asked, confused. The overseer drew a fat-bladed knife from a pouch at his back and pointed the tip at me.

"Cornwall is not part of that *sowznac* country, d'you see?" he hissed.

"Yes, master," I said.

We walked long into the evening. Kenver Kiet and the Africans showed little tiredness. It was only when Osca stumbled over a tree root that the overseer called a halt.

The slaves took out a bundle of canvas sheets – patched and stained pieces of sail – and threw one to each of us. Though their ankles and wrists were cuffed, they looked down on us as they made themselves beds on a mossy slope. Osca and I looked around uncertainly for a safe place to sleep.

"There's poisonous frogs here, Mincher," said Kiet unpleasantly, "and serpents, and wild hogs that have a taste for the flesh of man. If suchlike are nearby, there's no bed that's safe. Put your head down and sleep; I'll not permit you to hold us back tomorrow for lack of rest."

We laid down the sheets and tried to find a flat stretch of earth. The night grew swiftly cold, and the canvas was too stiff to wrap around us; I caught my breath each time the hard cloth brushed my still-seeping brand.

Osca's fearful breath kept me awake long into the night. Birds and beasts hooted and rustled, mocking us.

In the morning I was sore-limbed and starved of sleep. The trail narrowed as it wound through trees, scrambled over rocky ridges, forded streams; somehow, the slaves managed to stay on their feet and keep hold of their loads. Each time we left the forest, Osca's spirits rose. He picked leaves, sniffed bark, plunged his fingertips into the sullen mud, as if this heathen island were his home.

Towards noon, the way grew steeper. We struggled for footholds in the shifting soil as we passed through groves of tall grass, which shot up to twice the height of a man. Beyond the path, there was no room to move: all was clogged with trailing roots, dense ferns and boulders. My burned shoulder called out for rest, but I had to walk on, each step tugging at the wound.

When we stopped to eat, Kiet kept the slaves apart from us. I caught their eyes once or twice, but one of the blackamoors twitched his head, to warn me against speaking to them. We were given old dammy-cake: a gluey, leathery dumpling.

Late in the afternoon of the second day, we entered a strange misty woodland. The trees were stunted and mossy, overgrown with creepers that hung down across the path. I nearly stood in a patch of vivid purple mushrooms; as I shied away, I heard a man whistling sadly, a tune that went *High-low-didididi ... High-low-didididi.*

Then another, across the valley behind us: *High-low-didididi.*

"Piskies," said Kiet, pushing me onwards. "Sleep alone on this slope, they'll have your soul."

Osca crossed himself; I looked up into the branches to see if in truth a bird had made the sound, but there was no sign of one. Again the whistle came.

We made camp as dusk fell. Kiet had seen a column of ants scurrying for cover, and ordered us to prepare for rain. We gathered fallen branches to make a frame, and laid the blackamoors' canvas across it. The Cornishman made a fire and boiled up a mess of cassava porridge, which was flavoursome enough, even if it did pass speedily through my guts.

Asking permission, I went a little further up the path until I found a break in the trees. I could see far out into the valley we'd been climbing: all the way to the sea, where Port Royal's lights winked faintly. Jamaica's mountains enclosed me on the other sides, lush and beautiful in the dimming day, and the sea breeze calmed my thoughts. I thought to myself that, mission or no mission, I could find my way back to the port if I had to. I could survive.

The rain came suddenly, heavy and warm, and I ran back for shelter. It soaked the loose earth and ran in rills through our little open tent; at first, I squatted to keep my breeches dry, but in the end I lay in the mud and fell asleep like the others.

In my dreams I was still walking through the mountains. I came across a grove of bushes bearing dark red berries. Amidst them was a white house, and a girl painting a picture. Thunder barrelled down from the mountaintops. She turned and gave me that taunting smile.

Emilia de Corvis.

On the third day out of Port Royal, we stumbled for hours through a clammy fog until we reached an uphill trail. Ahead of us, the dusk air began to *shushush*, a whisper that became louder and louder until the trees gave out and we were surrounded by fields: thousands of crowded plants, taller than a man, their bladelike leaves rubbing against each other in the wind.

Sugarcane.

An African song came faintly through the gloom. The four slaves joined in, low-voiced.

"Alexandria," said Kenver Kiet. "Home, workdom, grave."

CHAPTER SEVEN

Alexandria

Third and fourth days of April

The cane rows shushed and swayed across Alexandria's irregular hillsides, ushering us through the lower fields. The path, overshadowed by forests, came to a split. Kiet let the blackamoors walk on, and led Osca and me to the bondsmen's camp. Two-score white men were lying in hammocks, arranged around a fire. A man stooped and blew roughly on the embers.

"Moses Severill," said Kiet, "this here is Osca. Find him a place to sleep. Mincher, you go get some firewood. I'll teach you what real labour is. And if you go near the black-amoors' polincks, I'll make a hole in your skull."

Severill stood back up. He was perhaps ten years older than me, twitchy and heron-backed. He nodded to Osca, who followed him into the camp.

"Now, Mincher," said Kiet. I judged he was about ready to strike me, so I headed off into the tangled woodland and waited for him to leave.

I sat on a tree stump to take off my boots, but my feet were too swollen after the long march from Port Royal. I tugged in vain for a while before giving up.

Moses Severill, who'd come after me and offered to forage in my stead, appeared with a double armful of sticks. I went to help him lay the fire. We knelt and blew, and soon the wood was sputtering and smoking wetly.

"Is there no better wood?" I whispered.

"It gives off fumes that keep the blood-gnats away," he answered in a low voice, peering into the fire to be sure it had caught. Ember-light shadowed his downturned lips. Moses' skin was young and unwrinkled, but his eyes were weary and his hair thin and patchy.

I clambered awkwardly into my hammock. It swung, making the tree sway. Another man, whose bed was slung from the same tree, grumbled under his blanket. Moses lay in his berth, his head not far from mine, both of us facing the mountain.

Collingwood had said that Montalbion would be there within weeks. When I made the attempt, I'd need to go back that way.

"Sleep now, fellow," breathed Moses. "Work begins before the dawn."

I closed my eyes. The scented fumes trickled into my chest.

Scratch. Tap-tap. Scratch.

Something cold and hard crawled under my neck and began to wriggle down my spine. Swaddled by the blanket, I struggled to free my hands. The bug buzzed away from my fingers. I caught its grape-sized body and crushed it inside the cloth, then sat up and flung the twitching carcass into the dying fire.

Tap-tap. Scratch. Scratch. I sat up carefully and swung my feet out of the rope-bed. The sound came from another part of the plantation, beyond the stinking piss-ditch that bounded our camp. I wrapped the blanket around me and took a step towards the noise. Moses' scarred forearm flicked out of his hammock. He took hold of my wrist and pulled me close.

"The blackies plant their crops," he whispered.

"But … in the night?"

"It's said such heathens have no souls, fellow, so they need no Sunday rest. And the hours of light belong to the masters here. Still, the blackamoors must eat, so they must grow their food at night. But it's a whipping if you go into their polincks."

Fifty paces away, the sounds of pick and hoe had died away. Faintly, a woman hummed, slapping the earth as each line of her song ended. I breathed out heavily.

"The days are slow if you do not sleep. Better to dream of your woman, if you have one to go back to."

I pried off Moses' fingers and got back into the hammock.

I did not dream.

Kiet woke us in darkness. My clothes were still damp from the journey through the mountains. We followed him to a little brick storehouse, where a grumpy Walloon bondsman was doling a porridgy mess into hollowed gourds. Under his breath he cursed each of us in French. It was my mother's language, but I gave no sign that I understood him.

We squatted to eat. The porridge was unsalted, lumpy with chunks of a white fruit that smelled of birch-bark but tasted as fresh as dew.

"Coconut," said Moses, watching me chew it cautiously.

Kenver Kiet came and stood over me.

"Day dawns and sugar wastes, Moses Severill. You're not a freedman for a few weeks yet, and your hours and body are mine. Quit dreaming of your ten acres, and get you a-boiling."

He purposely sputtered "freedman" over our food, marking the porridge with tobacco-brown freckles. I hesitated for a moment, then dug my spoon in, hungry enough to eat another man's spit.

Kiet struck me lightly across the crown with the flat of his hand. I stayed down, lowering my gaze.

"You've signed your name to work, Mincher, and work there is, enough even for a man of your size. Now, if you intend to dally at your food, I'll be obliged to take it for myself," he said, snatching the gourd from me. "Severill, take him along."

I got up and followed Moses through the canefield. The flopping leaves arched above our heads, filling the air with their whispered song. Far off, blades thudded into wood, and African voices rose in chant.

If I tripped or slowed, Kiet was at my back to poke me forward. He was quiet, listening to the blackamoors' work-song.

Grrrrummm. Grrrrummm.

A deep grinding rumble began. The canefield shushed, and Moses' elbows shook.

Grrrrummm. Grrrrummm.

The roof of leaves above us parted, and the path widened into a clearing, quarried out of the slope. Four brick buildings surrounded a hard-packed stretch of earth. In the middle was a single wooden post.

Grrrrummm. Grrrrummm. Grrrrummm. Grrrrummm.

The rumble came from the far building. Through its open arches, I caught glimpses of movement.

The other servants walking ahead of us had stopped in the yard, waiting for Kiet. He stood facing us, tugging at his damp shirtfront, and gave the men their tasks. Osca was taken off for fieldwork by a wiry foreman named Pelton. I gave the lad a cheery nod to bolster his spirits, as Kiet went on: "First boiler. Crushing-clerk. Third boiler. Striker—"

A hiss bubbled up from the midst of the servant-gang.

"I say Severill shall strike today, hear you that?" said Kiet loudly, unfrowning. Moses' shoulders slumped.

The man next to me whispered, "Kiet cannot bear that Moses will soon be free – striking is the hardest post, and the most punished."

Kiet went on with his task-naming. At last he came to me.

"Mincher," he said, raising an eyebrow. His left thumb stroked the butt of his whip. "Mincher shall—"

"Need one more mill-house runner," whispered Moses loudly. Kiet narrowed his eyes, but could not tell who had spoken. Slowly, as if the idea was dawning on him freshly, he turned and looked at the line of men waiting with their sugarcane.

"We are short a mill-house runner today, Mincher," said the Cornishman. He clapped his hands, and the servants walked swiftly to their posts. "Let Colquhoun here show you the duty. And mark you – spill not a drop."

He strode away towards the mill-house, slapping the post as he passed it.

Colquhoun was a toadish fellow. He smiled with only one corner of his sagging mouth, showing the blackness of his teeth; but the raw-knuckled hand he laid on my arm was friendly, and his voice was deep and singer-sweet.

"Moses done you safe there, my lad," he said, his London dockman's accent half-drowned in the wet corner of his mouth. "No danger in mill-house running 'less you spill."

Colquhoun pulled me into the mill. Two hulking engines, bigger than silk-looms, were being worked by a pair of blackamoors, sweating despite the early morning chill.

Underneath each engine, a stream of juice spattered into a funnel. Colquhoun showed me how to collect it with a barrow.

"Go now!" he hissed. Sweat blurring my sight, I trotted through the yard towards Moses, who was waiting at the open door of the boiling-house.

"In here, fellow. Quickly!"

I reached the doorway and gently eased the barrow over the raised threshold. Half of the building was taken up by a long firepit. Above it were hung five copper kettles, each stirred by a different white servant. At the end of the row of kettles stood a cistern, into which a giant blackamoor was carefully dropping a sticky steaming mess. The slave's wrist-cuffs clanged together as he worked.

Moses showed me how to push my load up a short ramp and tilt it into the biggest kettle. The juice bubbled and spurted.

"The first kettle must fill quickly," said Moses roughly. I nodded and left, nearly bumping into Colquhoun with his own barrow.

Behind him, Kenver Kiet leaned against the post, watching.

The air grew hot and sticky, and I was soon gasping for breath. I learned to take my rest in the sugar-mill, leaning on the handles of the empty barrow while I waited for it to fill.

At noon we ate a stew of black beans in the shade of the sugar-mill. Kiet stood apart, chewing on a long stick of dried meat. His forehead and nose were flaked by the sun; my own skin was red and itchy.

Kiet ordered a stuttering Cumbrian servant to cut him a length of sugarcane. Spit flowed freely in my dry mouth as I watched the overseer crunch and suck on the woody stalk with his eyes half-closed, like a cat in a sunspot.

"Not for us, that cane," murmured Moses.

Noticing my gaze, Kiet frowned and rose to his feet.

"Work," he said, tossing Colquhoun his whip. "Mincher, with me."

He led me round the back of the curing-shed. Across a lush lawn stood a solid stone building.

"That's the distillery, Mincher, but no need for thanks," he said, opening the door to an outhouse. "I'll not be letting you loose with the rum."

The outhouse's walls were stacked with firewood. In a cage at the far end was a snarling, shadowy mass.

He prodded me forwards. Three barrel-chested mastiffs wrestled and snapped over chicken carcasses, throwing off a swirl of down-feathers.

"Give me your hand," demanded Kiet.

I hesitated.

"Give it," he repeated. I thought of Simona, and put my wrist in his damp palm. The Cornishman dragged me forward and thrust my hand through the bars of the cage.

I took in a sharp breath as the dogs quit fighting and rushed over, teeth bared. My fingers curled, but I could not pull away. The beasts slid to a halt, inches from my fist, and sniffed, their meaty breath hot on my skin, growling all the while.

Kiet clicked his tongue.

"You can run all you like now, Mincher; my boys here have your scent," he whispered, drawing my wrist slowly back out of the cage. "Two *sowznacs* tried to break their bonds last month; we found 'em on the mountainside before nightfall. Not the first to try it, and not the first to be buried out there; that's why that grass grows so green. Now get back to work."

I was still weary from the long march from Port Royal and quickly out of breath, wheeling the barrow across the unforgiving yard. Soon we were ahead of the boiling-house men, and Kiet had to make the grinding-slaves stop their work lest the juice spill on barren ground. He did not address them in English, but struck them with the coiled whip, crying "*Brik! Brik!*" in his native tongue.

The overseer went to inspect the boiling-house, and came out cursing the slowness of Moses and the others. He beckoned us over. "You better help them, Mincher, else flesh will flay."

Bright-faced in the heat, the boilers were urgently stirring, scouring and ladling. Kiet made Colquhoun dump two more barrows of sugar-juice in the biggest kettle, nearly overfilling it, then shoved me to the end of the line where Moses was stirring. Next to him, the giant blackamoor slave was ladling a lump of molasses from Moses' kettle into a clay pot.

Kiet set me to helping Moses to stir. We were both dripping with sweat. My eyes stung from the smoke and heat, and I took off my shirt to cool down, revealing the branded "R". The blackamoor glanced at it, then looked back at his work.

We leaned into our work. Kiet suddenly flicked his whip at Moses' heels, making him topple towards the scalding sugar. I grabbed his arms and threw my weight sideways, and we collapsed on the big slave. As we all fell, a strand of boiling sugar spilled onto his chest and outstretched arm.

The blackamoor yelled, clutching at his burning skin. It stank of fire-ruined pork. The ropy mess clung on, scalding his fingers. He scraped his arm on the dirt until the bare skin began to break away.

I rose to my knees, thinking to help the man, but Kiet pushed me out of the way. He drew his foot back, squinted, and carefully kicked the blackamoor under the chin, knocking him out cold.

I grabbed my shirt, folded it thrice and pulled away the scalding sugar.

The big blackamoor's skin tore, leaving a flayed mottle of flesh eighteen inches long. I dropped the hot bundle on the ground before it could burn through the cloth. Pink blisters were already birthing in my palms.

"Be fortunate were this *brat* fellow to live," muttered Kiet, looking at the man's injuries.

He tossed Colquhoun a set of keys. "Colquhoun, call for the blackies from the mill! Tell Zuasheba her man's hurt. And bring Mincher a shirt from the stores – he'll work a month of Sundays to pay for it, mark you.

"Mincher, you take Kata's place. Spill another drop and I'll bleed you, I swear it."

Moses wordlessly showed me how to handle the thick sugar. It was sticky, and heavy, and my shoulders burned with the effort. Behind me, the boiler-men worked on, afraid to let the sugar spoil. Moses went back to stirring, his eyes turned away from the fallen man.

African voices boomed in the courtyard as the blacka-moors got word of the wounding. One of the slave-women had heard the man cry out, and she came in before the mill-slaves.

"Kata!" she exclaimed. Darting forward, she unwrapped a scarf from around her head, then wiped it on the sweat of her own face and neck to make it salt-damp. She knelt next to him and gently covered up the snaking wound.

"There's thirty guineas of man-meat a-dying there," snapped Kiet. "Burned to hell by a pair of twenty-shilling *scadgans*."

If the kneeling woman understood his words, she gave no sign. She beckoned the mill-men. They squatted and lifted Kata up, careful not to touch his arm. The woman kept the binding in place as they carried him slowly out of the boiling-house.

Kiet went with them. In half an hour he returned, holding his coiled whip.

"Moses Severill," he said quietly, "a man must account for his damages. Finish the load, all of you, and damp the fires!"

Moses' ladle skittered along the kettle-rim.

Kiet had gathered all the servants in the yard.

Colquhoun stood next to me. As we watched Moses go towards Kiet, he whispered, "Stay put, lad. You can't help the poor bugger now."

Much as I pitied Moses, I'd not have risked Violet's freedom against his pain.

Meeting Kiet's stare, Moses slowly took off his shirt. Lacy scars tattooed him from chin to waist, some barely healed and others violet with age.

He went unbidden to the whipping-post and circled his hands around it, leaning forward until his forehead rested on the stained wood. Trying to tell myself that I had not brought this on him, I began to wheeze.

Kiet shook out the lash. The forest grew into the dense clouds. The breeze had stopped, and the cane had quit its rustling.

"Pickaninny, out!" shouted the overseer. He had spied a little African water-girl squatting at the edge of the field, scavenging for dropped food. Kiet glared at the slave-girl until she ran away through the sugarcane.

"A black-faced bloody heathen may not see a Christian man punished," muttered Colquhoun.

Kiet planted his feet firmly, and slowly twisted his body round, flicking the whip again. We shuffled back, making the ring bigger. He stamped, and Moses flinched; but there was no blow. Moses began to breathe faster, arching his back.

"Could have been any of you men that Severill burned," said Kenver Kiet mildly. "Could have been Colquhoun here …"

"Lash him!" shouted Colquhoun.

"Lash him!" cried another servant, and then another. Moses glanced round at us, forgetting to brace himself. Kiet scythed towards the whipping-post, his feet grinding in the dirt. The lash hissed.

Cured leather burst flesh.

Moses shrieked and lost his grip. His head struck dully on the post, and he began to collapse. Kiet swiftly stepped forward and dragged him upright. Again Moses' knees buckled, and he let out a smaller cry as blood bubbled up along the crack in his skin.

"Come here, Mincher," said Kiet, skittering the bloody tip of the whip over the earth towards me. "You'll keep him stood."

I hesitated.

"Do as bid, fellow, else we'll all suffer," said Colquhoun out loud. "Kenver Kiet is for obeying."

"That he is, *sowznac*. He's for obeying," replied Kiet, letting go of Moses.

As I walked slowly over, Moses opened his eyes and shook his head a tiny fraction, begging me not to fight. Kiet clamped my hands over the stricken man's fingers, showing that I should not let him fall again. I could hardly make myself look as he took up the same stance again; it was as if I faced the scourge myself.

This time the lash struck Moses' thighs. He shouted and fell forward again, his breeches too worn out to protect him. As I gripped his armpits to keep him on his feet, I pressed against the edge of his first wound. He cried out and struck at me. I let the weak blow glance off my chest, seized his hands and pulled him back up again.

All around us, men who had once been free stared dumbly at the bleeding man. Though we were more than twenty to one, no one thought to strike at the overseer. Where could he run? Through miles of forest, pursued by Kiet's mastiffs and the parish militia? To arrive in Port Royal as a bond-breaker and runaway, there to be whipped, or hanged, or mutilated for sedition? Perhaps I might have tried it once, but not with Violet and Simona held in the Tower.

Kiet lashed underhand, a vicious stroke that opened flesh from lower back to ribs, and all along Moses' right arm. The knotted tail came last, curling over my hand and thumping down on my wrist. Now it was my turn to cry out, my voice wild above Moses' moaning. I let go of him so I could grasp my bruised flesh, but Kiet thumped me with the whipstock.

"You did your best for that blackie, Mincher; there's hope for you yet. Else it would be you in Master Severill's place here. Now keep that grip!"

I squeezed my eyes and yelled silently at the darkening skies. But I thought of Violet and obeyed, dragging Moses up, jamming my hands over his. I felt the lukewarm blow of rainwater on my head. Kiet came closer, pushed me back towards the other men and cupped his hand around Moses' neck.

"Ask to be sold, Moses Severill," he murmured, like a gambler asking for a loan.

"Go to Hell, Kenver Kiet," breathed Moses.

"Lash him!" yelled Colquhoun. This time, he was the only one to call out.

The Cornishman took four steps away and brought the whip down overhand, cutting straight through the wounds he'd already made.

Moses screamed. This time he did not fall, but pressed himself against the post, mashing his face into the splintering wood. Blood spurted onto the earth. Kiet lashed the dirt to dry his whip, then coiled it up and came to Moses' side again.

"Ask to be sold, fellow, else there'll be more of the same for you," he whispered, his mouth barely moving.

"No," Moses said. "Six weeks, Master Kiet, and I'll be free."

"We'll see," said Kiet, and those were the last words he spoke to Moses Severill. He hit him in the head, four, five, seven times; and when Moses fell he carried on beating him until the ground was soaked with blood.

"Put him in the earth," he ordered Colquhoun. "The rest of you, follow me back to camp."

Colquhoun obeyed. Ignoring Kiet's order, I went to help him.

The side of Moses' head had been staved in. His left eye was closed, and his right stared glassily at the sky. Rain bounced off his face.

We each took hold of an arm and lifted him. His wrists were slick with blood, and we had to grip them tightly. His feet dragged through the stained earth.

We took the body to the patch of lush grass beside the distillery. I folded Moses' arms over his chest while Colquhoun found us a pair of shovels. The mastiffs whined and scratched at the wall of the outhouse as we dug.

By the time we finished the hole, the rain had washed Moses' face. Naked splinters of bone poked out through his shattered temple. I held his head carefully until we had laid him in the earth, then closed the staring eye.

Kiet was squatting next to the outhouse, murmuring to his dogs. His face shone against the deep ocean green of the forest. "You'll go to the canefield tomorrow, Mincher. Bend your back to true labour, and you'll see why a blackamoor is worth twice a white servant. Or end like Severill there."

CHAPTER EIGHT

The Great House

From the fifth day to the ninth day of April

It was no accident that Kenver Kiet had chosen my first day to destroy Moses: he was trying to break my runaway spirit. He put me in the Great Gang, planting sugarcane with the slaves and the stronger, slower indentured men like Osca. Though I was long-limbed, I was less powerful than the others in the gang, and knew I would struggle with the work.

It was brutal labour. Last season's roots and crop-rot tangled our blades. We had to cut wide holes, delve down a shin's length, then fill the hole again a shin's length, ready for the slave-women to plant the stripling canes. Half a pace to the right, dig, pull at roots, dig, pile the waste neatly; move half a pace to the right and dig again. The cheap new shirt Colquhoun had brought me was ruined before nightfall.

All the while, the stoatlike foreman Pelton paced up and down, his eyes on the ragged row of men. Whoever was slowest drew the lash; whoever moved fast but dug too shallow, drew the lash; and so we worked as hard and true as we could, hearts pounding, backs humped with ache.

I looked across at Osca from time to time, always giving him a little jaunty nod, to show him that we should not be troubled by the labours. The lad had steel: his chin stayed up all through the weary day. I resolved to be like him until my chance came to strike.

I ate but half my dinner. I wrapped a baked yam and a piece of smoked fish in a large leaf and hid them under my blanket.

Deep in the night, the rains stopped. Blood-gnats whined busily around us, planting itchy kisses on my ankles and wrists. I looked around to make sure no other man was awake; tipped myself out of the hammock and made for the piss-ditch, keeping in the shadows lest a foreman should find me. I wanted to see if the giant blackamoor still lived, for I bore a guilt over him now.

The slaves' camp, forbidden to white servants, was on the other side of the plantation. I thought the fields might be guarded, so I pushed through the clinging forest to get there. There were rows of little huts, the roofs barely neck-high, the plots so small that I saw pairs of feet half-sticking out. Between the huts were furrowed food patches, deco-rated with shards of fruit-husk, feathers, mouse skulls.

No stockade was needed to keep these slaves in their camp: Kiet's dogs had their scent, too.

As I crept along the row of huts, I heard a shivery rasping noise: a man's breath, rough with pain and exhaustion. It wove in and out of a woman's low chanting. I reached the far end of the encampment and saw her squatting on the tacky earth, half-in and half-out of the last hut.

I hissed, not wanting to startle her by coming too close. Still chanting, she turned on her heels to see who came.

She took me for a free man at first, and dipped her gaze; but then the smell of me reached her, and she frowned.

I knew her face. She'd been the one who'd cried out when she came to the boiling-house: Zuasheba, the burned slave's woman. "Kata?" I asked, pointing to the places on my chest and arm where the sugar-rope had burned him. I showed her the rosy scald on my own palms.

Still chanting softly, she made her hand into a claw and slowly mimed ripping her own skin; rolled her eyes high into her skull. I unwrapped the fish and yam, and laid the leaf on the ground.

Alone among the huts, the ground next to this one was barely scratched. Nothing had been planted. I pointed, made the sign of digging. She clenched her teeth, as if I were another burden to her like the dying man; taking the food, she swivelled again on her heels and ducked inside the hut.

Without taking her head back out, she dropped some things on the ground and took up her chanting again. A broken-off hoe. Two little gourds, with different seeds in them. I began to work.

Tap-tap. Scratch. Tap-tap.

Tired though I was, tormented by the blood-gnats' bites, it was sweet to feel the hoe cutting into earth, an inch at a time. It was more than an hour's working before I could sow the patch. I pressed the seeds down and covered them over gently, the grainy soil rubbing on my blistered palm. When it was done, I quietly got up and left. The woman did not come out.

*

I had never been so dog-tired in my life. I found it hard to find sleep: my limbs trembled and my mind filled with the sounds of spade, hole, rain, spade, pounding away like a dozen looms. Then came fitful dreams of London, of Ty cursing me. Then Simona, puking in a cramped and tossing mule-deck.

Afterwards I lay awake, listening to my own faintly wheezing breath, and thought of how slight a thing it was to be alive. A musket ball, a strand of burning sugar, a master's lash: that was all it took to separate a man from his health, his hope, his very thoughts.

Rains came for the next two nights. We slept, walked, shivered in the same soaking clothes until labour grudgingly warmed us.

I took food to Kata's woman every night. He did not die, as I'd expected. His breath came steadier and stronger each time I visited, and I'd forget my hunger for a moment.

We made slow progress on the canefield. The earth became too soaked and heavy for any but the strongest blackamoors to shift, and so on the fourth day Kiet took me and the rest of the white men away from the planting-gang.

"Scudding is all you're fit for," he said, leading us past the mill and up towards the great house. The steep track had been topped with a layer of broken stones so that carts could pass in the wet weather, and it was a sweet relief to walk on steady ground.

"What's a *scudding*?" whispered Osca, and another man laughed at him. Not so shy now, the Irish lad knitted his brow and shook a pink-knuckled fist. The fellow who'd mocked him jerked his head away. There'd be no fighting so close to Kiet and his lash.

As we reached the crest, a hard, pale line began to form in the mists beyond the shushing sugar-leaves. The great house took shape, and I remembered who I was.

I am Calumny Spinks, I thought. *I must kill the man who rules this plantation. And then I must live. I must outrun Kiet's dogs, and live.*

Twenty paces off the path was a chest-deep pit. Two reeking mounds stood within it: the larger one of horse and mule shit, lumpy and steaming; the smaller one was mouldy and pockmarked by rain. We were still almost a hundred yards from the mansion. If I wanted to take Montalbion's life, I'd need to get inside it.

Kiet pointed to an untidy pile of barrows and shovels in the long grass. "This here field is near-barren, see? Two men to a barrow, one part man-dung to three parts horse. And you'll start at the far end."

Rain dripped from his thrusting chin.

"Mincher, if you stare at me any longer I'll crack your shell," said the overseer, pleasantly.

Which was to say: Scramble down into the shite-hole. Shovel deep into the horse dung. Swing full-armed up and into a barrow, held teetering on the pit's rim. Shovel, shovel; and then push, lemon-faced, into the man-shit, a muddy soup that clings heavily to your blade. Swing again – not too fast, lest it spatter in your eyes – and let it slide into the barrow. Spit, retch, and shovel again. First barrow filled, second …

I took a brief rest after the sixth barrow, and then the first man was back from the field, half-running, his shirt split redly by Kiet's lash.

Was this spadeful from Montalbion's arse? This one? Some patches were richer, filled with unchewed fruit-skins; but in the end, dirt melts with dirt, and we all go down to earth in the same foul pile.

Kiet kept me in the pit until I had carved a great hole in the horse-dung. I had given up on keeping my boots out of the shit, and stood ankle-deep in it, spattered head to toe.

The overseer himself was filthy from running up and down the field to drive on the men, and from standing too close to the barrow when I was shovelling, but he wore his stains proudly.

"Mincher, get you into the fields and spread!" he called out, when the rain had begun to fall more lightly. Perhaps two hours had passed. "You've had enough resting in the pit!"

He roared with laughter. Osca joined in, whinnying joyfully until Kiet poked him savagely in the belly with his lash. He shoved the boy over the rim, so that he landed arm-first in the horse-crud. Now the other men joined in the laughter, and Osca slipped further into the pit as he struggled to get up.

Seeing Kiet begin to unfurl his lash, I shouted in Irish, "*Shasiv, Osca! Shasiv!*"

Stand, Osca! Stand! I'd heard Violet urge Simona with that word enough times.

Osca wriggled around and dug his lumpen fingers into the pit's wall to pull himself to his feet. He looked up in time to catch the shovel that Kiet had thrown to him, and began to dig.

The field was two hundred paces broad and four times as long, and it stopped fifty paces or so from the great house. That first day, we spread the dung on the lower slope of the canefield, furthest from the house, but it was clear that the lord of the manor was still away. There were but two sentries, pacing idly up and down, and most shutters were closed against the driving rain. Only the lowest windows were lit.

By my reckoning it was now the eighth of April. Collingwood had given me until the end of June to kill Montalbion, and there was still no sign of him.

Stench aside, the scudding was not such bad work. Kiet made Colquhoun foreman and brought him up to the field to watch us. Colquhoun was weaker than the overseer, so we could slow our running to an amble, loiter at the pit rim to speak a word or two with the digger, watch the clouds boil and burst on the far hills. Soon, we were spreading dung closer to the house. We could hear the sentries burbling to each other.

I imagined what lay within that great house. Food, women, guns, secrets: all the beautiful pieces of a free man's life. Such thoughts were of little comfort; if I could not get inside the mansion, I would have to take some desperate action against Montalbion – to waylay him as he rode to Alexandria – which would likely mean my own death.

Being so near to my goal kindled my will. I asked Colquhoun how I might become a house-servant, but he only laughed grimly and told me that it was not a fate to be wished for; and that Kiet would never permit it, not with the master coming home so soon.

"So soon?" I asked. He clammed up, but I took hope. If I could not serve in the house, there might be other ways to enter the mansion.

Twice a day, a man would be sent to fetch drinking water from the well on the far side of the house. I was impatient for my turn, but Colquhoun seemed to smell my need, and always sent Osca or one of the other farm boys instead.

I finally got my chance that Saturday. It was around noon, and Osca was waiting for his next barrowload. The heat was worsened by the nipping of the blood-gnats in the steamy air; he grew dizzy and fell over.

"Water!" snapped the foreman. I did not wait for him to name a man to fetch it, but lifted the bucket and ran for the great house.

Three dozen windows stared gloomily at me, dark under the overhanging balconies that ribbed the mansion. Anyone who might think to take it by force would first have to cross a wide patch of bare oxblood earth that made a perfect killing-ground. From where we'd stood in the fields, the house's white frontage had seemed to gleam; but in truth the paintwork was peeling, and the plaster had flaked off the stone blocks in many places. The lowest windows were iron-barred, and flanked by gun-slits. I had slowed to a trot, trying to see which way I should circle the house. The militiaman on the highest balcony whistled and waved me around to my right. His eyes were on the forest beyond the sugarfields, not on me.

The well was at the rear of the house, shaded by a pair of listless trees. Beyond it was a row of low barrack-houses, in front of which two soldiers sat at a small table, one playing at cards and the other sewing. A sentry tramped along a balcony which reached round three sides of the house. None of them had seen me, so I ran quickly to the back door, the trees hiding me from the barracks.

As I drew close, cooking smells attacked the air: onions, pig-broth and a gamey scent. I'd grown used to hunger, but my belly tightened against this fresh assault.

"Save that piece for the men, Gallo," ordered a woman in a singsong voice. I crept up to the kitchen window and peered in. A white cook and two blackamoor women were at work on a vast pile of food. One plucked her way through a heap of bright-feathered birds; the second chopped up herbs; and the cook, her face bright with the heat, was turning spitted suckling pigs over a slow fire.

I backed away and tried the door handle, but it was locked. If I stayed longer, Colquhoun would grow suspicious; and besides, Osca needed water. At least I knew I could get close to the house now. Calling to the sentry not to shoot, I strode to the well and bent my back to the task.

The turning-handle was rusty, making it slow work to raise the bucket. By the time I got back to Osca, he was half-recovered. Colquhoun slapped me for slowness. It had not taken him long to become like Kiet.

CHAPTER NINE

Red Man

The first nineteen days of May

Kiet appeared at the head of a line of blackamoors. The scudding was long since done, and I was running the barrow again. Kata had returned to his post in the boiling-house.

"I'm bound for Port Royal, Mincher," said the Cornishman, brandishing his coiled whip. "And when I'm back, I shall acquaint you more with Kalken, which is the name of this here lash."

He led the slaves off down the track. It was such a large party that I was sure Montalbion would be coming back with them.

With Kiet gone, the plantation was quiet. It was Sunday, and when our work was done at midday, I could hear the distant thud of spade on moist earth. The air was taut, like the breath drawn before a scream.

"Going to hammock, Master Colquhoun," I called out politely, squinting as I stared into the sun's glare.

Colquhoun shrugged and flicked his head.

I did not go to the camp, but pushed on between the high rows of uncropped cane, trudging down the long valley of Alexandria. I felt the weight of each stem, the backbreaking labour that had planted it, the strength it would need to cut and stack and carry it across the cloying ground to the mill.

I had a baked gourd to give to Kata's woman, but the slaves' camp was empty apart from Kata, who was sitting next to his hut, letting the sun bathe his scarred flesh.

I hesitated. He jerked his head back, and I went to give him the gourd. He broke it in half and patted the earth. I squatted next to him, and we ate in silence, slowly, savouring the sweet burned flesh.

He seemed to be listening to the forest.

When we'd finished, he reached over and tugged at my sleeve, motioning that I should show him my shoulder. Remembering that he'd seen my brand in the boiling-house, I pulled open my shirt and showed him the "R". He reached out, wincing as his burned skin pulled, and touched a rough fingertip to the scar. It no longer hurt.

Something crackled in the forest, and Kata's eyes widened. He gestured urgently, bidding me to go into his little hut. I hid inside and crouched by the entrance, looking out.

Soon after, a line of blackamoors came silently into the slave camp. Their leader was a powerfully built man holding a matchet. He had a bandolier across his chest and wore ragged breeches, and his muscled calves were bare. Several of his followers wore rusty slave-cuffs with the chains snapped off. Four of them carried muskets, though I only saw two powder-horns between them.

Runaways.

"Eh, Quamin," whispered Kata. The leader came close and murmured a question, revealing teeth that had been sharpened to points. I held my breath. Kata touched his chest, showing where his flesh was healing.

A short, lithe blackamoor, who carried a bow instead of a gun, touched his leader on the shoulder, gesturing urgently towards the canefield. Quamin, though, had seen a few crumbs of yam lying on the leaf next to Kata. He asked another question, and Kata gave him a quick answer. The runaway nodded and rose to his feet, and within moments all eight of his party had left the camp.

Listening intently, Kata held up a finger. We waited for a long minute, and then he crooked the finger. I joined him outside again.

"Who are they, Kata?" I asked.

"No," he said.

"Do you understand me?"

"Yes."

"Who are they? Do they live in the forest?"

"No," he said. "No go. Dog."

Dog or no dog, I thought, *those fellows know a way out of here*.

I gave Kata a little nod of thanks, and headed towards the bondsmen's camp. As soon as I was out of sight, I doubled back around and followed the runaways towards the lower canefield.

The field was below the crest, hidden from the great house, but still I was cautious. We were forbidden to go beyond our camp, the field we worked on, and the millyard. More than one man had been whipped merely for speaking to the Africans.

I stopped and listened for a while to the faint thrumming of the slaves' work, far away, at the plantation's edge; then I carried on, swimming through a whispering sea of cane. There was no sign of the runaways.

By the time I found the work-gang, I was red-faced with heat, and I'd taken off my shirt to keep from soaking it with sweat. Beyond a field of uncropped cane, slave-men dug, and women planted in the raw, steaming earth. The foreman Pelton sat half-asleep with a small winesack on his lap.

I crossed through a line of tough shrubs with scarlet, saw-toothed leaves, and hid within the crops, watching the slaves. Some of the men were slipping into the nearby forest, one by one. They picked up leaf-bound bundles as they left the field. Each time one disappeared, one of Quamin's runaways replaced him, so that there was always the same number of male blackamoors at work. Pelton, who was side-on to me, would half-open his eyes every so often, mouth a headcount to himself, and let his chin slump back to his chest.

Stronger in the arms and shoulders than the field-slaves, the runaways would pretend to work each time the foreman looked up, and then sidle over to whisper to the slave-women as they planted the canelings.

Three more men went into the jungle; three came out. These last were slaves, their eyes cast down, their shoulders sloping. They seemed weak compared to the runaways, who were so intent on the women that I knew them to be their lovers. Scent and heat and alertness drew them together, even though they did not move close enough to touch – for to do so was to draw a beating from the foreman.

Quamin began to work next to Kata's woman, Zuasheba. He questioned her in a voice too low for Pelton to hear. She nodded, twice.

He dipped into his pocket for a battered silver pocket-watch, hiding it from Pelton with his body. Hissing through his nose, he called off his two companions, and they strode casually to the jungle's edge, whispering a word to the final three Africans who took their places back. I saw these men tuck strips of dried meat into their hole-ridden boots before coming back to work in the field. The runaways were helping the plantation-slaves.

I stayed to watch. After a while, Pelton rose to his feet as if he had not so much as closed his eyes. He rang a hand-bell and watched with his whip at the ready as the slaves came to eat their cold porridge.

My mind buzzed. I had thought of the forest's edge as a prison wall; but now I had seen free men walk in, claim their women under the noses of the foreman, and walk out again. Men who hunted their own meat; men who had broken their chains.

So there was a path into the forest. I wondered at first why the slaves did not simply run off, but I knew the answer. Any escaped slave would be hunted right across the island by Kiet and his mastiffs. It was the same for me – but these runaways seemed without fear. Could they offer me a way out, if I did kill Montalbion?

I made my way quietly after them. The trees arched high above me, their branches melting into each other to deny the light. Weakened by lack of food, weaponless and ignorant, I felt my own smallness.

I am Calumny Spinks, I thought to myself. *I've overthrown a king, and stolen a golden fortune. Death would be a blessing; to live would be a miracle; I cannot lose.*

Still, my balls twitched nervously as I went deeper into the silent forest. Even the gibbering insects were half-mute in the sweaty afternoon heat. I walked on, listening for the sounds of the runaways; but after a quarter-hour I could no longer hold my water.

Hiding between two fat-boled trees, I pissed, turning the clayed earth into scarlet pellets. My water smelled sharp in the heavy air, but I caught another, stronger scent under it. Man-sweat, stale tobacco, meat. I felt eyes on me, hidden behind the huge unnatural fronds of the Jamaican forest.

As I made fast my breeches, I heard the padding of feet. The shadows knitted themselves into the figures of seven or eight blackamoors, each carrying a wide-bladed knife or a musket. I was surrounded.

The runaways' leader stepped forward. Quamin. Stocky and as tall as me, his billowing hair made him seem huge. Drilled knucklebone rings hung from his earlobes, his calves were bound with leather gaiters, and a baldric was stretched crossways over his ragged shirt.

"Red. Man," he said. Though his voice was almost too quiet to hear, he made a great mime of each word, his eyebrows and lips stretching into mockery of his meaning.

I shrugged in a friendly manner, as if I spoke not a word of English. Quamin took out a knife and cut a sprig of hair from my head. I did not cry out as he held the copper strands to the light.

"Red Man," he mouthed again. "Why You Full Low?"

Follow, he meant.

Most of the runaways were dressed like him, with bare feet and cutoff breeches, shirts missing or wide-open. I noticed their powder-horns swinging emptily. One had a knapsack that bulged with the packages the slaves had given them. Their faces were lean.

"Tell Captain Quamin," he said, his voice drum-taut. He took a long knife that hung at his hip and sliced into the pus-stain at my shirt's shoulder, grunting with satisfaction when he saw my branded "R".

"You Run A Way. Captain Quamin Him Kill You, See?"

I tilted my head from side to side, letting the crack of my spine ring out in the hush.

"You've seven men here besides yourself, Captain Quamin. Only four have guns, and barely a thimbleful of powder between 'em. Nor do I see even a single bag of shot. Kill me if you like; and you'll stay weaponless. There's only one white man on this island who can arm your runaways here, and that's me."

"We No Run A Way!" hissed Quamin, brandishing my hairs at me. "Maroons!"

Widening my eyes suddenly, I snapped back at him in his own voice.

"No Drop Red Man Hair! Him Touch Earth, Fire Spirit Come Rise! No Drop Red Man Hair!"

Quamin was not alarmed by my play-acting; but his men scuttled back into the bushes. I slowly held my open palm

133

out towards the Maroons' leader. Taking care not to spill, he placed my red hairs in it. They all watched open-mouthed as I spoke a nonsense prayer in French, blew on the strands and tucked them inside my breeches. I grimaced, as if they were taking root and growing in my groin.

"Now then," I said, "let us speak of powder and shot."

Quamin and I squatted together. The others vanished into the trees, and birdsong began again; though it might have been the Maroons making the sounds themselves, a secret language that could be called across Jamaica without a single Englishman taking heed.

His right hand had sidled out of my sight.

"What for you come forest, Red Man? What for you help Zuasheba when her man Kata burned?"

So that was why I was still alive.

I pointed at my scar. Blood pearled where his knife-tip had brushed its ridges.

"I burn too," I whispered.

"You want run away, like Quamin say!" he said triumphantly.

I told him that I had indeed planned to run away again, but that Kiet's dogs had my scent. He parted his lips and gently rubbed his filed teeth.

"Same for Ashanti slaves," he said.

"Ashanti?"

The Maroon rapped his knuckles together.

"Ashanti best man fighter, worst man slavework. Maroons, them from Ashanti tribe."

"You ran away from Alexandria?"

"Not Lekandra, Red Man. Quamin long time free. Some Maroons live in mountain since grandfather time."

"Then you have come to free them—"

"Damn fool Red Man!" scoffed Quamin. "No powder, no shot, how we keep Quamin Town safe? How we fight white man soldier when him chase?"

I dropped back on my haunches. Ever since I'd seen the Maroons' empty powder-horns, I'd been trying to think how I might get them to attack Alexandria. I would need a great distraction if I were to kill Montalbion and escape.

"Can you not raid the militia storehouse?" I asked.

Quamin snorted. He had given much thought on how to do just that: he knew how many sentries patrolled the mansion when the master was away, and how many when he was home. He even showed me on his pocket-watch the times when the guards changed over. But the front of the house was protected by the razed earth, and the back by the barrack-grounds: it would be suicide to attempt either route. Only a white man could reach the storehouse unchallenged.

The runaways' captain spoke better English than he had first made out. While we talked, he scratched a plan of the house and barracks in the dirt. As he marked the slave camp, he gave a tiny sigh.

"The women?" I asked.

"Wives," said Quamin proudly, clenching his fist. "Ashanti women."

"Well, Captain," I said, "I'll be running away next time the Governor is at home. I'll help you take his powder and shot, but only if you take me with you."

"No go in mountain without Maroons," he shot back. "No go without powder, gun, ball. You bring, we talk."

"I cannot steal powder alone. The sentries must be distracted – attacked," I said calmly. In truth, my heart was skittering. I had been gone too long from the camp.

"Red Man must show he can pass sentries," he said, fastening the giant silver buckle at his waist. "Bring Maroons gift from house. Then talk."

"Too dangerous—" I began.

"Gift, then talk," he demanded.

"Well – how will I find you?"

"When Govnachief comes, Quamin will be here. You wait, Red Man."

He flashed me a grin, making the inky scars on his cheeks flare, then called his men back by chittering like a bug.

The short, wiry bowman was tasked with taking me back to the clearing where I slept. His name was Prussia and he bore a twisted back, making his right shoulder lower than his left. He looked as if he would happily slit my throat.

At the edge of the servants' camp, Prussia and I stood for a moment, watching the other white men wandering around the clearing. They did not know how to use their brief hours between labours. For that one blessed moment I was as free as the Maroons. I did not have to go back. I did not have to give up seven years of life. I could run into the jungle, keep running, and even if I died I would die free. But Violet, who had held and urged and listened to me for a thousand nights, stood surety in the Tower; and a sweet, rough-tongued bastard girl would be taken from her mother if I did not return – and I had given my name against this task.

Prussia tapped an arrowhead against my ribs, and then he was gone.

I walked slowly back into the camp, bent over as if with the belly-cramp. Osca, who had been looking out for me, gave a high-pitched laugh.

"You're meant to shit on the fields, Mincher! Colquhoun'll be beating you for wasting your dung!"

I groaned, making him laugh again, and went to my hammock. Closing my eyes, I imagined the Maroons flitting gracefully through the shadows. Quamin, climbing until there was nothing between his scarred face and the sky.

Nearly a fortnight went by without a chance to approach the house and get Quamin's "gift". The boiling-house was stifled by low clouds. Spitting molasses left dozens of tiny burns on our skins. The din of the mill, the clang of the sugar vats and the relentless weight of the sun made my head ache, from waking to fitful sleep.

Our toil was but a small part of a great worthlessness. In coffee, sugar takes away the bright bitterness. It robs men of their will: I'd seen tough traders with their tongs, snipping away at sugar-cones and sucking greedily at the little lumps, like spoiled babies on the teat; and lonely shopwomen, nibbling at sweetcakes while blackguard boys filched their stock.

What is sugar but a thief?

On the third Thursday after Kiet left, the mill and boiling-house were silent, the fires unlit. Colquhoun gathered the indentured men on one side of the yard, while Pelton assembled the blackamoors on the other. The slave-women were there, too, with a small mob of children. I'd heard the fears of rebellion when I was in Port Royal: the planters believed that the Irish were always ready to join forces with the blackamoors and murder them in their beds. And so they kept us apart.

The whispers began: Was one of us to be punished? Were we to be sold to new masters?

I kept silent. I'd seen the excitement on Colquhoun's face, and I knew that it was power that roused him. Alexandria's master was coming at last.

After we'd stood for the best part of an hour, we felt a faint rumbling beneath our feet, and then the murmuring of men's voices far down the forest path. Mules screeched. I knew it was Montalbion's party.

Kiet was on foot, dragging two mules by their halters, his leathery features peaceful despite the effort. Behind him came a dozen slaves, balancing hemp-wrapped bundles on their heads; then four white servants leading eight more mules, their saddlebags heavily laden.

Then louder noises: trumpets, chanting, rapid hoof-beats. The mules jerked forwards, dragging their drivers with them until Kiet managed to halt the train. Colquhoun ran along the line of servants, pushing us to our knees, while the foreman Pelton did the same with the slaves. I pretended to fall. While I was down, I quickly rubbed dust into my hair to conceal its true colour.

The noises grew louder and more shrill. A band of prancing, feathered Africans burst into the yard, stamping and yelling a praise-song.

Four trumpeters followed, blasting a fanfare. Then a troop of bluecoated soldiers, marching out of step but in neatish threes, muskets ported. The leader carried a regimental banner. It sagged, but I knew it anyway. A snake biting its own tail, looped around a harp and a sword.

He is here.

I knelt lower, tugging my fringe down, hoping the dust had dulled the redness of my hair enough. At least the hairs on my arms were blond now, faded by the sun. A stallion's steel shoes thudded towards us, then halted by the whipping-post. The dancers ceased their stamping and singing, and the soldiers drew up. With my face tilted down, all I could see was dust and leaf-smear on the neat rows of boots, and the gleam of the horseman's spurs.

Every man and woman in that yard held their breath. Kiet puffed and panted as he wrestled his two mules into stillness; and the rider's toe jerked angrily at the sound. Plumeria and musk oiled the air. I fought to keep my upper lip from curling as I remembered the last time I'd smelled that scent.

I know you, he'd said to me, and held his stiletto to my eye. Now I could feel the granite strength of his stare on my dusty crown. If he recognised me, I was a dead man.

Vincent de la Haye, Earl Montalbion, Governor of the Company of the Caribbean and natural son of King Charles the Second, turned his horse towards me.

"*You.*"

CHAPTER TEN

One Hundred and Twenty Thousand Acres

Nineteenth day of May

I kept my face down.

"Step forward, I say," said Montalbion quietly. Still I kneeled.

Kiet unfurled his lash, and Osca got up. He barged past me to stand before our lord and master, his feet splayed frogwise. His left knee yammered back and forth.

Montalbion did not dismount, but in that breathless pause I could hear the feathery caress of his riding crop on Osca's face. I glanced up through my untidy fringe; he tilted the lad's head left and right, poked his meaty breast.

"Wash it and send it up," said the earl, stepping his horse delicately back from the sweaty row of servants. Osca's knee began to shake more wildly, and I tapped his calf to remind him to kneel again.

"Captain Carver," said Montalbion, "your men have sailed far and fought bravely, and there'll be good meat for them tonight. You may make camp close by the house."

"Your Lordship," replied a firm Essex voice.

"But not so close that you frighten the parish militia!"

The soldiers laughed.

"Three cheers for His Lordship!" called out Carver; and the men obliged willingly.

Kraaaa! Kraaaa! The trumpets squealed; the dancers stamped; Montalbion and his troop passed between the boiling-house and the sugar store, and on up the slope to the great house. Kenver Kiet went back and checked the mules' harnesses.

As soon as the lord was out of sight, we got to our feet, yawning and stretching. Pelton had his arm around one of the slave-women. His long yellow fingernails idled on her chest.

"Colquhoun – take that *dobeck* to the great house. Nielsen, Mincher – I need you two great lumps for this. Step lively, spill not one bundle, and keep your stinking mouth-holes shut," ordered Kiet, leading the mules towards the mansion. Colquhoun grabbed a handful of Osca's hair and dragged him after, his right heel slapping miserably on the track.

It took a great effort not to wrest the lad free. I had seen what Montalbion did with his chattels: the empty eyes, bloodied skirts and stilled tongues of the damaged. I'd watched him sail down the Thames with Emilia de Corvis, once my lover, knowing he'd do the same to her. But I could not risk my freedom for Osca.

Nielsen was a lean, ill-tempered bastard of a Dane who worked in the curing-shed. He and I took over Kiet's two mules. Mine, a molly, gave me a guarded look. I quickly ran my hand over her mane to gentle her.

Kiet motioned Nielsen and me to join the four white muleteers.

"Now stay you behind me, and set no foot except where you are told. You are to go inside the great house. Touch ought, speak ought, or I'll have you against that there post before you can draw breath. Pelton!"

The foreman, who had been leading the slave-woman into the canefield, stopped and turned his head. His gappy mouth curled angrily.

"You'll follow us and take these blackies back to camp when they are done. You may break out two ounces of salt pork for each of them, for they've done twice the work of a white man. Two ounces each for you and Colquhoun, for standing in my stead."

Kiet tossed a key at Pelton's feet. *Salt pork!* Jesus' bloody feet, I had never felt so hungry until he spoke the words.

Pelton forced his fingers into the slave-woman's mouth, and then pushed her away. He peered past Kiet: Colquhoun was already out of sight and hearing, so I knew that it would be four ounces for Pelton and none for the other foreman.

Well, I thought, *no matter who gets that pork, it will still be on the scud-heap by dawn; but I'll be gone, or I'll be dead.*

Kiet ordered us to move. I smacked the mule's ribs and led her on gently.

"Walk fair and we'll be friends, beastie," I whispered.

Nielsen seized a double handful of his mule's mane and dragged the animal onwards.

Time moved faster.

The path skirted the canefield. A dozen yards beyond the dung-heap, the newly arrived bluecoats were making camp, grumbling that they had not been billeted indoors. Their bewigged officer stared at us calmly, judging how we held ourselves. Nielsen looked back boldly. I kept my gaze down.

We followed Kiet past the soldiers. The mansion's balconies and open shutters cast heavy shadows. Two militiamen in Montalbion's sky-blue colours stood on the highest balconies; as we drew closer, they leaned the guns against the railings. Round the back of the house, four more were seated on the well's rim, their flintlocks lying idly in their laps. Their arms were banded in velvet ribbons, stained with sweat and dust. Not one of them had the little flecked scars I'd seen on Captain Carver's cheeks: these fellows had barely fired a gun in anger.

Kiet ordered the blackamoors to leave their load beside the well. Pelton, who'd brought up the rear, led them away again. He did not have to threaten the lash like Colquhoun did: he was known for meeting disobedience with depravity.

We tied up the beasts and undid their loads. Nielsen lost his balance and nearly dropped a bale on the ground, catching it just in time. Kiet flicked out his lash at the Dane's leg, splitting breeches and skin. I offered Nielsen my neckerchief; he took it with a nod and knotted it round his calf.

"Kitchen," said Kiet to the sentries at the well. "And tell Lieutenant Sharples that we're coming – I know what a nervy sort *he* is."

One of them got up wearily and went to knock on the back door while the others watched us. He gave a password to another sentry inside, too quietly for me to hear it. The bolts were thrown back, and I made sure I was first into the house, blinking in the cool dimness of the passageway. I thought I heard a snatch of French song.

A witches' brew of scents seeped from my bale: cinnamon, nutmeg, cloves, the tickling kiss of pepper, and other smells I did not know. One was like Violet's arm-sweat in the morning; another was a fiery itch, like the dried rosehips I'd once dropped down the shirts of my enemies at Sunday worship.

The sentries stood well back as I turned into the kitchen. One pointed his gun towards us at shoulder-height while the second loaded his. Such carelessness gave me hope.

The kitchen was glorious. The hearth was big enough for a short man to step inside without ducking. A dozen knives and choppers were lined up on a huge, sturdy-legged table. Hunks of smoked meat hung from hooks, side by side with copper pans of every size and shape. Cupboards lined the walls.

A sleek orange-and-white cat sat on the windowsill where I had peeked inside, weeks before. Its eyes were half-closed but its claws were out.

The cook came in through one of the two low doors on the other side of the big fireplace. Flushing despite the unlit fires, she was holding her blouse's neck open to keep herself cool. Her uncapped hair stood out from her face like a spent dandelion. A little chin she had, and a snub nose; yet she was handsome enough, and held herself straight as she stared me down.

"What's this?" she demanded.

"Spices, miss," I said, flattering her with the gentle title in as deep a voice as I could make.

"Miss!" she scoffed.

I stepped closer, taking the bale from my shoulder, and her eyes crinkled as the scents clouded her. The smell of her armpits and tangy underparts, the reek of onions, all had stewed into the spices. I started to grow giddy with lust. It did me little credit; though I excused myself with the notion that it might serve my cause.

I backed into Nielsen so I could pretend that he'd barged me. This gave me an excuse to tumble against the cook, wrapping my arms around her to keep from falling. I let my nose drift across her jaw and cheek, and into the soft corner of her eye, while cinnamon puffed out of the bale and dusted our faces.

Nielsen cursed in his clog-nosed language. I let go of the cook and set the bale on the table. Seeing the tall Dane staring at her knives, she bustled past me, gathered up the blades and stowed them in a small cupboard.

White servant, black slave: they feared us.

"Miss," I said again, tapping Nielsen to make him leave with me. Still he stared around the kitchen; he'd been a buccaneer for ten years before he was caught and indentured, and he was reputed to make free with other men's property.

"Master Kiet shall hear of your clumsiness," said the cook. I threw her a smile to show I knew it was a hollow threat.

Nielsen and I had to step back from the doorway to let the other servants in. Kiet glared at us suspiciously when we returned to him.

"Take the hog-legs to Mistress Diggott, you *emmets*," he ordered, showing me the heavy oilcloth packets. Nielsen and I needed Kiet's help to lift them onto our shoulders, one to each man. The smell of smoked flesh teased me as I carried mine into the kitchen, the greasy cloth trailing against the passage wall.

Two other servants, men I did not know, were making slow work of unpacking their bales. Sacks of flour, bundles of red and orange roots, pots of preserves, dozens of prickly fruits with leaves so sharp that you could cut a finger on them; smoked fish, smoked pork.

"Where d'you want these, mistress?" I asked sharply. She glanced across: pig-fat had soaked into my dirty shirt.

"Enough, you gadabouts," she snapped at the Irishmen, threatening them with a ladle. "Go about your work."

One of them grinned as they pushed past us.

"In the cellar," said Mistress Diggott, pointing at the door next to the fireplace. She took a lantern off a hook and led us downstairs. The crossbeams rested on giant tree-stumps, still rooted in the earth. Her stores made a kind of room around us, but I could see from the glistening reflections of the candle flame that the cellar stretched the breadth and width of the great mansion. Voices echoed faintly from other parts of the ground floor: it was a low chamber that reached from one end of the house to the other.

Vegetables and meats were hanging on the nearest beam. We carefully unwrapped the hog's legs, lifted them and spiked them on the hooks. The cook watched our shirts tighten around our straining shoulders.

By the time we came upstairs again, the Irishmen were back, this time bearing gamebirds wrapped in sacking. The feathers were bright: they must have been hunted by Montalbion's guards on the way back from Port Royal. As Mistress Diggott went to oversee the unwrapping, Nielsen and the others stared at her; and so I had time to poke my head around the door that the cook had come out of earlier. It was her sleeping-room, a little cell with a hammock slung from corner to corner. In truth it was hardly a room at all. It had been carved out of a stairway; the far wall, where her clothes were hung up limply, was but a curtain. Through a gap, I saw steps leading upwards.

I turned quickly and ushered the other men out, as if to help the cook in her work. I still did not have a "gift" for Quamin.

Outside, Kiet pointed to three sturdy wooden cases. As we hefted them in pairs, metal shifted and clanged heavily. We were soon puffing as we shuffled past the kitchen door.

The great hall was chiefly taken up with a braggart, overlarge staircase. The floor was of neatly laid slivers of dark wood.

"Lieutenant Sharples," said Kiet to the soldier standing nervously at the end of the hall, by a double doorway, through which I could see a long mahogany table. His flintlock was loaded and cocked, but he seemed unsure which way to point it. There was fine wood panelling on all sides and above; two marble busts on pedestals, and glassed cupboards protecting Spanish silverware: nowhere a misfired ball could go that would not cost him a whipping.

From above came a high muffled drone: Osca, asking a question.

A silence, and then he asked again in a slightly higher tone. Someone stamped and laughed in a high voice; a door shut heavily; and then nothing.

Nielsen and I carried our case into the dining room, the Dane wincing each time his cut leg hit its reinforced corner. The wall opposite me was heavy with pride and gold leaf: paintings of lush English forests and fields, ornate round mirrors, a sideboard with inlaid ivory and marquetry, bearing inscribed silver goblets. The room faced east, towards England, but slatted blinds kept out the morning sun.

Two more soldiers stood between us and the window. A youngish house-servant wrung his hands as he watched us. Sweat trickled from under his wig and mingled with powder, gathering on his badly shaven chin like a Covent Garden molly-boy on a rainy day.

"Set those there loads down," ordered Kiet, softening his voice as if it might scratch the table. It was the first time I'd seen him a little cowed: if one piece of treasure went missing, no doubt it'd mean his Cornish head on a pike. He pointed at a low trestle next to the pink-faced servant lad.

We obeyed and then stepped back to watch the servant crane over the packages. He wiped his face with a cuff, took out a fat-bladed knife and clumsily cracked open the first case. The wood was old, and a sliver of it split off, flying against the panelled wall. The servant drew out a long silver platter stamped with a coat of arms. Kiet crossed over and knuckled my forehead.

"Out! Eyes off the master's silver, if you want to keep them in your heads."

But he was slow to lead us out through the great hall. His neck bulged as he looked lingeringly at Montalbion's wealth. Struggle makes men strong, but it is a rare man who can endure hard labour when he sees his master idling in the shade. And Kiet was not that man.

I let the others push ahead of me, careful not to show my intent to the militiamen, who were following us out. It would not be easy to enter the house a second time, let alone climb to its lord's chamber and take his life. I let my heart slow, as Mister de Corvis had once taught me, and counted the dangers.

Primo, the patterned floor clacked and shifted under my feet, its slivered boards pushed up by the swollen joists beneath. Too noisy to cross unheard.

Secondo, I'd seen two watch-chairs in the hall, one in the lee of the staircase and one on the landing halfway up: *ergo*, at least two sentries within the hall, and most likely a third outside Montalbion's room.

Tertio, the house was hollow: parts of both upper floors were open to the hall, with balconies that ringed the staircase. If I reached Montalbion's chamber, he had only to yell with the door still open, and the alarm would be heard by every jack in the place. Therefore, my way upstairs lay through the cook's little bedroom.

Quarto – but Nielsen had noticed me falling behind. He turned and gave me a sudden slap to the neck, cupping his hand to make it loud. At my back, Lieutenant Sharples had seen me gaping upwards, but the Dane distracted him.

"Country boy," he said, rolling his eyes, and pulled me a step or two by my nostrils. I brushed his hand away, blinking to show him thanks. Sharples laughed, grabbed my collar and pushed me along from behind. I pretended to trip. He was so busy snatching his musket out of my reach that he did not feel me tug the wooden powder-keg away from his belt.

The lieutenant kicked my thigh and shooed us down the passageway. The kitchen door was open again: I caught Mistress Diggott's eye, and made sure she saw me gaze into her little bedroom. I followed Nielsen out into the blinking light.

Walking past the bluecoats' camp, we had to clear the track to allow a closed carriage past. The horses' hides frothed, and the driver was humped angrily in his seat. Two of the soldiers deliberately turned their backs on the coach; its curtain was pulled shut before I could see who was inside.

I counted seven tents: that meant perhaps four-and-twenty soldiers, and a pair of officers. Dust-stained uniforms were slung carelessly over the taut roof-ropes, and hats perched aslant on pairs of boots: a peevish complaint at having to stay out of doors when a large house lay half-empty nearby. I marked well that the tents were all facing away from the scud-heap.

I was ready; as ready as I could be.

Colquhoun set us straight back to work that afternoon. Our spirits had been raised by the mansion's cool, wealthy air, and the molten sugar felt much easier to stir.

The boiling-house door was always kept open to release the steam, giving me a clear view across the yard. During that long afternoon, seven or eight horsemen passed through on their way to the great house. I recognised Michael Hicks, Sir Fergus Ordene and Colonel Flowers, the planter who'd sold Francis Coyle to Kiet.

What business did they all have here? That knowledge could perhaps be worth as much to me as taking Montalbion's life. And the cellar offered me a chance to acquire it, if I could get underneath the dining room when Montalbion hosted the Port Royallers.

There are no clocks for indentured men. We crushed and ran, stirred and struck until long after dusk. As the dark gathered, Colquhoun and Kiet strode from mill to boiling-house to curing-shed, cursing and driving. Not one of us dared to complain of the lengthy day. We knew the reason: the master was home. Fires must smoke and crushers must creak, so Lord Montalbion could go to sleep knowing that his wealth would be greater when he woke.

I had tied the soldier's little triangular powder-keg into my shirt-tails and tucked it into my breeches. Every time the bellows-slave blew sparks out of the firepit, I cupped my backside to keep from a fool's death.

"I do believe Mincher has birthed a great *fist*," said a boiling-house man named Figgot, leering from the uncut side of his face, "and is afraid it will burst into flame."

Seeing Colquhoun come in, I quickly made a play of shovelling my wind at Figgot. The foreman laughed, and for a breath we all joined in; but then he frowned to show us Kiet was close by, and we went back to our tasks.

*

It must have been close to nine o'clock by the time we quit working and went to our hammocks. I lay awake, waiting for the others to fall asleep. The English stars had slid to the edge of the sky, bullied out by foreign constellations.

From the great house came music, swept into discord by the gusting wind. I thought on Montalbion, and the College Secular, and Tyburn Pettit. Why were they risking the College's good name by sending a fool like me to assassinate an earl? I pulled the mould-stained blanket down to my waist and tried to reckon it all.

If I were to succeed in killing Montalbion, I would most likely be caught and tried; and I would surely tell the court that de Groot and the College had told me what to do. Montalbion's supporters would revolt against the Crown; even if I escaped, they would likely rise up anyway.

And if I were to fail, then Montalbion would likewise know that an assassin had been sent: he'd have no choice but to rebel. Either way, it was war; but a war that would seem to have been started by Montalbion and his followers.

Then there was the rumour that Collingwood had started: that Montalbion was to be recalled to London. It was all of a piece: de Groot and the College intended to force a revolt in Port Royal. But why?

It did not help me to know that I was expected to fail. Killing Montalbion was the only way for me to free Violet and Simona, and to escape my own bondage; there was no choice but to try.

My spirits sank to the murky depths, touched their toes to the freezing clay, and began to float upwards again.

*

It was not long before I was the only man left awake. Time to find Quamin: for all I knew, Montalbion would be gone in the morning, and with him all my hopes.

It is no easy thing to roll from a hammock without making a sound. The sapling at my feet swayed, its bladelike leaves shushing against each other as I swung my feet out. I pulled on my boots, their seams gaping where the stitches had burst, and slipped between the trees without a backward glance. Bugs chirred, complaining as I invaded their lands.

I was not halfway to the slave huts when I saw the tree shadows stir: Quamin, waiting for me. Perhaps he had been close by, watching me, the whole fortnight.

I tugged the powder-keg out of my shirt-tails and gave it to the Maroon. He led me to the edge of the canefield, where he complained in a low voice, "No shot."

"If it's of no use, I'll have that powder back off you, Captain," I replied sharply. "There's proof that I can pass the sentries; now it is time for your side of the bargain."

He threw me a look and slipped into the cane rows.

The great house was a blaze of light. Long-poled torches edged the strip of razed earth, which was patrolled by two pairs of sentries; half a dozen musketeers were posted on the high balconies. The music came more loudly as an arrogant blast of trumpet and drum took over from the wishful viols. It blared and fell silent, leaving only the soft tramp of boots on earth, and conversation dribbling through the dining-room shutters.

"When Govnachief is gone, best then to attack," said Quamin. His eyes darted from sentry to sentry, timing their paces, reckoning the distance for their guns.

"While these soldiers are here, there'll be thrice as much powder," I reckoned aloud, "thrice the shot. Enough to last your men ten years, perhaps. Well, it shall be plenty enough for me and my lads."

Which lads I meant, I did not know – but it gave the Maroon something to chew on. The cane leaves above us dipped and rustled as we watched the musketeers.

"Thrice?" he asked at last; but I knew he'd understood me. Without answering, I led him off towards the scud-heap, keeping the bunched rows of cane between us and the sentries.

At the side of the field, I showed him the bluecoats' camp. Quamin tilted his head as he watched the pickets patrolling the tents. Blooded in their raids on New Spain, these soldiers were more watchful than the militia who guarded the house. Though we were out of sight, the sentries seemed to sense that they were being watched. They whispered to each other. Two fixed bayonets while the others loaded their guns; we shrank back into the field, and returned to the forest.

Only when we were at the far edge of the field, beyond the ridge, did I touch Quamin's back to make him stop. He turned, took hold of my wrist and pulled me down into a squat opposite him.

"See? The governor-chief has more soldiers: more powder, more shot," I said.

Quamin folded his neck until chin almost touched collarbone. Cane-leaf shadows striped his face. He was utterly still. His massive fingers dug into my wrist, and I felt my flesh thumping slowly against his. I knew what he was about: a lying man's heart flutters. But I had only hidden a part of the truth.

At last, he smacked his lips open, grinned joylessly and began to speak.

The Maroon captain was no fool. His plan carried much risk for me, and a good deal less for him and his men. True, Prussia was to join my attack on the barracks, but I knew he would push me to the fore of the action.

Quamin also intended to free some of the slaves to bolster his numbers. It would slow us down, but I felt a savage joy at the thought of Kata and Zuasheba escaping the plantation.

I tried to close my mind to what awaited me if we did succeed. With a runaway's brand, I had little chance of boarding any English ship; nor, despite our contract, did I truly expect Ty to let me go free if I survived my mission. Yet the only chance for Violet and Simona was if I met him in Naggle Bay, as instructed.

Quamin took out his pocket-watch: it was a quarter to ten. He showed me the shape the hands made at two o'clock. I nodded, and then he was gone.

Cautiously, I made my way back to the bluecoats' camp. The sentries were on patrol, casting the odd resentful glance up at the house.

I waited until the guard changed at ten o'clock, and darted across to the nearest tent while the sentries went to rouse the next watch. I crouched among the guy-ropes. Inside, a man muttered a prayer in his sleep.

The new sentries huddled at the other side of the camp, unwilling to go their separate ways into the night. I crept towards the furthest tent, which still had several uniforms draped over it.

"Six months at sea, and now he is withholding four-fifths of our prize-money!" complained a high-voiced fellow.

"Well, we have a receipt for it," replied another, mildly.

"A receipt! He's kept our portion for that scheming harpy. We've not enough even to pay Kiet for a go on one of his black bitches. Oh, he promises double when we return to England: who'd believe that?"

"What's your complaint?" snapped a crisp Essex voice: Captain Carver. "If you'd your coin already, half would be in a whore's purse, and you'd have pissed the other half into Port Royal harbour. The Governor's done you safe."

"If we ever reach England," said a third man, his voice muffled. Grabbing the biggest uniform off the last tent, I ducked into the shadow of some scrubby bushes.

"Who said that? Yarrold?" demanded Carver. I dared a glance above the tents. As tall as me, his black curly hair shot with lines of silver that caught the distant torchlight, Carver stared angrily at the watchmen.

I pushed through the spiny bushes, making my way to the edge of the dungpit where the company could not hear me. Choking on the stench, I put the uniform and boots on over my sweaty rags.

Torches lit the killing-ground. I could not cross it without being seen by Carver's men at this end, and by the house militia at the other.

The tiny determined cogs of time ground on. I counted to a hundred, two hundred; Carver's sentries paced back and forth, alert. Quamin had promised to distract them – what was taking him so long?

Noise came crackling through the canefield. Four raw-tongued birds burst upwards from their shelter in the field, and the sentries formed up quickly, with their captain snapping orders. The Maroon was keeping his word.

A man must sometimes move before he thinks. While the bluecoats' backs were turned, I stumbled out of the bushes and across the razed ground, making a play of doing up my breeches.

The racket grew louder, thundering towards Carver's men. I threw a glance over my shoulder and ran towards the house, waving my hands at the militia sentries, who by this time were pointing their own weapons at me.

A great hog plunged through the last rows of cane and bore down on the line of guards.

"Split ranks!" shouted Carver, fifty yards behind me. His men quickly raised their muskets again, scattering so the animal could run through them. Laughter rang out from the balconies as the house-sentries saw that the soldiers had been making ready to fight a pig.

I smiled foolishly at the nearest sentry as I slowed and walked past him. "Captain Carver's respects to Lieutenant Sharples—"

"Hold!" said the militiaman, fumbling with his flintlock.

"—and I've orders for your quartermaster besides," I finished in a gentlemanly drawl. It was enough to make the fellow doubt his place: he lowered his weapon again.

"Sea-rat," he grumbled to his companion, who had already joined in with the laughter. Without waiting for permission, I carried on round the house, out of sight of Carver's company.

One man stood guard at the well, an ancient of perhaps sixty years. He held himself more like a soldier than the others did; and though he wore the same bright blue uniform, his hat and baldric were of the oldest fashion, such as my father used to wear. I touched my hat respectfully.

"Good night, sir," I said gruffly.

"To you," he replied, not changing the grip he had on his weapon.

"My father wore such a hat," I went on, nodding at the short leather thong that kept the front brim raised, "but I did not know they had made them since the Lord Protector's day."

It was a risk to speak of Cromwell, whose head had not long since been on a spike at Westminster Hall. But I had judged it right: this was an Old Stander.

"Landed here with Venables in fifty-five," he said, pulling on his neatly trimmed beard, "fought with Doyley, earned my acres. God bless you for a right-thinking man."

I nodded and looked at the ground modestly.

"Quartermaster?" I asked after a breath or two.

He planted his musket stock in the dirt and pointed at the second barracks hut, which had a steel-banded door at one end. I glanced up at the scrubby slope behind it: no sign of Prussia. If he was not there, this would be the shortest night of my life.

The house-soldiers who were not on patrol were ensconced in their huts. Their voices were bleary with booze. A pair of men stood in the shadows of the far-most hut, sharing a tobacco-pipe. They ignored me entirely as I went to knock on the quartermaster's door.

Two bolts slid roughly back, then a key rattled clumsily, and he came out. Thick eyeglasses blurred his expression. With the carelessness of a man over forty years of age, he'd not even remembered to challenge me first.

"Captain Carver requires powder and shot, fellow," I said, rudely looking over his sloped shoulder into the little storeroom behind. An oil lantern burned near the entrance, but I could see little beyond him; I kept myself in his shadow so he could not see the rags I wore beneath the stolen uniform, nor how my wrists poked out from the too-short sleeves.

"Requisition."

"Very well. Captain Carver *requisitions* powder and—"

"I mean, where is your requisition? Signed and sealed?" he snapped.

"Sent here two days since with the other orders from Port Royal," I replied wearily. "Have the *gentlemen* of your *militia* mislaid the entire packet? We're twelve pounds short and must quit this estate before dawn."

"*Twelve* pounds? Do you intend to shoot every hog on Jamaica?"

"Every Spaniard in these seas," I said, "and any Englishman who knows not his duty."

He was not to be cowed.

"I know my duty," he said, "and it is to withhold His Lordship's powder and shot against a duly signed requisition. Good night."

I put a friendly hand on his arm, which made it harder for him to shut the metal-bound door.

"If I'm to ask my captain again, I'd rather have a full belly. D'you have any salted pork in there?"

The quartermaster shrugged my hand away, took off his eyeglasses and cleaned them carefully with a corner of his tunic. He gave a little nod to the old fellow by the well.

"Our meat is weighed and stamped and docketed; it's not for me to share out. But Mistress Diggott is still about her work" – he pointed his glasses at the kitchen window behind me – "and may allow you a scrap or two. But not twelve pounds of powder. Twelve pounds!"

Tutting, he closed the door and slid the bolts home. As I returned to the old man at the well, I glanced at the scrubby slope again. I kept the light of the kitchen at my back so the sentry had to squint.

"I'm to ask the cook for leavings, sir," I said quietly, "and ... well, I am shamed to ask your discretion ..."

I rubbed my chin awkwardly.

"You're a sinner, and an arrogant one besides," he answered. "I doubt Mistress Diggott has encouraged your thoughts of fornication."

"I cannot be both," I said with a little smile. "If I sin, it will be because my confidence is merited; and if it be foolish arrogance, why then no sin is possible."

I picked at a knife-scar on my neck. An old soldier cannot ignore an old wound: he pulled a face and pushed me towards the back door.

He knocked, and waited for the sentry to come to the other side.

"Whitlock," said the old man to the door, "with one of Carver's popinjays for the kitchen."

The guard inside sighed roughly. "Watchword, Master Whitlock?"

"Fitzroyal," snapped the ancient. The password signified that Montalbion was a king's bastard.

A key jiggled in the lock. The door had swollen damply and jammed in the frame, and the soldier on the other side had to force the gears to turn. I held my breath.

As I'd hoped, the guard had changed within the house. A pigeon-toed, shambling brute opened the door. He had not even bothered to bring his flintlock, which was leaning against the wall further up the passage. Ignoring Whitlock, he glanced at my face and nodded for me to squeeze past him. I did not look back at the Old Stander, but went into the kitchen while the sentry struggled to lock up again.

A good, honest fire warmed the room. I closed the kitchen door behind me.

The cook and her two slaves were almost hidden behind a mountain of food. The sturdy table bowed under its weight: huge salvers of chopped fruit, pink and green and yellow; cakes of bread, dripping with oil and crusted with more salt than a London family might eat in a year; roast hogs whose slit bellies leaked the feathers and claws of gamebirds; a giant tureen that was nearly emptied, soup slittered down its silver side; brains, livers, kidneys, half-raw on beds of shiny jungle leaves; a dozen ravaged cones of sugar, each on a little brass plate with its own pair of sugar-tongs; piles of dumplings; and a stack of spitted baby birds slathered in treacle, piled up on each other like carcasses in a plague pit.

And that was not even the whole feast: the other half of the table was covered in dishes yet to be served.

One of the slaves caught sight of me. Inked scars marked her cheeks: perhaps an Ashanti, like Quamin. Without stopping her work, she clacked her filed teeth to alert her mistress.

The cook stood on tiptoes to look. I had the soldier's hat pulled low over my eyes; she did not recognise me.

"Away, or I'll have you whipped," she said, and dipped back out of sight. I'd never heard a woman speak to a soldier so.

I strode into the kitchen, snatched a sweetbread from the tripe plate, and bit into it. The soft earthy meat melted deliciously on my tongue. I licked away the snail-mark of grease that trailed across my upper lip, desperate for every morsel, and reached out for more, but the cook had rounded the table. She rapped my fist with the back of a cleaver.

"I said begone," she said.

I took off my hat. Her eyes widened, and she drew breath to cry out.

I swiftly opened my coat and shirt to show her the branded "R". Perhaps a man would have given the alarm nonetheless. But she did not: she let out her breath with a faint waft of sugar.

"If you wish to break your bond," she whispered sharply, cradling the cleaver carefully against her chest, "it is customary to run *away* from your master's house, not *into* it."

She used genteel words, but under them was a Kent accent.

A few years before, I might have put a hand on her waist, said a flattering word, clamped her against my groin; but now I knew that such gestures could break a woman's trust. As for Violet, I could serve her better if I forgot my vows for an hour or two. A little wiser now, I took a dumpling from the table, waited for her to nod permission, and bit into it.

"Caraway …" I said, tightening my nose and throat in the Kentish way, "… salt, cinnamon – Jesus, but this is good – sheep's lard – not pig's … sage …"

"Not sage. That's a herb they grow here, which has no English name."

I took another bite. I had told the truth: the dumpling was delicious, still a little warm, dripping with herb-scented fat. She looked at the piles of food, tapping her fingers on the cleaver's flat blade. The slaves had slowed down to watch us, and she shot them an angry glance.

"You've work to do," I said warmly. "And all I'm asking is to taste fresh meat, and sleep for an hour indoors. Let me wait in your cellar for now: if that's too much to ask, I know my way."

Her frizzy hair wavered in the heat from the fireplace.

The door handle banged downwards. Hatless, my uniform open to the belly-button, it was clear I was no true soldier. Mistress Diggott quickly wrapped a hand around my head and pulled my mouth down towards hers. The cleaver was pressed between our chests.

It was well done: the sentry laughed out loud as he took a heavy step into the kitchen. The cook moved her mouth back a little, reaching for my tongue with hers in such a way that the militiaman could see it. He laughed again, less comfortably this time, and backed out of the room.

"I am Calumny Spinks," I said. "That's whose life you just saved with your quick wits. And quicker tongue."

"And I am Lessie Diggott. I kissed you for kindness, not encouragement. I shan't weep if they hang you, Master Spinks."

The slave-women were murmuring in their native tongue. Lessie banged the cleaver flat on the table to remind them of their duties.

"The cellar," she said firmly. "But if you touch one case of flour, or lighten one flagon, I'll have the sentry back in."

"How long must I wait?" I asked.

"An hour and a half at least. Midnight."

"And then—"

"And then I shall decide. You won't be the first beast to be swallowed up in this kitchen, and your tired bones spat out at dawn."

She grinned wolfishly, showing pink gums and long yellowed quarter-teeth, and for a brief moment I was no runaway, no assassin, only a lusty fellow with a promise from a strong woman. Anger, teeth, curious tongue, powerful belly, wrestling thighs: that was how I'd once filled my empty heart. Before Violet.

The cellar door was next to the hearth. She lit a candle-stub and thrust it into my hands. I had barely set foot on the stairs before the door closed, bundling me downwards. I cracked my forehead on a cross-beam, nearly dropping the wavering candle.

I rubbed my head and knelt to steady myself. The floor was nothing but pressed earth: as I touched it, my fingers drifted over a tiny seedling.

All wealth is built on mud. One day this island's vines and weeds would split the boards above my head, reach up through the staircase, and pull the walls down. Holding out the flame, I stepped carefully over the seedling. I would do nothing to delay that glorious revolution.

Murmurs and footbeats echoed through the gloom. An hour and a half, she'd said.

I ducked under the hocks I'd hung earlier, then wriggled between two stacks of wooden crates. There were more stores behind: piles of porcelain dishes, pewter flagons left higgle-piggle on the earth, three sets of fire-pokers and rakes. Behind them were discarded steel breastplates and helmets, too hot for Englishmen to wear on this island.

To my left was a passage between two beams, leading towards a glow that seeped down between the ill-sealed floorboards: candlelight from the dining room. If I did not reach Montalbion tonight, I could at least learn his guests' secrets. Rooting the candle in the ground, I moved carefully through the cellar towards the falling light, passing under the great hall.

The floor creaked and grumbled. Footmen trotted in and out of the room. Chairs squeaked as the well-fed guests wriggled and farted, trying to make room for Lessie Diggott's dumplings. A silver plate clattered to the floor.

It was hard to make out the voices at first: only one came through clearly, that of the first footman snapping orders to his underlings. I realised that I was under the doorway, and had to duck under a joist to get myself beneath the dining table. I was waiting to hear Montalbion's voice, but he was not there.

I let my breathing slow, and listened to the banter and taunting in the room above. I knew some of the voices: Sir Fergus Ordene; the trader Michael Hicks; Flowers the plantation owner. Some of the others were planters, by the sound of them: slow and pompous of speech, familiar with the servants, insolent to the Port Royal men. Yet they were not sat on opposing sides; they had been mixed together like friends, trader next to planter.

Perhaps an hour passed with nothing of consequence being said. Most of the talking was done by the Port Royallers. Boasts of privateer expeditions, complaints against the Royal African Company and its monopoly on slaves, grumbles about the press-ganging of sailors from private ships.

I was thinking of retracing my steps when Montalbion spoke from the doorway.

"So now you sail no longer."

He had not raised his voice above a murmur; but the man was used to addressing crowds, and his words stabbed clear through the parquetry to reach me.

"Well, Your Lordship," said Ordene, "our new ship is—"

"Privateer ships clog up England's most valuable harbour. Eight of ten of them have not been careened since the great treason against my uncle. Their crews live aboard, shitting in the dock, and their captains scavenge a living from occasional hog-hunts. Which are *illegally* pursued in forests belonging to the Company of the Caribbean."

Every voice in the room was still. The servants moved softly out of the room. Montalbion's heels rang solidly overhead, and then the doors boomed shut.

"Of which Company," said a planter, "His Grace is the Governor-General."

I noted well this "Grace" business: a title reserved for a duke or higher, not an earl such as Montalbion.

"If I may, Your Grace?" asked Michael Hicks with calm authority, in his Liverpudlian voice. His chair squeaked on the polished floor as he stood.

Montalbion must have nodded, for Hicks went on confidently, his voice dry and persuasive. "Our lives are threatened daily, gentlemen. There are more indentured men and malcontents than honest Englishmen on this island, and even more blackamoors; it cannot be long before they confederate, and seek to murder you all on your plantations."

"Hicks, it is better to live free for a short while—" blustered another man.

"Free to return to England, Warriner? Free to spend your wealth on English land, to end your days near your family? Not you, who fought against the Dutch usurper in eighty-eight; and not Sir Fergus Ordene here, who has lands he cannot claim in Ireland. I doubt that more than two of us around this table – I regret that I must count our planter brothers in this – are free to go home. Else why should we be here?"

The silence this time was longer, nastier.

"Eat, gentlemen, I pray you," urged Montalbion, and clapped his hands. The doors opened, and the floorboards rang with the bustling tread of footmen. Plates were lifted, fresh dishes put down.

"What's this?" demanded Ordene.

"Spiced goat, sir, buttered yam, palm-wine syrup—" stuttered a footman.

"Not the damned food! This paper we've all been given."

"An order from His Majesty," replied Montalbion. Another clap, and the servants left again. Michael Hicks began to read aloud.

"Order ... etcetera etcetera ... to the acting Lieutenant-Governor of Jamaica, and to the Governor of the Company of the Caribbean ... All pirates, which shall encompass all privateers to have taken English ships into action in excess of their letters of marque ... in the event of doubt to be taken to *England* for trial ... to be hanged, and all properties and coin forfeit to the Crown ... etcetera."

"Now I am *certain*," said Montalbion, walking slowly round the dining table, "that not a man here has exceeded his letter of marque. I am *persuaded* that no witnesses, foreign or English, could be found to testify to it; else I should not have invited you to set foot here. This house is Company property; it is most heavily guarded within and without; and it would seem ill-mannered to hang a man when his belly is full of my food."

Two men stirred violently.

"Sit, Warriner," said Hicks sharply. "His Grace does not threaten."

"Besides, I have not brought you here to speak of piracy and hangings," continued Montalbion, as if there had been no interruption. I could not help but admire the man's charm, how he condescended to these rough, insolent fellows. "I merely share His Majesty's wishes. I have summoned you because I am concerned, as I rightly should be, with the inefficiency of our sugar industry, which naturally concerns us all … as *loyal* Englishmen.

"It seems to me that we have too many smallholders on Jamaica – and Barbados, and Saint Kitts, and all of our territories here – and not enough landowners of substance."

"Not least," said Hicks quickly, "because seventy thousand prime acres are put aside for indentured men to take when their time is served; and another fifty thousand are already in the hands of such freedmen. If we gain honestly, whether from letters of marque or hard labour in our fields, then we are forced to buy scrubby land, far from port; yet these thieves and ruffians are given some of the finest parcels, though they are ill-equipped to work them."

"And they do not sell at a fair price," grumbled Flowers, "but sit stubbornly on their fallow soil until they die."

Anger rumbled round the room, muffled by eating: appetites had returned. Noisy complaints belched through mouthfuls of liver and dumpling. I looked up, suddenly aware of a change in my surroundings, but it was simply that the candle-stub had guttered out, leaving me alone in the darkness.

"Yes, Mister Warriner?" asked Hicks; he was Montalbion's chosen spokesman.

"That's a hundred and twenty thousand acres for those indentured buggers. And twelve loyal English gentlemen around the table …"

"Indeed," said Montalbion, as if he had never contemplated this sum.

"Why then …" said Warriner, and slurped his wine vigorously. Ten thousand acres had made him forget the noose that he had so recently been menaced with.

"Mister Warriner!" snapped Hicks. "Those lands are *Crown* lands, and the King himself has promised them to those who serve under indenture. Lord Montalbion here is a peer of the realm, His Majesty's trustee. You cannot ask him to consider such a thing."

"Not the *sole* trustee," said Ordene crisply. "There is a Lieutenant-Governor in Spanish Town, is there not?"

"The *acting* Lieutenant-Governor is similarly bound, I'm sure," said Montalbion, "and I will leave you to your debate lest Mister Warriner condemn you all out of his hasty mouth."

"Ahh ... Your Grace, forgive—" sputtered Warriner; but the doors had closed again.

Montalbion's footsteps stopped immediately outside the door.

"Mr Hicks," said Ordene in an offhand way, "is not the Governor the son of our late King Charles the Second? A monarch who tolerated all manner of religion and commerce?"

"So it is said," replied Hicks. "Do pass Mister William-son the stuffed quail; his plate is but three-quarters full."

Ordene continued, "Does not this noble lord have more right to set laws on this island than a Dutchman? It does strike me that our duty as Englishmen—"

"Englishmen!" cried out Warriner, thumping his fist on the table.

"—would be to raise a banner for His Grace, and declare him Governor of the whole island. After all, the Assembly cannot meet while we are awaiting Inchiquin's replace-ment, and the Council is a toothless beast."

"Not enough," said Hicks swiftly. "King of an island is a nonsense, when it is England that strangles Jamaica. And I believe the rumours are true: William has recalled Lord Montalbion to England, so there is little time for us to consider this."

"Well," said Ordene. "Since we cannot restore the blessed James to the throne …"

"Why then …" began Warriner; but not even he was foolish enough to speak treason aloud.

Knives clattered on silver. I heard their gullets at work even through the floorboards. I could picture the uneasy silence well enough: the planters avoiding each other's eyes; Hicks' gaze flickering from face to face, weighing up the resolve in each; Ordene staring back at him.

More footsteps from outside the room. Montalbion whispered, then took a pace back. The door opened.

"Ah," said Hicks, "allow me to introduce Monsieur Samuel Grulle."

Warriner sprang to his feet, his chair thundering to the floor. Steel scraped on steel.

"I know this fellow! A bastard, cowardly shore-pirate!"

"Calm you, gentleman," soothed a French voice. "I let you live, is it not? And if you lost your gold … Well, the sea is a cruel mistress."

"Warriner, I beg of you, put away that sticking-needle," said Ordene mockingly. "Let us hear this fellow's story: if it sits ill, we may cut him open as an enemy of England."

Hicks spoke soothingly and at length, casting a lawyer's sleepy spell over the company. "If certain *loyal* gentlemen were to take ship against *tyranny* … if an *ally* were to provide fleets and victuals ... then certain *ports* and *estates* could be made *available* in the ensuing peace ..."

"Give this Frenchy plague-rat our English lands?" demanded Warriner.

"I am not conscient of making such a demand," answered Grulle politely. "I am here as a man who wishes to be an English subject himself, and comes with gifts to make amends for past fights. We are all gentle landowners—"

"Not yet," muttered Ordene. I only heard him because I was directly below his feet.

"Gifts?" demanded a planter; and with that word, it was as good as done. Handful after handful of coin poured onto the table.

Montalbion burst in.

"Gentlemen! I trust the melancholy talk of land seizures has ceased ... But what is this, Mister Hicks? Coin, at dinner? I had thought you gentlemen of better breeding. And who is this? A Frenchman, by the look of him."

A Frenchman who sings and sleeps under your roof, I thought.

"Forgive us all, Your Grace," said Sir Fergus Ordene, rising to his feet. "We – Well, we thought ... Mister Hicks?"

"We thought to raise a subscription, my lord. Since you will need to return to England with the treasure from your remarkable attacks on New Spain, we believe that a considerable body of men and ships ought rightly to be sent to guard your person and your fleet. We expect that lawbreaker, Colonel de Groot, to make an attempt on you when the Navy ship *Mordaunt* arrives in June. It would perhaps be best if such a body were assembled by

Saturday the twenty-eighth of May: it is easier to bring men into Port Royal on a market day. Certainly, de Groot will not anticipate a strike so early; and we do already have hundreds of loyal militiamen in the port."

I held my breath. I had been listening for more than an hour, and no such subject had been discussed. Yet no man dared contradict Hicks.

"I had not considered the matter, Hicks. A pretty thought, indeed."

"And if we were to raise perhaps two thousand men more—"

Ordene coughed loudly and sat down.

"—then we should need more ships than can be found in Port Royal. And so we thought to charter vessels from independent captains such as Mister Grulle here, a foreign gentleman who seeks to be made a natural Englishman. At midnight it will be the twentieth of May, and so there is little time to lose."

"A rather curious escort ... I must consider this ..."

A coin slipped from the pile of gold and landed loudly on the floor.

"Very well," said Montalbion brightly. "I have no fear of pirates or foreign fleets ... yet I cannot refuse your loyal generosity, nor your solicitude for the Crown's treasure."

When he talked of treasure, it was that of "the Crown" – by which he meant himself. Ty and Collingwood had been right: he proposed to invade England from the West Indies, and by allying with that devil who'd murdered my mother's family, Louis of France.

"Gentlemen, let us toast your proposed escort in Spanish brandy before we all retire to our rooms. You there – remove the plates. I think perhaps my guests have eaten well enough already."

CHAPTER ELEVEN

Vincent

Nineteenth night of May

It was treason he spoke – and grand larceny he planned. Thinking of Francis Coyle and Moses Severill, of the years they'd toiled for land that would now be seized by Montalbion and his allies, I sank into a rage I had not felt since the Revolution.

Lessie would soon know that the meal was done. I scuttled back to the cellar stairs, holding my hand out front to keep from hitting the beams. Sure enough, I had barely settled myself on the bottom steps when the kitchen door opened, spilling light and gamey air.

"Quick!" hissed the cook. I went to her, and she bundled me towards her little room. The two slaves were cutting the last slivers of meat off the bones, arranging them on simple wooden trenchers. They kept their faces down, avoiding my eye. This was not the first time they'd seen their mistress take a man to her bed. One of them dropped a bird's carcass, earning herself a slap from the cook, and I grabbed a knife while Lessie was distracted.

"Wine," I said, dragging my feet. I needed her to sleep soundly: if he kept his word, Quamin would be attacking in two hours' time.

She pressed a hard knuckle into my lower back, shoved me into her room and shut the door. It was just in time: the footmen had entered the kitchen. As soon as they were safe inside, they began talking loudly, clanging down platters, goblets, knives, salvers.

"Threatened that Ordene with the noose! Gave him a paper …" sputtered one fellow through a mouthful of pudding.

"A warrant, I'll be bound. But why does His Lordship—"

Lessie Diggott spoke up. "Not in front of the blackies, you halfwit jacks!"

"They can barely make out a word, Lessie," protested a footman.

"If you want your share of leavings, you'll abide by the rules," she answered firmly.

There was no more talking as the servants fetched the rest of the dishes. It took them a good long while to finish bringing the feast back to the kitchen; and even longer for them to finish flirting with Lessie and picking at the leavings. She scolded them for stealing the wine dregs, and shooed them out of the house. The slave-women followed.

I listened to the cook tidying up. Locking the passageway door; sealing the meat-lockers; sweeping bones and feathers into sacks; clattering plates into piles for scouring in the morning. I stowed my hat under her hammock, hiding the knife beneath it.

"Open," she said, and I went to let her in. She had two goblets, brimful of jewel-red wine, wedged between her fingers, filled with the dregs from the table no doubt. Her cap was off, and her eyes were heavy with tiredness.

We sat side by side on the hammock, laughing quietly as it rocked under us, threatening to spill our wine. I remembered the last time Violet and I had eaten together. How we'd talked of coming to the New World. Praise the angels, she was thirsty, and drank three gulps for each one of mine. I was careful.

"A night indoors, a bite of meat, a pillow; and then you'll be off. They'll catch you for sure, Calumny Spinks," she said, holding the cup to my lips.

I sipped, looking at her over the rim, then put it down, so I could embrace her with one hand and pull her skirts up with the other. She leaned in to my embrace but tried to wriggle away from my exploring hand. Too late: she breathed faster as I found the soft flesh of her thigh; she reached for my breeches, but I shrugged her off, kissing her neck. I was ready for her, and no mistake, but I needed that rage in me, not the sleepy forgiveness that comes with release. And Violet had shown me how to give a woman pleasure.

Violet. Despite it all, I did not want to betray her trust.

I found Lessie's venus. I leaned closer, biting her gently from ear to chin to throat while my other hand made finger-kisses on her. Slow and soft, slow and soft until she began to pull my uniform open.

I was rougher with her now, her skirts so high that I could grab handfuls of her belly, clamp her thigh, tease her; and then return to my task, each time bringing her closer to the edge. She fell further and further back until she was lying in the hammock. I was caressing her neck with my free hand. I kissed her mouth, keeping the fury inside.

She bucked and dug her fingernails into my forearm. Held the noise within, as all servants must in their master's house. Pressed her lips into mine and then pushed my wrist away.

It took a good long while for her to stop crying. Not tears of joy; I was not so gifted a lover. She was comfortless, a woman who had left her family and would not birth another.

I crouched awkwardly next to her hammock, one arm across her shoulder, the other cradling her head. She kept her back to me, but did not shrug away my touch. From outside came the occasional murmur of sentries. I knew it must be long past one o'clock, but could not leave her yet. If Quamin attacked before I reached Montalbion, I would lose my chance, once and for all.

At last Lessie slept, falling fitfully into a dream. Her hands and feet scrabbled under the thin blanket I threw over her. I took up the knife and watched her for a moment, then slipped through the curtain that covered the servants' staircase. She did not wake.

The staircase had been built so that servants could bring trays of food to the higher floors without entering the great hall. At the top, a door led onto the balcony that girdled the house. I clasped the knife and waited, listening for the sentries, but they must have been on the same balcony but round the front of the house. I knew that Quamin's men were in the canefield, from time to time making the noises of forest beasts: enough to distract the militiamen, but not enough to draw fire. Beyond them, the field-slaves had begun to sing.

After a minute, I decided to take my chance: I opened the door and darted along to the corner of the balcony, staying low to keep out of sight of the barrack-huts below.

The side of the house was also bare of sentries; there was one window, opened, with a gauze curtain swaying in the fitful breeze. Still I listened and waited. Quick steps; I ducked back around the corner, and a sentry came from the front part of the balcony, standing outside the window for a while.

"Vincent sleeps," he said in a cheery low voice, and went back to his post at the front of the house. I wondered that he had dared call Montalbion by his given name.

Now was my time. Thinking of all the people who'd suffered and died because of the man I sought, I took a dozen soundless steps and went over the windowsill head first, landing lightly in a crouch.

I had expected to see Montalbion asleep. But this was not his bedchamber: the largest piece of furniture was a cot four paces to my right, far too small for a man of the earl's height. Ten paces to my left, a door gave onto the balcony at the front of the house, and another doorway ahead led into the heart of the house. Faint sounds came through a third door, to my right. Clearly the earl was awake within his chamber at the back of the house.

I took a step towards the cot, and tripped on a wooden object. It clattered across the floor.

"Your Grace?" asked a sentry from outside, and before I could reply, the balcony doorhandle began to turn. I strode over and jammed my foot against the door before he could open it fully. I could see the tip of the man's nose, smell his pig-flesh breath: he had been feasting on Lessie's leavings.

"Guard," I ordered in a whisper, adopting Montalbion's husky voice.

"Sir …" he whispered back.

I waited, keeping in the shadow of the barely open door.

"I mean, my lord – Your Grace—"

"Go tell the gangmaster to keep those filthy savages quiet. And take that other villain down with you, his damned stamping will disturb my sleep."

I'd mimicked his master well enough. The guard closed the door and spoke softly to his comrade. They marched away, heels soft on the balcony floorboards.

I took a deep breath.

He dies, or I die.

He dies, or they lose their freedom. Violet, and … But I could not slow myself down by thinking how I'd ruined their lives.

Grasping the knife, I closed the balcony door and stared into the gloom. I was now used to the weak moonglow, which crept dustily onto the room's peaks and ridges: a rocking chair before a small fireplace, the low cot against the wall with two framed pictures above it, and a messy pile of objects on the floor. The blade ready to strike, I walked past the little bed. The pile on the floor grew clearer: a painted horse, some wooden balls, and a doll made from patterned cloth, its button eyes watching me.

In the cot was a small shape covered in blankets. It twitched and snuffled, worming its way into the plump pillows. A witchy dread pulled at my gut as I leaned over and gently pulled down the blankets. A child, perhaps three years old, was lying on its side, its face wrinkled in the terror of a nightmare.

The infant's dreaming faded, and it rolled onto its back with a whimper. As it calmed, its mouth pursed in a way I had seen before, the sharp ridge of its nose so familiar that I could not help but look more closely.

It opened its eyes. Too pale for its black corkscrew hair, they flared angrily in the moonglint, and then I knew who this was. Those were my mother's eyes. That was Emilia's mouth.

The child's mouth split into a terrified scream. My wits deserted me; I did not even try to cover its mouth or pick it up. All I could think to do was slip under the cot before it opened its eyes again, and hope it thought me a bad dream.

It screeched on, as wild and relentless as one of my mother's rages.

The door to the bedchamber banged open, and I watched a pair of bare feet stride towards the cot, flanked by the hem of a silk nightgown. Long, slender and tattooed with veins, the feet came to a halt close by my face. The child's screams faded as the man reached down.

"Devil man a come!" it sobbed.

"Vincent," said Montalbion gently, "I have commanded you not to speak that dirty pidgin. Now tell me, were you dreaming?"

"*Hiuuu*," whimpered the infant, his voice muffled. I held the blade as high as I could under the cot, staring at the spot on my enemy's foot where I should stab him, then bring him to the ground and cut his throat.

In front of my own son.

I had got the boy on Emilia de Corvis, I knew it now: that one time we'd lain together. And now it was Montalbion who held him, comforted him.

"Did you dream, my angel?" he whispered, rocking the boy in his arms. He stepped slowly out of my reach, his bare feet clinging damply to the floorboards.

"Smelly devil," said Vincent. "Fire on his head, like Mimma says—"

"Mimma knows nothing," Montalbion cut him off. "She is not to tell you island stories … but a stinking man could be … Guard!"

There was no reply, since I had dismissed both the sentries. Still holding the child, Montalbion sniffed the air. He must have seen my dirty footprints by the door, since he walked carefully in that direction. He was far enough away that I could see him draw the long stiletto from his deep nightgown pocket, keeping it hidden from Vincent with his body. I would have to wait for him in his bedchamber; kill him when my son was safely asleep again. And after that, God only knew what I'd do.

"Guard!" he barked, yanking open the balcony door.

Holding my breath, I rolled out from under the cot and dashed towards the other door. Behind me, I heard Montalbion speaking to a sentry in the grounds below, demanding to know where his door-guards were.

I slipped into the next room.

A four-poster bed, its drapes half-closed, took up much of the room. To my right were double doors leading to a dressing room, peopled with cloth mannequins wearing uniforms, feathered hats, sheeny visiting-clothes. Opposite me was a chest of drawers, under a small round window. At the foot of Montalbion's bed was a pallet, a nest of sheets and blankets.

Sitting bolt upright in it, her hands cuffed and chained to the bedpost, was Emilia de Corvis. Despite the dimness, I could see that her skin was darkened by the Caribbean sun, and her hair was untamed, more African. She stared at me silently, twisting her wrists.

I listened at the door, looking at Emilia. Behind her, the covers stirred, and Osca's head emerged. His eyes were open but empty, his loose lips bruised and wet.

"Where is the devil-man?" asked the boy, Vincent. Montalbion was coming back, guessing that a man of flesh and blood had disturbed his son's sleep. I showed Emilia the knife, but she shook her head, eyes imploring. *I have no choice*, I told her wordlessly; hide in the bedroom and I was trapped, but if I took Montalbion unawares as he entered the room, we might all escape.

The cot creaked as Montalbion put the boy back into the cot.

"Shhhh …" he said, making Vincent believe it was a game.

"Shh …" replied the child.

Still Emilia stared at me, her bound hands turned palm upwards. I hesitated, listening for Montalbion's breathing as he drew close to the other side of the doorway. The thudding of my heart sounded louder than the marching of guards outside.

Drumbeats echoed across the plantation valley. Then the wild uproar of the Maroons' war-songs. A gun cracked from far off, and there was a cry from the balcony.

Quamin's men were attacking at last.

"Two men in here!" ordered Montalbion loudly. "Guard the boy."

I took two steps back from the door just before he pushed it open. He saw me and attacked immediately, driving me towards the window with feints of his knife. I slashed wildly to keep him at bay.

The windows in Vincent's bedchamber shattered: a lucky shot from Quamin's men. Guns roared as the militia returned fire.

"Guards!" yelled Montalbion, but the noise was too great. He hesitated: the infant was in the line of fire. In that moment, he saw my face for the first time, and shook his head contemptuously.

"They sent *you*," he said.

"Traitor," I replied. His eyes widened, and he backed away towards the door, slamming it between us. I followed, but Emilia blocked my way, trying to grip my legs with hers.

"You shall *not*," she whispered furiously. By the time I'd wrested her off and opened the door, I could hear the sentries returning to the balcony. Montalbion was carrying Vincent through the door that led inside the house.

My chance had passed. I closed the door, turned and ran back through the bedchamber, hurdling Emilia's legs. I clambered onto the chest of drawers. The round window turned on its middle, leaving a narrow gap that I thrust myself through. It was a ten-foot drop. I twisted in the air to land neatly, feet first, and then I was away, racing for the high ground. Men were tumbling out of the barrack-huts, their attention on the gunfire on the other side of the great house, and I reached the scrub without challenge.

I had barely crouched down behind a spiny bush, weapon at the ready, when a strong hand seized my wrist, and my throat was caught in the crook of an elbow. I struggled to release my weapon, but an African voice hissed, "*Daabi*!"

The man who'd seized me loosened his grip. I fell down, wheezing for breath, and turned my head to see Prussia's tense face as he began a fierce whispered argument with four other Maroons. He looked to see if I was unharmed; I nodded to show I was not, and without pause they ran, crouching, down towards the storehouse.

Dozens of guns were now firing from the front of the house, and English voices were raised in confusion and alarm. As we'd planned, Quamin's rustling had drawn Carver's company into the canefield. When the Maroons fired their first shots from the field, the nervy militia at the great house had fired back, making the bluecoats believe that they had enemies on the balconies. Meanwhile, Quamin's men were making for the slave camp, continuing to loose odd shots to stop the Englishmen from realising their error.

I still had another part to play. Slipping in my ill-fitting boots, I bumped past the Maroons, who were waiting in the bushes. I took a breath or two at the edge of the scrub to button my uniform.

Twenty or so men had formed up in three lines next to the well, straightening their flintlocks against their shoulders. Whitlock seemed to have taken charge: he led them around the side of the house and towards the battle.

Still more voices came from within the huts; there was no time to lose. I darted to the door of the storeroom, knocked loudly, and gave the password in the dry voice of the ancient: "Fitzroyal!"

As the quartermaster came out to meet my challenge, holding his gun with one hand, a slender Maroon darted round the corner. He thrust a broken bayonet through the man's throat. I seized the quartermaster's musket and hat, and we bundled him backwards into the storeroom.

All the pickets had abandoned their posts and raced to the front of the great house to attack the Maroons, little realising that half the gunfire came from bluecoats. Now came shouts from further away, beyond the fields, and smoke billowed into the air high above the mansion: Quamin had set fire to the sugar-mill and distillery.

I stood guard at the storehouse door, carrying the quartermaster's musket, his hat pulled down over my red hair. Another little knot of soldiers raced from the huts to the front of the house: I waved the gun at them, comrade-like.

Men are blind once shooting begins. In the fear and noise, a white face and uniform were enough to make me a trusted friend, no matter that the quartermaster's blood had spurted half across my face.

I glanced up at the window I had jumped out of. It gaped blackly, like a hole in a sugar-eater's teeth. Down the side of the house, I watched Carver's company come out of the field, shouting and waving at the house-sentries. The shooting ceased for a moment; and then the Maroons in the field set up another volley, shattering more windows. Ordene, Flowers and three others ran to join Whitlock's band of militia.

Montalbion appeared at a window to yell at his blue-coats – God rot him, but the bastard had courage.

"They have but half a dozen guns, you dogs! Carver, send your men to help Kiet hold the slaves! And you gentlemen there, come round the back: there is an assassin close by. Look for his red hair."

The house blocked most of the battle from my sight, but I could see the English soldiers running back towards the sugarcane. Ordene and the others conferred briefly, then turned towards us. I urged the Maroons to leave. Each man carried two kegs of powder, and had a sack of shot and a musket slung around his neck.

The canefield caught fire with a roar. Quamin and his men were racing through the rows, making a wall of flame between themselves and Carver's company of bluecoats.

I used the quartermaster's bayonet to puncture a keg of powder. Kata pointed at the back door of the house, but I shook my head: Lessie was within. Instead, we ran a trail of gunpowder from the storehouse up the slope, each of us carrying two muskets. We were hidden by the sickly smoke coming from the field.

Shots were fired in the plantation, and a Maroon cried out. Quamin's men were badly outnumbered.

From a hundred paces off, Ordene saw us and called a warning. Our pursuers were carrying pistols, and they were too far away to hit us: their first volley came nowhere close.

Kneeling next to the powder-trail, I pulled my gun's doglock right back as my father had once shown me. I pushed the frizzen down, turned the gun sidewise over the powder-trail and pulled the trigger, but nothing happened.

Ignoring Ordene and the others, who were now but fifty paces off, I fired again: the pan was empty, so the sparks were free to fly into the powder trail. It flashed instantly this time, singeing my ear and eyebrow. The flame, throwing out white smoke, rushed towards the store-house. I grabbed the two nearest Maroons to pull their heads down towards the dirt, and the others followed suit.

A moment later, the powder store exploded. We were knocked onto our backs by the blast, the flare blindingly bright. A giant's finger and thumb gripped my temples. Burning timbers flew high into the air.

Prussia was on his feet before I could even see again. Seizing the muskets we had stolen, he half-dragged me up the slope and into the scrub. We could see clearly across the house. Our pursuers had been knocked flat, and Montalbion's bluecoats were in disarray: half of them were running back towards us, and the remainder were calling out to each other in the field. Quamin's men had taken advantage of the explosion to disappear into the forest. The wind had protected them, filling the cane rows with smoke; but Flowers and Ordene were on their feet, and had seen us again. Shot thudded into the earth around us. I gasped for breath as we scrambled over the ridge.

Further off, I saw a thin line of indentured men come running with buckets to pass from the well-head to the burning mill and boiling-house.

It was time to run, laden as we were. We ran the opposite direction to Quamin and his Maroons, skirting wide around the house and plantation.

*

It is a curious thing, to be far from home, to be hunted and sliced like a beast, and yet to be free. To taste the wild and distant sea in the air, to feel the rough force of your heart flinging itself against its cage, to know that nothing is asked of you in that moment.

I followed Prussia's wild wake through the forest, falling further and further behind.

Freedom sharpened my wits. I felt I knew where the tangling roots were, could sense when to run and when to slow, could hear Prussia's breath far ahead of me. He was leading us uphill, further into the mountains.

As the air behind us stilled, my guts plunged, and cold sweat mingled on my forehead with the warm.

I had not killed Montalbion. I had not kept my part of the bargain, and Ty would know of it soon enough. That meant transportation for two that I loved; capture and a runaway's punishment for me. At best, they'd cut off a hand or foot, and give me a beating. At worst – but my man-parts shrank to acorns at the thought.

Prussia was waiting for me in a clearing. He crouched with cocked head, his splay-tipped fingers to the earth. The half-moon clouded over as I drew near, dimming its firefly reflection in his eye. Small though he was, he'd outrun me for three hours or more.

A bat blattered over my head, circled Prussia, and was swallowed by the darkness beyond the clearing. I narrowed my eyes until I could see the shapes of the other four Maroons, just behind the treeline.

The air was drenched with the spicy perfume of the forest, but I could still smell the tinge of gunpowder from the kegs they carried.

Quamin loomed out of the darkness. Behind him came almost a dozen others: by burning the canefield, they had given themselves time to free at least some of the slaves. Among them were Kata and Zuasheba. They sat down, breathing heavily, Kata clutching his belly.

"Red Man him bring powder," whispered Quamin hoarsely. "Where him go now?"

I pretended to think about his question, but there was only one place I could go. I had to warn Ty about Montalbion's attack, and hope that he would show mercy in exchange.

"I need a ship—"

"Quamin Town," snapped Prussia.

"Naggle Bay," I countered, tapping a toe against one of the powder-kegs to remind them that I'd kept my side of the bargain.

"Plenty of soldiers hunting," replied the Maroon captain. "Red Man come to Quamin Town. Then talk. Mayhap new bargain to make."

"Mayhap," I replied reluctantly; Montalbion would be ready to strike in a week's time. "But we must be quick."

He patted my back and ordered his men to rouse themselves. Kata did not get up.

CHAPTER TWELVE

Quamin Town

Twentieth, twenty-first and twenty-second days of May

Quamin drove us on through the dawn, into the cool of the Blue Mountains. Four of the Maroons carried Kata's body, which meant more muskets, powder and shot for the rest of us to bear. We slowed to a trudge.

The Maroon captain was distracted and angry. He'd lost a man in the canefield, and had only freed seven Ashanti men, two women, and two other Africans from Alexandra. And Kata was now dead.

By mid-morning, we could hear dogs baying; by the time the sun was overhead, the pursuers themselves were within earshot. We began to run, a steady lope. I marvelled at the stamina of the men carrying the huge corpse.

Quamin called a halt in a clearing. Prussia took Zuasheba, the other woman and the two Africans up ahead. The other Maroons and the Ashanti men went into the forest to collect vines. They quickly wrapped me in the creepers, showing me how to keep my knife free, and where to lay my musket so I could fire when needed. "*Ambush*," whispered Quamin.

Within two hundred breaths, the whole company of Maroons was cloaked in vines, invisible in the undergrowth.

Quamin pointed to the spot where I was to stand, right by the path.

Covered head to toe, blinking away sweat, I could barely see through the vines. The noon heat pounded us, and I blinked away sweat. The dogs howled: they were almost upon us.

Where Quamin had crouched, I saw only a shadowy shrub, half a man's height. The clearing was utterly silent. Had the Maroons left me to face my countrymen alone?

I am already dead, came the reply from within my chest. Let them rip the flesh from my bones, I'd run no more.

Kiet's three great mastiffs appeared, dragging Pelton and a pair of sour-faced militiamen along behind them. Behind them was Captain Carver. I counted twelve in all, mostly bluecoats, against six Maroons and six male slaves. And me.

The hounds whined deep in their throats, pressing their snouts into the dirt as they drew close. I clenched the blade's handle, waiting for the soldiers to loose the dogs, but suddenly there was a wailing outcry from the women, further down the path. Just as Quamin had planned, it drew the attackers on.

Without a thought, Pelton and the two other dog-handlers rushed down the path, holding onto the leashes. Captain Carver came cautiously after. Still Quamin gave no order.

The bluecoats spread out into the little clearing. Some soldier's instinct brought Carver towards the tree I was pressed against. I held my breath as he came forward. He did not stop until he was within two feet of me. I looked beyond his shoulder at the bush Quamin was hiding in. Three soldiers surrounded it, peering into the gloomy trees beyond.

Carver saw the whites of my eyes. He opened his mouth, but I thrust my blade deep into his belly, and he gasped. Across the clearing, Quamin fired two muskets at once, then sprang up, slashing at an English soldier's throat. Another Maroon, just on my shoulder, darted into the middle of the clearing, cut at the backs of two soldiers' legs, and rolled away before they could fire.

Carver gasped and seized my blade. Without a thought, I let go of the handle and rammed my musket-barrel into his windpipe. We fell together. The Maroons fired a ragged volley and rushed down into the clearing with wild cries. They knew how to jink and duck around the soldiers' fire, but two of the freed Ashanti slaves did not, and they fell. Carver pushed against me, trying to turn his gun so that he could shoot into my guts. Gritting my teeth, I seized the blade again, ramming the handle down so that the point was guided into the captain's heart, and leaned on his chest with my other hand until his struggling stopped.

The remaining soldiers broke and ran, rushing back up the trail. Two of the Maroons yelled and began to run after them, but Quamin halted them with a harsh word.

Leaving two men to cut the throats of the wounded bluecoats, Quamin led his band down the path. I did not follow: my hand was knife-bound to the dying officer.

I'd killed a man once before, but that man had aimed to destroy my father and the master I loved. From his name,

I guessed Carver to be a craftsman's son like me, a soldier who'd come here for duty and a handful of coin, and I'd cut him open with a heathen trick.

More musketfire from deeper in the forest, as the soldiers tried to shoot their attackers. I could see in my mind's eye how the arrows came from the darkness, how blades met flesh, and I did not need to hear the last man's trembling plea to know that they were all dead.

I went a little way down the trail. Two dogs lay on their sides, pierced with arrows, their throats cut. They'd had the scent of Maroons in them, and could have led any man on this island to us. Further on was Pelton, one of Prussia's arrows in his throat. He was still alive, but Zuasheba, whose foreman he'd been, had seen him. She drove a matchet into his eye.

Quamin stormed towards me, blade in hand. Four of his tribe had died since the attack on Alexandria.

Waiting for him to strike, I passed a bloody hand across my forehead. He pushed me back into the clearing, gesturing that I should help myself to the possessions of the dead.

I stripped Carver of his uniform, gorget, stockings and breeches. His waistcoat was ripped and soaked in gore, with the blade still pinned deep between his ribs. None of the fallen soldiers was as tall as I, so the waistcoat I took – from a man with a Maroon arrow in his throat – was tight around my chest.

One by one, the other Maroons went up to Quamin, carrying boots and muskets and powder-bags. Some dropped little handfuls of copper and silver coin at his feet. The Maroon captain did not look down.

As I folded the uniform into a soldier's knapsack, Quamin kicked Carver's ribs.

"Take *afana*, Red Man," he said, meaning the knife. I tugged at the straps of the knapsack instead of replying. He placed his heel on the dead man's hip and pulled the weapon out with one hand, sucking out a handful of slivered guts and belly-meat.

I took the handle from him. Sunlight glistened on the English captain's innards. The wiry archer, Prussia, put his bow down and gave me a piece of soft bark to clean my blade with.

"*Abeng*," ordered Quamin. One of his men brought him a cow-horn, pierced at the closed end with a small hole. Putting it to his lips, the Maroon captain gave a blast that raised my hackles.

We reached Quamin Town the next morning. Nestled in a flat-bottomed valley, lacking palisades, it was little more than a camp: three dozen huts with dried fronds for roofs, open firepits that smouldered through the day, and a patch of ground where women worked. Beyond the camp was a strip of tilled land, almost the length of Silk Street. Yellowing leaves sprouted sparsely from the earth.

Quamin yelled a greeting as we came out of the treeline. Three girls quit peeling yams, and were joined by a whelming rush of women, some carrying babies on their hips. They were in faded loincloths. Strings of feathers and bright snail-shells were laced through their hair, and polished pebble necklaces hung between their bare breasts. Among them were Quamin's two wives, one as old and scarred and powerful as he, and the other short and doe-eyed.

A moment after greeting their men, the women were upon me, wide-eyed and suspicious. Three naked infants ran among us.

"*Eho fitaa!*" cried a girl. She pinched my white skin, pushed my chest, stared at me.

"*Owo ti hwi kokoo!*" replied Quamin, pulling my head down to show them my red hair.

Some of the men who'd stayed behind in the village came to take Kata's carcass from their comrades. Zuasheba and the other slave-woman followed. I turned to watch them, ignoring the patting and pinching that bedevilled me.

The Maroons lifted the corpse by his arms, speaking quietly to him as if he were simply too old to walk. As they went towards the biggest hut, two of them took off their bone necklaces and hung them around the dead man's neck.

"Kata will speak tonight," said Quamin.

"How will he speak?" I blurted.

"*Hawilapiki! Hawilapiki!*" mimicked one of the younger wives. Prussia tugged at my sleeve.

"Water," he said, pointing to the stream that ran round the lower side of the valley, and made a loop with his hand to show that I should not cross the trunks that marked the women's place.

I shrugged and went, alone, to drink.

Perhaps I had expected to be praised and feasted; or, more likely, to be killed. But I had not expected to be ignored.

My pride prickled: had I not stolen the Govnachief's weapons and blown up his barracks?

I made for the shallow stream, where I took off my boots and lay down on the pebbled bed. The water rippled warmly on my skin, bathing the scratches and sores of a night's forging through the jungle.

I listened to the children playing.

Finding the boy Vincent had changed everything.

Montalbion had seen me, and I'd lost my chance to kill him. Which would mean leaving Emilia and our son in the middle of Montalbion's war.

I closed my eyes, letting the water caress my skull, and then crawled out of the stream to sleep.

I had a son.

Kata's body had been laid out on a trestle next to Quamin's house. The Maroons had rigged a frame, onto which two women were laying huge leaves to shade the dead man. He was ornamented with linen, a cloth that was strange to see on a half-dressed runaway. His ankles, wrists and brows were pinned with trinkets of carved wood, teeth and shells. Little pearl-like seeds were fixed to his ears. Zuasheba was sleeping on the ground next to his bier.

I had slept well into the afternoon, and now I was dizzy from the heat, a rash bubbling up on my neck and throat. One of the Maroon women watched me: Quamin's younger wife. Her hair was clumped and matted, and she bent her shoulders and elbows awkwardly as she lifted a bundle of leaves for the other woman to lay. Her loincloth sat ill on her hips, and had twisted around so that it barely covered her venus. I looked away and let my gaze fall on the cadaver, which had begun to smell.

"*New-come buckra he get sick* ..." sang Quamin's wife, just loud enough for me to hear it. The other woman snorted.

"*He tak fever, he be die*," I sang in the jay-caw of the Port Royal canoe-women.

"Ehh, Pheba! No *buckra* here!" laughed the woman who was atop the frame, reaching down and batting Quamin's wife, whose name I took to be Pheba, with a leaf-stem. She smiled, trilling through her teeth.

Quamin and his elder wife appeared in the doorway to his hut. She frowned at Pheba, who twitched her nose, shrugged and went back to work.

"*New-come buckra he get sick*," I sang softly. "*He tak faver, he be die* ..."

"Red Man," said Quamin. "Not sing. Talk."

I rubbed at the red patch on my throat.

"Naggle Bay," I said. "You'll take me there tomorrow; I've kept our bargain."

Pheba and the other woman rustled away at their thatching. The elder wife stared at me as Quamin's bare toes curled into the earth.

"Wait you, Red Man. Tonight we sing to Kata with *obi* man. Then you-me talk."

I looked at Kata's corpse.

"We sing," I agreed. Quamin tapped his full powder-horn.

He led me to the mouth of the valley, where some of his men had gathered on a dusty slope to practise. These were the warriors who'd stayed in Quamin Town, and they were sparring with the fierceness of men who have just missed a real fight. We sat down a stone's throw away to watch them.

"Sombah," said Quamin, pointing to a burly fellow standing at the lip of the slope.

Sombah held a spear and a matchet. Two other Maroons came at him with their spears, jabbing and swiping, driving him down the slope as he slapped back with his blade. Twice their thrusts went past his guard; they pulled back so as not to pierce too deep, but still they cut his flesh, and soon blood ran from his arm and side.

Sombah was no weakling. His calves bulged, the sinews standing out from the backs of his knees as he dug into the shifting earth, twisting this way and that to invite his opponents downwards. At last, after he had retreated five paces, he drew them into lunging at him at the same time, and clinched their spear-tips between his two weapons. His opponents were caught off balance, and he threw himself onto his back to pull the others down the slope beyond him. Now they were skidding, their grips on the spears loosened. Sliding down in pursuit, he dealt each of them a cracking blow on their scalps with the flat of his matchet. The watching Maroons hooted.

As the sky grew more bloated, each warrior took his turn at fighting a pair of men at once. Three were defeated swiftly, unable to parry the dancing blows of the attackers. Prussia was next, his bow and quiver strapped tightly to his shoulders. Slender and spring-limbed, he wove and leapt his way around the spears that jabbed at him. He crabbed across the slope, slicing at his opponents' feet, yelling and shrieking to throw them off. He grabbed a low-hanging branch at the edge of the forest, flung his feet skywards and swung his whole body up into the tree.

Instead of chasing him, the other two stayed back, jamming their spears into the earth.

"Prussia, him *katawud*," said Quamin. "Them Maroons cannot follow. Prussia hide in trees, then *whoosh* – arrow in throat from high."

I ignored the unspoken threat.

"What is *katawud*?"

"We are all *katawud*. When slaves run away, they *kata* into the forest. *Kata*, you mind? Like … "

He took a handful of earth, crumbled it between his palms, and dusted the ground before us.

"Scatter," I said, sounding just like Ty when he tried to teach me something. "*Scatter*wood."

"You *katawud* now," said Quamin impatiently, digging his forefinger into my side. "Better you learn quickfast how to fight them *buckra*."

Now the Maroons began to run, up and down the slope, darting and ducking from side to side; crouching to make themselves small; sliding to raise dust. This was how they had dodged the soldiers' gunfire. Quamin insisted that we do the same on our own patch of slope. We raced each other, stumbling on the shifting ground until the other Maroons were laughing and the air was filled with rain, drops as big and leaden as musket-shot.

It was still raining lightly when the ceremony began that night. The whole village squatted in a ring that began and ended with Kata's bier. Within the circle were four firepits. A casket of woven bark was placed at the dead man's feet, and one by one the Maroons got up from their places to drop in an offering. The two Africans who were not Ashanti – contemptuously called Bongos by the Maroons – sat outside the ring, staring at their own feet.

There was no start or finish to the funeral. One moment there was the bubble of voices, and the next there was music. Drums seemed to rise bodily from the earth. Between the firepits, a pair of Maroons thrummed on a hollow trunk. Dancing outside the ring, three men rattled sticks on hacked-out blocks.

At first the drummers seemed to beat against each other, out of time; but then the women began to hoot, high and low, in a darting rhythm that charged and shied away and charged again. *RrradadumradaDA, rrradadumradaDA, rrradadumradaDA*.

Slumped on my side, my thighs too tired to squat like the Maroons, I felt the music spark the gathering. Quamin's senior wife stood, taking up a gourd that was strung like a lute. She went to Kata's altar, plucking at the highest string, her finger sliding up and down the weeping neck. Others played on cooing nose-flutes.

Zuasheba remained at Kata's side, staring into the fire.

Quamin rose and danced around the nearest firepit, close enough for steam to rise from his skin. He sang, *Fai-oo, fai-oo*: Fire.

Fai-oo, fai-oo, fai-oo,
Fai da bun oo, fai rakita

Fai da bun oo, fai rakita
Fai-oo, fai-oo
Fai da bun oo, fai rakita

He beckoned. Though I refused at first, Prussia took my hands and dragged me to my feet, leading me in a wild dance around the fires; and all the while the noise and music rose. We were playing out the burning of Alexandria.

When we reached the middle of the ring, the archer stopped cold. He pinned my elbows against my sides and widened his eyes to say that I should stay still. Then he stepped back.

With a scream that pierced the smoke, a man with his head bundled in cloth rushed at me, brandishing a matchet. He chopped at the air above my head, then whirled around me, snatching at my clothes. I twitched but I held my ground, holding Quamin's gaze. This was the *obi* man.

The sorcerer yelled a chant as he slashed at my wrists and arms, each time stopping just short.

"*Obroni!*" he shrieked.

The *obi* man flung his blade into the ground between my feet, making it shudder. Crossing his legs, he kicked backwards, making himself stagger and twirl, arching his shoulders and flapping his arms like a great bird. "*Opete! Opete!*" chanted the crowd; and Prussia grabbed a spear, spiking two huge embers from a firepit.

The *obi* man seized the coals in his bare hands. Prussia ripped my shirt open to the navel so the sorcerer could press the coals to my chest, rolling them down from collarbone to breastbone. I gasped at the stinging touch, but it was not followed by pain. Looking down, I was astonished to find that my flesh was unharmed. Rain fell like a blessing on the pink heat. The *obi* man threw the coals into the air, catching them close by my face. He flung them far outside the ring, into the tilled fields beyond Quamin's hut.

One of the drummers hooted. Another man cut a chicken's throat and spattered its blood on me. Quamin led the freed slaves into the ring, and within moments the whole village was dancing and singing. Even Zuasheba, who had stumbled all the way to Quamin Town in silence, joined the song, her voice raw and insistent.

Outside Quamin's hut were placed clay drinking-pots, big leaves bearing a yellowy mash, and pieces of yellow fruit. Now the dance had begun, we were free to eat a little, drink a little; and the booze was as rough and hot as a night upstairs at the Spanish Dogg. I gasped at my first gulp; laughed at my second; staggered full into Pheba with my third.

I was no Maroon, yet I was part of their tribe. I was drawn to Kata. The smell of his body was masked by the teeming cold rain and the fire-smoke, earthbound in the damp air. The dead man's eyes had shrunk back into his skull, but his lips still seemed pursed on the edge of speech.

I watched Quamin dancing. He whooped as loud and jumped as high as any man; he took his turn at the drums; he poured a portion of his drink on the earth, as they all did; yet there was a pretence in the way he moved. He did not believe.

He felt my eyes on him, and jerked his head. *Watch me not, Red Man*, said his expression. He called an order to the drummers, and soon a new rhythm beat the air, making the flutes and stringed gourds fall silent. The village squatted in a ring again.

RrrradadaDA. RrrradadaDA. RrrradadaDA.

The cloth-headed *obi* man stood by the drummers, shaking and stamping in time. He held himself differently, like a warrior, his back twisted so that one shoulder drooped lower than the other; amid the smoke and darkness, he could have been Kata himself.

"Kata! Kata *a prandes*!" called out Quamin.

"Him go home," said Pheba, who was standing close to me. "Go home in Africa."

Kata's spirit now grew inside the *obi* man. He strode from fire to fire, jabbing like a spearman. Then he lifted an invisible musket to his shoulder, aiming it into the forest; then danced across the ring, pointing it at the Maroons. Zuasheba knelt down next to Kata's body, looking away from the *obi* man's performance.

The Kata-spirit did not speak, so Quamin spoke for him, a stream of words in his native language, which Pheba gave to me in English.

"Kata him never can go *a prandes*, home in Africa … Kata say Quamin him make *prandes* this place, then Kata-spirit can live with Maroon people."

Quamin spoke louder, faster; and the drumming rose, beating the rain back up into the sky's womb until it ceased falling.

"Kata him say too many Ashanti women *buckra* slave. Maroons him take them women, take powder, take more men, make this place whole *prandes*. Take hundred hundred Ashanti man, woman. Make Maroons' spirit strong."

Now Kata's spirit pointed at me, thumping his chest with his other hand, showing the Maroons where the glowing coal had not harmed me. The rum made my senses swirl.

As Quamin ranted on, Pheba whispered, "Kata say you *buckra* no more. You white-skin Maroon."

So that was the bargain Quamin was thinking of. He would use his tame *buckra* to free more slaves; and perhaps then he would let me go. Perhaps.

Well, I'd play that part if I had to. But I would get to Naggle Bay, with or without his help.

I tore off my shirt and went to the firepit, spinning to show my runaway brand. More drink was pressed on me; I grabbed a piece of hog-meat, and then the dance seized my legs, and I was Calumny Spinks no more.

I woke in the depths of night, half-naked and cack-throated. The air was loud with rain, hurling itself down to all sides of where I lay. I rolled to one side, cracking my skull on solid timber, making the roof two feet above me clatter.

I rubbed my forehead, squinting queasily into the pouring rain. It was the coldest time of night. I realised that I was under Kata's bier: it was his death-gifts of shells and beads that I'd rattled.

My eyes grew used to the gloom. Bones and drinking-gourds were scattered across the churned ground. At the far side of the ring, spears had been thrust into the ground and draped with vines, making the shape of a green man. His chin thrust upwards, and he leaned forward as if greedy to swallow his own future: they had made a copy of me, about to stab the *buckra*.

The drink and the feast still warmed me from within. I remembered Quamin, using the dead man's spirit to promise that his village would become a homeland for his Maroons, that he would fill the mountains with freed slaves and build a stockpile of powder. That was the work of months and years, and I had but days to spare.

I turned onto my belly and wriggled towards the rain, holding out my cupped palms. The water tasted of thunder, and waxy leaves, and the scent of Jamaican soil. It was a flavour I knew well: it was the essence of the coffee I'd roasted in London. Somewhere on this island was my old master's plantation, which had once yielded a rich crop.

I had to warn Ty that Montalbion's rebellion was a month earlier than he'd expected, otherwise he and de Groot would be taken unawares. Perhaps I could win Violet and Simona's freedom that way, even if it would cost me my own.

But I could not get to Ty without risking my life for Quamin's ambition. And time was pressing. It was now May the twenty-second: less than a week before the planned uprising.

I lay awake until the sky began to lighten, then went to Quamin's hut and called for him. Pheba came out and scolded me in her tongue, but the Maroon captain was not long behind, and put an arm around her waist to ask for peace.

"Kata's spirit wants you to free more Maroons, Captain Quamin," I said, as if I had just been sharing a glass of port wine with the cadaver.

Pheba curbed a smile.

"Kata says that I am no longer a *buckra*. I am a white-skinned Maroon. So let me fight for you."

I folded my arms and waited. Quamin grunted and stepped past his wife into the dawn light.

"Red Man no fighter," he said.

"True enough," I replied, "but I'm willing to strike a blow or two if you'll take me to Naggle Bay afterwards, and without delay."

"*Crakka Juba*," he said under his breath, and went back inside.

"You crazy somebody," said Pheba, scratching the tattooed scars on her cheeks.

Quamin came out with his matchet and led the way over the tilled field into the forest. We took a well-masked path that led up the steep end of the valley, alongside the stream. Rocks had been wedged along the path with boughs, in such a way that fleeing Maroons could dislodge them to crush their pursuers.

The stream became a pool under a waterfall. I snatched a handful or two of water from it before following him, up the path, which climbed steeply next to the cascade. The clouds burned away.

Near the top of the hill was a little grassy platform which had a sheer drop to the waterfall below. Here Quamin stopped and turned, showing me the vast forests that clothed the mountains. Far away, the ocean was a wavering haze of promise and threat.

He pointed down the valley. The village could not be seen, but thin wisps of smoke were rising.

"Them fires bring danger," said the captain. "Show *buckra* Quamin Town from far away."

He looked up. I knew these sinewy peaks: they were on the painting I'd stolen from Emilia, a picture that showed her father's hidden coffee plantation. If the angels smiled, it was still in Port Royal, folded up and locked in Hoopy's chest.

The mountains' shape was different from where we stood, but close enough that I believed myself to be within a day's walk of where she'd made her picture.

"Red Man," Quamin said quietly, one hand in the small of my back. "Why you go into Govnachief house? Why you not tell Quamin all the truth?"

The waterfall roared on below us. Standing on the precipice, I did not risk a lie.

"To get something I needed."

"Gun? Coin?"

I tapped my head. "What's in here, I must take to Naggle Bay. And then—"

"And then you free."

"And then I'll be free," I agreed. "And my – my wife and daughter too."

The Maroon smacked his lips.

"No more lie," he said. "Red Man free Ashanti men, Red Man can go Naggle Bay. Red Man lie …"

Quamin lifted his warm palm from my spine and went to shake a tall slender tree. Four or five green-skinned fruits plummeted from above. He caught two in the air and threw one to me. He showed me how to peel the lizardish skin, and we bit into the soft nutty flesh. It was oily and delicious. We threw the round stones into the stream far below.

I pointed out over the forests. "Where do you want me to go?"

He squatted, ripping out dewy handfuls of grass until he had cleared a patch of earth. Pointing at the mountaintops, he drew a copy of their outline with his stubby finger, and then made marks here and there. "Fever tree place," he said, pointing. "Stony Fall River; Kincaid place; *Lekandra*" – by which he meant Alexandria – "Button Farm, close by hog-hunt forest."

"How far is Kincaid's?" I asked. It was the easternmost of the plantations he'd named, which meant it was on the way to Naggle Bay.

"One day, one night ... Bad river cross, maybe ten-twelve Ashanti, many more Bongo slave ..." He shook his head.

"I know that place," I lied, despite his earlier warning. "I can make the *buckra* open his door to me."

"Ha!" coughed Quamin, putting on his pretence of bad English again. "Red Man Talk Big. Man Talk Big, Fight Small."

"Naggle Bay," I insisted. "If I open Kincaid's place to you—"

"Then Quamin take you. Naggle Bay."

I held out my hand to seal our bargain. The Maroon flattened his nose, looking at my *buckra* gesture as if I'd offered him a turd.

A hound bayed in the valley below. Quamin leapt to his feet.

"How many dogs did you kill before?" I asked quickly. "The *buckra* had three, but I only saw two bodies—"

He was already racing down the hillside, matchet in hand.

I stayed at the summit; my skin was not my own to risk now. Minutes later, a musket fired from beyond the village, and then another. The dog bayed again, but the sound was cut short. And then the whiny snap of English voices.

The burly figure of Sombah came running up the path, followed by the Maroon women and children, and the two Bongo slaves. Gunfire crackled below.

By the time they joined me, the sky was smudged with soot. The Maroons had set fire to their village to blind the attackers so we could flee, while Quamin and his warriors drew the English off in the other direction.

Once everyone had reached the top, Sombah led us all in a wide circle down the back of the ridge. I went last, following Zuasheba, whose eyes were wide: she knew the penalty for recaptured slaves. We could no longer hear the fight, only our own ragged breathing as we descended the rough path.

At the bottom, Sombah plunged shin-deep into a pebbled stream and skidded on downwards. The women and children followed, gasping at the chill of the stream; but not one complained.

After half an hour, the stream joined another. Quamin was waiting for us there, carrying three muskets. Some of the men who stood with him were carrying two guns: three more Maroons had fallen. With Kata and the others, that was seven dead in all. They would all be alive if I had not encouraged them to attack Alexandria.

As Quamin began to speak, the bowman Prussia translated for me: he spoke English as well as any Limehouse tanner.

They had fought off the white men again, killing their only dog; but some had escaped, so now the valley was no longer safe.

Since they were short of fighters, Quamin told his tribe of his decision to raid Kincaid's and free more Ashanti, but Sombah was not content. He rumbled angrily in his tongue that we should make for the Mandingo cave, which was a hiding-place for runaway slaves on the coast.

Quamin waited for his men to have their say. His power was more like a buccaneer's than a lord's: it sprang from his followers' will, not from right of law.

Sombah had his way. The burning of the village had quelled the Maroons' appetite for raids.

We set off eastwards. There was no path in this direction: the Maroons had to push their way through shrubs and creepers. They could have cut them easily enough, but that would have left a trail, and so we trudged on, swiftly falling into a weary *pad-pad-pad*, eyes always downwards, trying not to trip on vines and roots.

Sombah was leading the party, and he stopped every few hundred paces to listen, sniff, feel the thrum of the land beneath his feet; but there was no sound of pursuit. We did not sleep until near dawn the next day, when we were sure that the soldiers had lost our trail.

I knew I was of little use to the Maroons now.

Later that day, we came to a deep, fast-running stream that led to the Mandingo cave. I was not permitted to see it, but made to wait with Quamin while Sombah ensured that it was safe.

"Captain," I said to Quamin, "I ask for a new bargain."

"No more bargain, Red Man," he replied.

Prussia watched me, quietly shuffling the arrows in his bark quiver.

"I know of a place. A farm. It … it belongs to me. And it can be a safe place for Maroons: hidden. Enough money to buy powder and shot and food. Enough land to plant new provision-grounds. We can share it all."

Quamin knelt by the stream, took a double handful of water and threw it over his head. Drops clung to his hair like jewels.

"More lies," he said.

There was a long silence. Sombah reappeared higher up the stream, waving, and Quamin gave the command for the Maroons to go to the cave. Only he and Prussia remained. The bowman nocked an arrow.

"Wait," I said. I knelt next to Quamin and began to draw the blue mountains of Emilia's picture in the sandy soil. A rough curving peak like an Italian's nose, two others sheltering beneath it, and a jagged ridge clawing at the sky.

Quamin tilted his head. He looked at my drawing, and then up the valley at the distant mountains.

"Turkey Head," he said, pointing at the biggest peak above us, and then at the noselike jag on the ground. "Fallen Child. Mouth Bone ... How you know this place?"

"I told you," I replied. "I have a painting. A map of this place."

Prussia put down his bow and spoke at length in Ashanti. Quamin grunted once or twice.

"What do you want?" demanded Prussia.

"If you take me to Naggle Bay, there is a man ... He was my friend ..."

Quamin sucked his teeth.

"Now not your friend."

I nodded and said, "After I see this man, I need your help to get away from him and find my map, which is in Port Royal. I must be there within four days: will you take me?"

"Runaway in Port Royal! Red Man, you *Crakka Juba*," said Quamin.

But he knew I was not mad; he could see that I spoke the truth. Emilia's painting was the map I spoke of: the position of the mountains would show us how to find the hidden de Corvis plantation. Within an hour, ten Maroons and the two Africans were ready to leave for Naggle Bay. The rest of the tribe would wait at the Mandingo cave.

CHAPTER THIRTEEN

A Letter

London, tenth day of January

Citizen Pettit,

    It gives me no small pain to inform you that Calumny Spinks is not with you as a Volunteer; he has no care for the College's mission; he is a Criminal and Thief. He is in truth the man who stole the Gold that should have been your father's, and that would have paid for your fuller education. By way of proof, Master Collingwood will give you the Ingot in question. Irrespective of any Sentiment of Vengeance, I trust that your Reason alone tells you that he should pay.

    I do regret to inform you that his Paramour, Violet Fintry, and her daughter are to be transported unless he discharges his Obligation to the College. C. Spinks believes that his mission is confined to Investigation and Spying, but in truth he must attempt to assassinate Lord Montalbion, and thus draw the earl into open rebellion. The Crown requires such a casus belli: *If Port Royal burns, the Charter for our Colony will be signed.*

    I know you to be a man of Conscience and Independent Thought, and capable of preserving your quondam Friend against the College's needs. Therefore, contemplate the following:

If you warn C. Spinks, or if you do not brand him as instructed, then the Fintry woman will be separated from her child, and both transported.

If he does not try to silence the earl, they will be separated and transported.

Live or die, if he makes the attempt by the end of June – which means that the Navy ship Mordaunt *will be in Port Royal – then they will be freed, my solemn word upon it. But you must understand that it is most likely that he will fail: Lord Montalbion will recognise C. Spinks, which is why we have sent him. We must provoke a reaction.*

If he fails in his task and returns to you, he must be sent back into indenture. That is the contract.

I know that you will do your Duty.

You are likewise reminded that the Republic Secular has an absolute and pressing need of funds, if we are to secure our Colony. The College urges you to use ALL MEANS NECESSARY, including the planned salvaging of Wrecks using the Device, to meet that need. Should you be successful, you will be named Warden pro tempore *of the Colony.*

I have no doubt that your late Father would have pride in your Accomplishments. Be resolved; and once decoded, destroy this letter.

Citizen J. P. Northmoor, Provost of the College Secular

CHAPTER FOURTEEN

Naggle Bay

From the twenty-third day to the
twenty-fourth day of May

Prussia became my shadow on the journey to Naggle Bay. I decided to make use of his wits and learn something of the Maroons' language. He was a willing teacher, demanding in return that I tell him of Port Royal and London, of the white men's alliances and betrayals and ways to wealth.

He'd been a slave to a hog-hunter before he escaped, and he knew the forests as well as I knew Silk Street. As we walked, he would point at a tree, or a great red bug, or a cutlass-beaked bird, and give me its name in English and Ashanti.

Late on the first day, Prussia opened up a twist of torn cloth that hung at his belt. Inside were two shiny, ancient-looking apples, and a tiny gourd that had been plugged with bark. I reached out to take one – but the Maroon snatched the bundle away.

"Don't touch, Red Man," he snapped. "This is manchineel fruit ... Poison. A little serpent that will bite you from inside ..."

The little gourd held the sap of the manchineel tree, and was used to poison the Maroons' arrows.

This lesson did little to lighten my thoughts. By stabbing Captain Carver, I had become a different kind of man. No more flitting between Heaven and Hell; I was of the earth now, and in the earth I'd rot, a killer.

I'd once helped a merchant cut away his rotting warehouse floor in the docks: you chop into the wormy joists and soft boards until you see the cold, drowning Thames shivering in the darkness below. There's power in looking at nothingness, in knowing that you are no more than a beast that eats, breeds, fights and dies.

The first night, we slept on beds of cut ferns. I drifted in and out of dreams. Out here in the jungle, there was none of the teasing and boasting I'd seen in the village: the men were silent and unhurried, laying down to sleep without ceremony.

The next day was May the twenty-fourth, four days before Montalbion's planned uprising. We crossed the lowlands, staying in the shade of the forest. This was a rough country: we had been heading south-east, and the plantations we skirted were small and ill-shaped, the sugarcane limp and sparse. Ten acres was a great deal of land in London, but out here it carried pitifully few crops. These were smallholdings of the sort I'd earn, if ever I survived my indenture.

Eventually, Quamin stepped out of hiding to hail a pair of poor planters. One was Irish; the other a Londoner who'd been in the Caribbean so long that he now spoke in a singsong Creole way. I stayed hidden, mindful of the runaway's brand I bore, but Quamin waved for the Bongos to step forward. The Irishman offered him a pair of silver dollars for one of the men, but Quamin shook his head angrily, saying only that the Bongos' freedom had been bought in blood.

The Londoner took out a moneybag and shook a few gold pieces into the Maroon's palms.

One of the Africans saw the gold and wailed a warning to the other. They turned and began to run into the forest, but Prussia and the other Maroons were waiting for them, flintlocks cocked. The bargain was struck.

Quamin gave one of the coins back, and the Irishman handed him a package of food. I watched the two white men lead the pleading Africans away at gunpoint. The Maroons did not follow, but shouldered their muskets again, hooding their eyes.

Prussia saw me staring at Quamin. I glared back at him. We did not speak for the rest of the morning.

That afternoon, we descended through a narrow rocky valley. The path came out high above secluded turquoise waters, then dropped steeply along a cut in the cliff. I joined Prussia at the top.

"Naggle Bay," he said. The stony half-moon beach was piled high with jetsam. Waves battered at the great toothy rocks which protected the bay; beyond them, in deep water, was a two-masted ship at anchor. Its deck was busy. More than a dozen sailors clustered around a scaffold that was slung out above the water; there was a rope at its tip plunging down into the sea.

It was the *Esperance*.

Wind plucked at our sweaty clothes. I shivered, and without asking Quamin's permission, I set off down the cliff-path. Prussia followed me; which was just as well, because I stumbled halfway down, and would have fallen twenty feet to the strand if he had not grabbed my musket-strap and dragged me back onto the path. Walking more carefully now, I looked at the rocks below, which were littered with pieces of bleached wood. Many a ship had foundered in this bay.

Once the Maroons had joined me, I asked Quamin to keep them hidden in the bushes that lined the bottom of the cliff. He needed little persuading: being seen would present no small danger for him and his warriors.

I went further along the beach and waved at the ship, but every man on deck was intent on the scaffold. Ty Pettit's Nereid Device was being hauled out of the sea, swaying despite its great size. The scaffold bucked, and though I was half-blinded by the sun flashing on the water, I could see the strain as the sailors pulled back on the ropes. A man's body fell from the Device, and two sailors jumped into the waters after him.

I watched as the Device was bound to its scaffold again. The body of the man who'd fallen was pulled out of the water. Richard Collingwood was watching from the rail, smoothing his hair.

I took a deep breath and waved again. He saw me and turned to give an order. Before long, a boat was lowered from the ship. The Master Secretary climbed down into it with four oarsmen. As they rowed carefully around the jagged rocks, I pointed Collingwood out to Quamin.

"I must go aboard. Grab that big fellow. If I do not return: kill him."

"More trouble, Red Man," he said.

I went down to the surf to watch the Master Secretary leap out of the boat. He and his men had not finished dragging it ashore before they were surrounded by ten armed Maroons.

"You'll hang for this," said Collingwood furiously.

The oarsmen were allowed to return to the *Esperance*. The Maroons held back from the boat, eyes gloomy with remembrance. Many of them had been shipped to this island in yawing darkness, a press of bodies slick with puke and piss and blood, unable even to sit upright.

Prussia, who'd spent years on boats, made to join me. To his disappointment, Quamin ordered him to stay onshore.

The sea was bright and patterned, but it was no relief to be among the *buckra* again. In the coxswain's calling of the oarstrokes, I heard the pitiless beat of Kenver Kiet's voice.

Up on deck, the crew was busy making the Device fast. Puddles of water shrank into salty stains. On the poop deck, the surgeon who'd sealed my brand looked down sombrely at a trestle bearing a dripping wet shape: the body of the man who'd fallen from the Device.

Next to him, a shorter, slender fellow, dressed in a full suit of black gabardine despite the heat, sat at a low desk, scribbling on a loose sheaf of papers that he held down with his elbow. He dipped his quill irritably in a pewter pot: *tok-tok-tok*.

"Ty," I called, but my voice cracked. He turned in his seat and stared at me. Then he bent back to his writing, batting an outstretched arm. It was an order to the coxswain, who took me into Ty's little cabin under the poop deck.

"Sit," said the coxswain, roughly pushing my shoulder. It was as if the brand had never healed: the "R" clenched at his touch.

"Where's Francis?" I asked him. "I did not see the diver, Francis Coyle?"

The sailor shook his head. "Nor will you again. That fellow today's the third to drown in that infernal bell. We warned Mister Pettit about the undercurrents, but he will only speak of mass and inertia—"

He snapped his mouth shut and closed the door.

While I waited for Ty, I looked around the cabin: the chests under his bed were padlocked, and there was no food to be found. His Bible had been left on a shelf. I opened it, and a paper fell out. At the top was row after row of numbers, broken into little gangs of four; at the bottom was a letter from the Provost of the College Secular, written out in Ty's handwriting: it was a decoded message. I had only read the signature and the date when I heard Ty's footsteps outside.

I tucked the paper swiftly into my shirt, sat down, and waited for him to come in.

"And?" he asked coldly, closing the door behind him. He remained standing.

"And Montalbion lives."

"So you've broken your bond and abandoned Violet" – he cleared his throat – "and now kidnapped Master

Collingwood. If it weren't for my affection for the Master Secretary, I'd have you drowned."

Wavelets slapped weakly at the *Esperance*'s hull. The serpent carved by Ty's father leered at me from the wall.

"Which you won't," I said quietly, "and I'll take no words on duty from the man who sent me into that monster's chamber."

Ty frowned. "Do you mean to say that you found him? That he saw you, and knew you intended to kill him?"

I rapped my knuckles on his Bible. "I was as close to him as you are to me now. And he intends to attack Colonel de Groot's force—"

"That's well done, Cal!" interrupted Ty, and for a moment he became the excitable boy I'd known in London. "Violet and Simona: they will go free now."

He held out his hand. I kept mine on the Bible.

"As will I," I said, but he had backed towards the door, blocking my way.

"No, Cal – you're still bonded to the College … You signed a contract, did you not?"

"God damn you, Ty!" I exclaimed, jumping to my feet. "I have more intelligence of Montalbion – at least trade with me—"

Ty shook his head. "Cal, if you run away this time, then you are a condemned man. Six and a half years is not so long, and we will all be together in the Rep – in the new colony. In time, forgiveness may—"

"To Hell with your forgiveness, Tyburn Tree Pettit. I know that you intended for me to fail – that Montalbion should see me and have me killed. I'll be damned before

I bond myself to you again. I know what you've done to Francis, and all for your bloody College."

Furious, I did not tell him how soon Montalbion had planned his attack.

"The Republic Secular," said Ty, "is worth some sacrifices. The Provost says—"

"Your Provost knew my father for forty years, but he had my warehouse broken into, and Violet arrested. Did you know that?" I demanded. "Now let me go, or Collingwood dies."

Ty closed his eyes. He fiddled for a moment with his charcoal quiver, then opened the door and led me out.

On deck, I saw two more bodies under canvas. An indigo-stained hand, with one finger missing, was poking out of one of the shrouds.

Ty came back to the beach with us. As we stuttered over the wind-chopped waves, I watched him gripping the tiller. If I but spoke the word, he'd take me to America to serve my bond. The time would pass soon enough: at twenty-seven I'd be free to take my acres, and have a chance to make amends.

"They go free, no matter what I do?" I asked him.

"I swear it. And once Montalbion is taken, come and find me in Port Royal. I'll sign your manumission myself."

"Tell Violet … Tell her …" I began; and then I had no words.

When Quamin saw that I was safe, he pushed Collingwood towards the boat. The Secretary stumbled, cursing like a mercenary.

"Come now, Collingwood. The revolt has been sparked: we must meet Colonel de Groot at Fort Charles without delay," called Ty, with a warmth I had not heard since his father died. Collingwood obeyed, giving me an evil glance as he passed. He clambered heavily into the boat. Oar-blades scraped on pebbles, the iron-bound keel squealed, and the rowers dug powerfully into the sea to back away. Ty called the stroke over the dim rumble of Collingwood's voice.

"He's counted your men and your guns," I said quietly to Prussia, holding back from the other Maroons. "You need to leave this place."

"Why does that other man hate you?" asked Prussia, loud enough for Quamin to hear.

"His father died for me," I said.

The Maroons gathered around us in uneasy silence as we watched the *Esperance* weigh anchor. Once it had set sail, Quamin demanded to know what had happened on board the ship.

"Now I need to go to Port Royal," I said.

The Maroon captain grabbed hold of the front of my uniform. It crumpled, showing a corner of the paper I'd stolen. Quamin snatched it out.

"Read aloud!" he demanded. As I read the Provost's decoded message, the Maroon made me point to each word as I read it, so that it would be harder for me to lie about what was written. I'd no doubt I could have fooled him, since I'd lied all my life: to field-girls and lords, to men holding pistols to my head, to my own father. But this time there was no need.

"*Citizen Pettit ...*" I began.

*

Prussia interrupted me every now and then, asking for a long word to be explained. I could not tell him what *casus belli* meant, though I could guess at it. It was the mention of Port Royal burning that I stammered over.

When I had finished, Quamin asked, "You kill Govnachief?"

"I tried," I said. "And I know what that has cost you, Captain."

He nodded, very slowly.

"Port Royal will burn?"

"Yes."

"Then we had better move quickfast, or your bloody map will burn, too," said Prussia.

Quamin returned to the Mandingo cave, leaving Prussia and two others to escort me: I would keep my promise, or it would be an arrow in the throat. I could hardly blame the Maroon captain for it. Seven men dead, and his village burned: that was what I'd brought him so far. One more debt to pay.

We walked for the rest of that day, cutting across hilly country towards Port Royal. Prussia did not seem to bear me a grudge. He was an adventurous, bloodthirsty fellow, and he chattered away until I decided to tell him my true story. What did I have to lose? At first he did not believe me, but by the time he'd felled a pair of bright green birds for our dinner, he was fascinated by what I intended to do.

"They sold you in Port Royal. And now you go back there?"

"The best time to advance is when your enemy thinks you have fled," I said.

The other two Maroons, who spoke but poor English, stared at me. Prussia grinned and began to lay a fire.

After we'd eaten, we talked about Port Royal: the fortresses, the King's House, the wharves. I scratched a rough map in the dust for him, and he looked at it from all sides, shaking his head. Since the Crown's forces controlled forts on all sides of the town, we could not see how Montalbion could hope to win a battle there.

I read the Provost's letter again, and my heart sank. Ty had not branded me for revenge, just as he'd told me that night. He'd done it to protect my family – and now he was sailing to Port Royal, not knowing that Montalbion was gathering an army that would greatly outnumber de Groot's forces. It would strike in four days' time: I had to warn him, for Violet's and Simona's sakes, as well as his own.

I slept little, and dreamed less.

CHAPTER FIFTEEN

Kalken

Twenty-sixth and twenty-seventh days of May

Two days later, we crested a ridge. A deep green bay lay before us, bounded by a long narrow spit. Port Royal was a fragile shimmer at its tip.

We reached the shore the next morning. Leaving the two other Maroons at the edge of the forest, Prussia and I collected water from a stream and braced ourselves for the weary miles along the Palisadoes. Since no man but Kiet ever walked them – it was less than an hour's row across the bay – we were alone with the spiny plants, the butterflies and the buzzing heat. Every so often, a hidden bird sang *Wee-oo, shwee-oo.* We no longer talked.

Late in the afternoon, I trudged towards the town gates in my filthy blue uniform. Prussia followed two paces behind, as if he were my slave. I told the guardsman that I was the last of Captain Carver's company, which had been slaughtered by runaways in the Blue Mountains, and that it had taken me almost a week to get back.

"Has Lord Montalbion returned to Port Royal?" I asked him.

"No sign of him, friend – but some of his household arrived at the King's House yesterday. Militia, bondsmen, even that vixen – saving your pardon."

He ushered me through with a friendly pat on the back. Prussia followed, carrying a sack with his bow and arrow in it.

I could not risk being seen by one of Montalbion's soldiers, so I hid the blue coat in Prussia's sack and led him cautiously into Port Royal, making sure my ragged shirt covered the branded "R". There was a bustle about the place: more militia than I remembered, gathered in gangs of twenty or more. I avoided Thames Street, going instead around the back of the King's House. Keeping my face down, I passed the church, a tumbledown building that was scaffolded for long-abandoned repairs.

I made for Lime Street and went to knock at Hoopy's lodgings, but a round-shouldered fellow was mounting a whore in front of the doorway. She was bent on hands and knees, trying to stop his thrusts pushing her fingers into a pool of piss. I waited to one side, impatiently watching his scrawny buttocks go faster and faster.

He was taking handfuls of her flesh, kneading her like dough. Every fifth stroke, he'd pull away and plunge his stubby crooked pimmy into the other part of her, then back again after five more. He stank of slavery: of airless decks, the bloody flux, and death.

Juddering, the man finished. He laced his breeches, spat to one side and tossed a silver coin into the piss-pool for the doxy. I waited for him to clear the doorway, but then he looked me full in the face: it was Edwin Foulkes, the man who'd sold me at auction.

I hesitated.

"Watch!" he shrieked. "Call the Watch on a runaway!"

There were no Watchmen in Port Royal; but the call runs deep in all Englishmen, and I did not get far before I was caught. Fat-bellied buccaneers who'd not drawn a sword in years pinned me to the ground. Prussia got away, at first cowering like a fearful slave, and then wriggling through the mass of men. He scrambled onto a warehouse roof, a flash of purple-black against the moody sky.

"You'll be needing those," said Kenver Kiet, running the butt of his lash over my hands.

I knelt, barefoot, in the servants' yard. The chain between my wrists had been nailed to a stump. My feet were tied to a post behind me so that I could not curl up.

He tapped my skull. "You'll be needing that, too. Ten years at least you'll have to serve now, runaway."

I knew none of the men in the yard. A score or more of them, drably dressed in calico, or cast-off cloths that had been sewn into patchwork. Standing with arms folded, mouths downturned, chests rising and falling faster than the cool day deserved. No man wants to see a beating, but few can look away from one.

Kiet brought the butt of the whip down on my back. Then twice more, lower down, pummelling the breath out of me. As I tried to draw breath, he dealt me a crack across the throat, leaving me gasping. My forearms had been driven into the stump's rim, scraping the skin until it bled.

Like a child, I tried to hunch my back against the blows, but no more came. Only the slow pacing of the Cornishman around me.

"Break a bond, break a bone," he said to the watching servants, wagging the lash. "Any man here wishes to forswear his indenture, and speak with my whip Kalken here?"

He shook out the lash now; raised a puff of dust. The whip's tip lay in front of me, trailing through the dirt like a thirsty river.

"Why'd you run again, Mincher?"

"I was taken by the blackamoors—"

"Why'd they take a white halfwit when they could have freed a hundred of their own kind, eh?"

Slowly, the whip slithered back along its dusty groove. I raised my head to watch as Kiet gently lifted his elbow, snapping it down, eyes on my hands – but he rolled his shoulder at the last moment so that the lash fell brutally on my calves.

This time I yelled. I'd not known how tender that flesh was. Three times more he hit me, coming around to strike at the backs of my knees, my thighs, my backside. I'd been on the march for more than a week by then, and every ounce of me was tender and bruised. My chest tightened. My tisick had taken hold – I rolled to one side, dragging my feet and hands against the piniored chains, wheezing and choking on dust.

Pain came and left, came and left. Foul air clogged my throat, and I kicked and bucked, tearing my wrists and ankles on the bonds.

I would not faint. My mother had died the last time I'd let myself fall under; I'd not let it happen again. I had to warn Ty. I commanded my heart to slow, my voice to quit screaming, my throat to open.

Time slowed.

"I was took, Master Kiet," I rasped, desperately trying his Cornish accent. "I was took a slave like your forebears, I ran back to the *sowznacs*, I am here for my bond. Beat me or not, I've broken no law."

In the silence that followed, I could hear the gulls crying far overhead, the grumbling of porters on Thames Street. My own heartbeat, slow as sin.

Kenver Kiet laid the lash down, curling it before the stump. The indentured men curbed their breath: it was not over. The overseer took an oiled knife from its worked-leather sheath at his belt.

"Runaway pays a runaway price, Mincher," he said softly, dropping to his knees in the dirt. One hand clamping my right wrist, he placed the tiny point of the dagger just below the first knuckle of the pointing finger. I jerked away, but his fingers were like steel, and I could only scream as he drove the knife into my flesh, pressing down with all his weight so that the blade slowly, slowly cut into the bone. My sight was blasted white. Gore sprayed against the Cornishman's open shirt. My finger twitched for a moment after it left me – I had no time to mourn its loss, for he had tugged his blade out of the stump and driven it into the middle finger.

Another scream. Whiteness flared once more. A cold void took me under.

*

Charred hog-flesh. Rattling in the darkness, like coach-wheels on cobbles. Carking of gulls, and a spice in the air …

"Take him out of here before my husband sees," snapped a woman, her singsong voice bound up with steel. I was blind. My arms flopped as strong hands lifted me – a ravaged hand brushed on hard wood—

Tallow guttered. My eyes rolled open. A black-spotted candle stood in a small pool of grease. I was lying on my left side, my other hand cradled on a pile of rags in the hollow of my belly and lap. The skin of my right arm was tight.

The stink of charred flesh.

Deep bruises pounded across my ribs as I lifted my head to look at the mutilated hand. Two stumps, seared pink, twitching under my gaze.

I dropped my head again.

"Be thankful. It could have been the whole hand – or both of them," came a whisper from the darkness.

Ignoring the fierce ache in my ribs and bones, I carefully leaned towards the candle, pushing it to one side with my wrist so I could see who spoke. The two remaining fingers dragged through the tepid tallowmelt.

Emilia de Corvis stood with her back against a door. Her face was drained, her eye sockets puffy, but there was still that wild challenge in her expression. She was dressed well, as if she were taking the air in Westminster, and not hiding with a bondbreaker.

We were in a small storeroom. Casks were stacked neatly up against one wall. On the other side was a pile of sacks, one of which was slowly leaking powdered spices.

I tried to raise my head, but I did not have the strength at first. Blinking, I tried to clear my thoughts.

"Be grateful, Calumny Spinks," she said, "that I had those wounds seared. Else you'd have the fever by now."

"But ... you're free?" I said.

"Why should I not be?"

"Montalbion. You were tied ..."

She shrugged. Had she allowed him to bind her? It was too much: I closed my eyes and waited for her to speak.

"You tried to kill my husband. And now you think you can try again, that I will let you?"

Husband. Christ's blood! The gate-guard had complained of a "vixen". "Harpy", Carver's men had said in Alexandria: they meant Emilia. Montalbion's woman.

"I want our son," I said, getting defiantly to my knees.

"And where would you take him?" she asked mockingly. "To Fort Charles? Tomorrow it will be smashed to pieces; and there isn't a captain in this port would defy Lord Montalbion. No, Calumny Spinks, you will not be taking *my* son."

Sharp pain from my missing fingers gripped my arm and chest. I doubled up, my breath whistling in, and she took a hurried step towards me.

"Cal—"

But she cut herself short, waited for me to recover, and began again.

"By coming here, you've brought danger to me and my little B – My little Vincent. I should have let Kiet cut your throat."

She flung something hard at me. It bounced off my leg and into the darkness.

"Run from here tonight, Calumny Spinks, and you had better keep running. My husband will rip this island apart to find you. But do not leave this room for a quarter-hour at least."

She closed the door behind her.

Chin slumped, I began to count my breaths. By the thousandth I was on my feet, groping my way towards the dim outline of the door. I found what Emilia had thrown: a heavy iron key. Keeping my maimed hand against my chest, I felt for the latch with my left hand.

It was unlocked: I lifted it, stepping awkwardly back to open the heavy door.

It led to the yard I'd been beaten in, empty in the horned moonlight. There was the stump, spattered with my blood. An arched gateway leading through to the main yard. Beyond it was Thames Street: that was my path.

A boy cried out, "Devil-man a come!"

I looked up at the King's House. Far above me, an infant of about Simona's age was sprawled half-out of a window, his belly pressed on the sill. Curly black hair, bright eyes, and the twisted lip of a boy who is always ready to tease and demand. Vincent, unafraid, pointing a crooked finger at me.

Two men appeared, their arms full of kindling. One of them challenged me.

Vincent screeched at them, "Go away, you!"

Meekly, they touched their forelocks, scurried past me and through another door, slamming it behind them. The boy turned his head, as if someone inside had said something; he snapped back at the other person, but ducked back inside without another glance.

Well – I knew where the little bastard was now. I could not let myself think of him as a son.

Warn Ty, I thought. *Warn Ty.*

I began my slow, painful walk to the archway. I was close to fainting with the pain of the lash-cuts and my maimed hand.

I stopped at the arch. The courtyard beyond was filled with voices. I slid the key into the door and turned it, thanking the angels when it clicked. I opened it cautiously and slipped through, hiding in the lee of two shrouded hulks. After waiting for a minute, I peered out.

At the far end was the main gate, guarded by four soldiers of Montalbion's regiment. Planters in martial dress were waiting in line to see a bluecoated army officer, who was writing at a field-desk. The colonials' uniforms were bright and varied: canary yellow with blue armbands, white with grass-green frogging; some wore the gorgets and spurs of cavalrymen, rakish feathered hats, boots polished to a shine. There were three or four officers from each militia, bantering and arguing with each other, faces pink with heat and excitement.

Two little blackamoors ran from man to man, each carrying a sack of port wine. As well as the officer, there were five other bluecoats standing guard.

"Colonel Ganner's militia, eighty men," announced a yellow-coated fool to the officer at the desk.

"Condition?" he asked coldly.

"Armed, drilled …"

"How many muskets? How many horses? What drill?"

"Forty guns …" answered Ganner, flushing. "Eight horses, and the monthly drill … Well, every second month for gentlemen and landowners … which is to say—"

"Which is to say: no arms, no drill, no horses," said the soldier. "Just like every one of your milkwater militias. You'll have to subscribe for the rest – silver, mind you, none of your letters of credit. Another dozen horses, ten muskets … You'll need to pay for a section of musketeers besides. See the Comptroller inside there."

He nodded in the direction of the main house, where a double door stood ajar. Ganner, trying to put a proud face on it all, jangled a sack of coin at his waist as he strode off.

Blood pounded against the seared stumps of my fingers. I watched the other militia-commanders give their names and dispositions and go in to see the Comptroller. In all, more than five hundred men were spoken for that hour. Five hundred men, not to mention Montalbion's own regiment; de Groot's garrison was heavily outnumbered.

I hid until the militia-commanders said their good nights and the lantern was doused. The bluecoats disappeared into the King's House, leaving the four men who guarded the main gate. Unsure whether to enter the house or try to trick the guards, I waited; which was just as well, as three more men were still in the yard, and had gathered around the second hulk.

I crawled around to watch them peel back the covers from a curious cannon. It was like no gun I'd ever seen: its mouth gaped upwards at the stars, and its belly bulged like a woman with child.

Two of the men were army officers, and the third wore a leather jerkin and broad-brimmed Puritan hat.

"We must conclude this before His Grace arrives. You said it could fire over a thirty-foot wall," snapped one of the bluecoats in a low voice.

"And so it can, Lieutenant," said the leather-jacketed fellow calmly, taking off his Puritan hat and running a hand through his sweaty thinning hair. He had the contented, fat-cheeked look of a man with knowledge all his own. "Yet a parabola's apogee is determined by its amplitude. It is not *absolute*."

"Speak English, damn you," said the other bluecoat, hand on his sword pommel.

"What I mean," replied the engineer, gently prising the officer's hands away from the cannon-mouth, "is that to vault a thirty-foot wall will require Baron van Coehoorn's mortar to be within two hundred feet of the same. It is the great catapult of our age, but it is made by man, not God. Natural law must circumscribe its reach."

The lieutenant made the engineer explain what he meant, twice more. His fists clenched as he listened: he had the manner of a man who must share bad news with a tyrant.

"Christ's nails," he said at the end, "we cannot get this engine to within two hundred feet of Fort Charles! There's a hundred *yards* of killing-ground from the end of Church Street to the walls. We are dead men if we cannot explode the powder-store. We must strike it direct, blow up those Dutch invaders, and then the other forts will surrender. If not, we'll have four hundred men and thirty cannon at our throats."

"Chocolata Hole at dawn," replied the engineer, stooping to lift the canvas back over van Coehoorn's mortar.

"What d'ye mean?" demanded the officer.

"Not here," said the Puritan, leading the soldiers towards the door of the great house: he was in command now.

So goes the world. Lands are conquered with powder and steel; but it is men of mathematic and letters who govern the world.

Fort Charles: Ty had told Collingwood that he'd meet de Groot there. Could this Coehoorn cannon truly vault its walls?

The stumps of my lost fingers clenched painfully. How was I to get out and warn him? The gatehouse was manned by four guards with muskets. Two on the parapet above, one on either side of the door. Emilia had been mistaken: there was no chance for me to escape through the gate. I would have to find a way through the great house before Kiet discovered that I was missing.

I waited for the gate-guards to settle down into sleepy boredom, then slipped through the shadows and up the steps to the door of the King's House. It was not fully closed. The engineer had been the last fellow through: as I followed his trail, I praised the angels for the forgetfulness of intelligent men.

The panelled hall within was unlit. I waited for a moment with my back to the door, peering into the gloom. Loud voices came from behind a closed door to my right: the militia and army officers, drinking and debating. On my left, a stairway spiralled up to a landing.

I took off my boots, tucked them under my arm and darted up the stairs. The house stank of tobacco, souring my tongue. A pair of high-backed, three-legged chairs were placed against the banister, separated by a round table. On it were two sugar-cones and two sets of pincers. One of the cones was half-hollow: the eater had scooped out the middle, where the sugar was still soft, leaving a shiny crust for the flies that crawled on it. The other cone had barely been touched, nor the dish of coffee alongside it.

I was out of breath already, my head reeling. Two half-open doors led from the balcony, but I needed to gather myself before pressing on: I had not eaten since morning.

With my unhurt hand, I clumsily brushed the flies away and plunged the pincers into the untouched cone. I found a soft kernel of unfouled sugar, dipped it in the dish of cold coffee, and sucked it off the pincers, sighing at the drink's dark caress. The sugar melted in my throat, a stinging sweetness that woke me fully.

I took another scoop, and another, until the core had gone and I was chewing through the fly-shotten crust, cramming it into my mouth with dirty fingers. The coffee in the dish was scummy with melted sugar, and the black dregs trailed down my arms, staining my shirt still further.

Below me, the main door banged open.

"Barsby!" shouted Lord Montalbion, striding into the centre of the hall. He was flanked by officers. "Ganner! Flowers!"

There was a brief hush, and then the air bubbled with the noise of boots on wood, and the extravagant greetings of the plantation owners. I peered down through the railings: Montalbion, resplendent in a silk sash, gorget and pale blue costume, held up a hand for silence. Behind him, six or seven privateers and merchant captains filed in silently, led by Hicks and Ordene.

"Where's that God-damned armourer fellow?" he demanded.

"Thomas Cattle is my name," said the Puritan, "and I am an *engineer*, Your Lordship."

Montalbion glared at him.

"... Your *Grace*," Cattle corrected himself.

"Are those weapons ready to fire, Cattle?" asked Montalbion. "They look as if they would explode within themselves."

"Indeed not, Your Grace," Cattle replied, failing to hide his injured pride.

"I do hope not. In any case, you will be placed with the firing-crew, so you will share in our risk as well as our reward. Now, gentlemen ..."

The planters and bluecoats shuffled a little closer.

"We all know the injustices that my *Dutch cousin* has brought to England, as well as to our blessed colony here. A standing army, paid for with new taxes; continual war with the French; terrible restraints upon our freedom to trade. Like you, I have suffered and served in silence, because I love England, which my own father once ruled."

A fly buzzed around the despoiled sugar cones. One of the officers glanced up at the balcony. I shrank into the shadows, faint with pain again.

Montalbion went on: "But injustice has led to outright crime. Half our gains from the Spanish tyrant to be taken by the Excise. And then they send an *assassin* for me ..."

A buzz of voices. Montalbion raised his voice.

"Yes, an assassin. A heretical thief from England, a man who once tried to violate my own wife, shipped in by the Dutch Jew who lords it over our Port Royal. He was in my own infant son's bedchamber, knife in hand, when I found him—"

Now there was uproar in the hall below me. Though these men had seen rape and slavery and murder, they felt true outrage at what I'd done; and in that moment I could almost have joined them. If a devil-man had come to my son's chamber—

"No more," whispered Montalbion throatily. "No more tyranny."

"No more!"

"His Grace is ready to rule England as his father did," declared Sir Fergus Ordene. "And with nearly six hundred men, and the advantage of surprise—"

"De Groot expects us to do this," interrupted an officer. "Indeed, I believe that his entire plan was to provoke His Grace into rebellion. We must reduce the two principal forts before he can turn their fire on our forces. Fort James is poorly defended on the landside, and Fort Charles has a powder-magazine that we can destroy."

"Impossible," said one of the militia commanders: the planter, Flowers. "Any attack must come down that neck of land by Chocolata Hole: they can fill it with shot from dawn to dusk."

"Not impossible," began Thomas Cattle, but he was interrupted by a noise from outside: Kenver Kiet, shouting raggedly for His Grace.

I did not need to hear more: he had found the store-room empty, and would know I could only have escaped through the main yard. Once Montalbion heard that a redheaded runaway was loose in the King's House, it was over for me.

I turned quickly and ducked through a doorway at the back of the balcony, which led to a short hallway with a door on either side. At the end was an unshuttered, mullioned window. I ran to it, and looked out.

To the right, beyond the mare's nest of homes, taverns and warehouses, I could just see the flash of moon on sea. Directly before me was the scaffolded church. This part of the King's House was perhaps only eight feet from the edge of the scaffolding.

Voices came from the balcony behind me. One of them was Emilia's.

"Someone has touched the sugar ... heard any noise?"

"Perhaps Vincent ... nothing ..."

Still she protected me. I had no time for gratitude: I undid the latch and swung the window inwards. As I climbed up on the sill, an officer called out, "Forrester! Come here!"

A salty gust of breeze. I prayed they did not feel it on the balcony as I balanced on the narrow sill, closing the window with my good hand. I flicked the latch up at the last moment so it fell back into place. My sugar-sped heart pounded as I looked over my shoulder at the scaffolding. A sliver of light inside – the hallway door was opening – I twisted and leapt across to the wooden tower. It bucked against the long nails that bound it to the old church, but held firm. Ignoring the pain of the wounds Kiet had given me, I scrambled around the side of the church, keeping in the shadows.

A man carrying a lantern went into one of the side rooms, flooding it with light. He rattled the casement, but it was sealed shut – and in his haste to find the runaway, he forgot the hallway window.

From the yard beyond came more voices. Soldiers banging doors, demanding answers. Shouting, running, and the alarum bell ringing from the gatehouse. Boots on the streets of Port Royal.

Now was not the time to warn Ty. I could only flee upwards. Before the soldiers reached the churchyard, I got to the highest part of the scaffolding, lifted a pair of loose roof-slates and dropped inside. Sanctuary: a gift not from God, but from my own wits and battered body.

CHAPTER SIXTEEN

Ordnance

Twenty-eighth day of May

Montalbion's men searched the port for more than an hour, whispering to each other to avoid alerting de Groot's men. Doors were rattled, locks tested; but the church was sealed, and the lower ladders of the scaffolding had been stolen long since.

I knew they would have to give up soon: at dawn, de Groot's men would see the bluecoats and know for sure that Montalbion was in Port Royal. Once the sounds died away, I climbed to the bell-tower. The weak moon glistened on the timbers of the King's House before me.

To my left was the sweep of the Thames Street warehouses. Beyond them, the dark bay was unnaturally still, with barely a lick of white foam. I saw the *Esperance*'s curious tilted masts in the busy harbour.

At the west end of the port, close by Fort James, the *Swan* was drawn up on the careening ramp. The fort's ramparts had been rigged with blocks and tackles, and I could see that a pair of ship's cannon had been heaved up to cover the town. But it was clear that they had no notion an attack was coming so soon: Montalbion had slipped into Port Royal unseen.

Left of Fort James, past the end of Church Street, stood Fort Charles, a star-shaped castle whose guns covered the entrance to the great bay. In the lee of its unarmed northern wall was the Chocolata Hole, a grubby little mooring for fishing-smacks.

Fort Charles also had a block and tackle on its ramparts, and in its centre was a round storehouse with enough gunpowder to bring a mountain down. They thought it was safe behind the doubled stone walls.

I could see clear up Church Street and the High Street from the bell-tower. Quietly, in threes and fours, a large company of militiamen slipped through Port Royal, keeping to the shadows. It took a long time: there were hundreds of them, gradually filling up the alleys between the Thames Street warehouses, until they were all within charging distance of Fort James.

Creeeooommm. Creeeooommm. Creeeooommm. Creeeooommm.

A small band of men pushed the two covered Coehoorns out of the King's House and directly onto the wharf opposite. Two ships were waiting for them: swiftly, quietly, the mortars were dragged up the gangplanks and lashed to the decks. It was perhaps four or five o'clock in the morning, and the port was dead quiet.

I recognised the tall man captaining the first ship: Sir Fergus Ordene. He waved an arm; two small sails were unfurled, and the ramp was drawn back on board. The *Blessed James* slid out into the flat waters of the bay, followed by the other ship.

Out of my sight, in the courtyard of the King's House, I fancied I could hear a hundred men drawing breath together. And then the high, brutal voice of Vincent de la Haye, who'd once held a blade to my eye and given orders for my friends to die. I could not hear his words, but I knew that priest-of-war tone, the song of a man who glorifies death for those about to receive it.

No more time to watch and wait. The Coehoorns would fling their missiles; Ty and de Groot would die, and my contract with them; Violet and Simona would be lost. If I did not reach Fort Charles quickly, this city would burn.

I took one last glance at the bay. Ordene's vessel was already rounding the headland, and the second ship had anchored a hundred feet off Fort James. I stumbled down the staircase to the attic. Back out through the broken tiles, onto the scaffolding, clinging clumsily with my uninjured hand as I climbed down to the graveyard. I leapt down from the last platform, landed safely and rolled behind a large headstone. No cries of alarm. I was up and running in an instant, leaping the low stone wall and racing up Church Street. Montalbion's combined forces had vanished into the warehouses, and I only saw a couple of drunks sleeping in tavern doorways.

Dogs ran in the other direction, tails between their legs. It was the first time I had seen the beasts do anything other than sleep or beg. I slowed for a breath, forgetting my haste, and fell over a man's outstretched foot.

"Mincher," drawled Kenver Kiet, "you're a hunderprice now, a thrice-runaway. You've had the lash, you've lost a finger or two. Now your man-parts are forfeit."

He aimed a punch at my head. I rolled away, catching a glancing kick on the ribs. I seized his foot, but he was slippery and shook it free, lashing out at my head again. I ducked and sprang to my feet. I backed away from the Cornishman, who was blocking the way to Fort Charles.

"Hunderprice is theft, see?" said Kiet, taking out a large knife.

I'd been cut enough for one lifetime. With my good hand, I took a handful of dust and flung it at him. Slitting my eyes, I barged him aside and ran towards Lime Street, hoping to find the Maroon. Kiet was hard on my heels, slashing at my back with the knife. I had not my usual speed, and he drew closer, cursing me. The sound drew three drunk privateers from the Dogg. The middle one snatched at his sword. I could not slow, and was barely four strides from them when Kiet gasped.

I turned in time to see him fall, clutching at an arrow that pierced his chest. Up on the roof of the Spanish Dogg, Prussia dropped his bow and ducked out of sight.

"We are under attack! The French attack!" I shouted, pointing at the Cornishman. His ribs had been pierced by an arrow, not a French musketball, but most men will fight or flee before they ask the wise question.

"Alarum!" yelled the man who'd drawn his sword. He and his companions began rattling on doors until the cry was taken up from within.

I shouted to Prussia in Ashanti: *Stay up there!* Kenver Kiet was staring at me accusingly, his cheek pressed into the dust. The arrow had been dipped in manchineel sap, and he was near-gone already. I took the knife from his feeble fingers and left him there; I hated him right enough, but I did not rejoice in his death.

Dawn had broken, and Fort Charles' guards raised their guns at the sight of me. I raced towards the gates, waving my arms at them.

"Colonel de Groot!" I yelled. Glancing out at Chocolata Hole, I saw that Ordene's ship had its nose in the little bay already. Half a dozen men were gathered around the Coehoorn, which was still shrouded. Among them was the engineer Cattle. He was holding a device to his eye, which he angled up at the fort's ramparts, then down to its base. The fort's cannons had been shifted from the bayside to point at the town, which meant that none of them could be aimed at the *Blessed James*.

"Colonel de Groot!"

"Take him!" ordered the Dutchman, who'd been on the walls, overseeing the the raising of Fort Charles' guns. He leaned over the parapet, the sunrise glistering on his sweaty forehead. Two of the guards stepped forward. I dropped the knife and let them seize my arms.

"Take me inside!" I demanded, glancing at the *Blessed James*. Ordene's men were busy furling sails.

"Hold," snapped one of the guards, a set-jawed stocky fellow with a Frenchy accent.

"Huguenot?" I asked, trying to catch my breath. "*Nom de Dieu – il faut qu'on entre directement!*"

God's name, we must enter now!

Nothing moves a Frenchy like his own language. The Huguenot guard ushered me in.

Ty was waiting with de Groot.

"What d'you mean by this, citizen?" demanded the Dutch commander, furious. "The orders were clear: no disturbance must be made before the ship *Mordaunt* arrives—"

"Ordene has his mortar aimed at us, not two hundred paces from the armoury," I burst out. "Delay, and we are all dead."

Ty grabbed de Groot's shoulder and whispered urgently, hiding his mouth with slender fingers. The Dutchman nodded twice, stepped forward and yelled his orders.

"Grenadiers to the gate! The *Swan*'s western cannon party cease raising; transfer sakers to northern gunports! Third and fourth companies to the muster-ground! Engineers draw water, prepare for fire!"

I had never seen such speed in a band of men. In fifty breaths they had obeyed. Dozens of soldiers drew up at the gate. Behind them were scores of bareheaded, cold-eyed fighters, in double lines from the fort's main well to the round armoury tower. De Groot berated his company as they struggled to swing a cannon into a gunport that overlooked Chocolata Hole. No English soldier I'd seen had ever moved so fast or complained so little: this was something new, a weaving of men and ordnance. Our new king had made a machine of his army.

Richard Collingwood joined us at the gate. He spoke a word to the lieutenant of the grenadiers, who nodded brusquely. They set off for the fishing-wharf together at a trot, leaving me alone with Ty.

In the bay, the *Blessed James* had dropped its anchors, and was lying still in the scummy water. The Coehoorn's covers had been taken off, and two men were packing powder into its greedy mouth while the rest of the crew lined the railing. They watched Collingwood and the boarding-party take possession of half a dozen boats that were drawn up on the pebbled beach. The grenadiers wore furred caps with coped crowns, giving them a fierce look. Each bore a sack of green glass grenades.

We stood aside as de Groot marched the other two companies past us, taking up station a hundred paces from the fort, ready to move on Port Royal. I followed them.

"Cal, you should stay here," began Ty, coming up behind me.

"You'll have to shoot me," I said.

"If you run, then Violet—"

I began to run. I shouted over my shoulder, "Ty, if you love Violet so much then you should marry her yourself. My son is in Port Royal. When he's safe, I'll come back."

"Ah. The boy," he said quietly. I stopped and rounded on him. He was holding a pistol.

"You knew? Jesus Christ, Ty, you knew Emilia was alive? That I had a child?"

"When I first came back from the Caribbean, I tried to tell you that Emilia was involved. You didn't listen." He pointed the gun at me. "For Violet's sake, for Simona's sake, if you run I will shoot you in the legs."

We were between the town and Chocolata Hole. The fort's defenders had managed to raise a single cannon on the side facing the attackers: with a loud crack, it fired on the *Blessed James*. The shot landed far out in the bay, and I could hear de Groot's yelled commands as his men worked to raise the gun's base and lower its muzzle.

On board Ordene's ship, the powder-loaders had finished, and four men were levering a huge shot into the Coehoorn. Collingwood and the others were rowing hard, but the *Blessed James'* musketeers fired a volley. It ripped through the oarsmen.

From Thames Street, there was a great roar, and then hundreds of muskets fired at once: Fort James was under attack by land and sea.

Ty's pistol wavered.

"Too late," he whispered. "All our hopes, Cal: the colony, Violet …"

We watched in silence as fire was put to the Coehoorn. The explosion clouted the sky. The shot flew upwards, hung in the air, and landed within the fort's walls, not far from the brick powder-magazine in the middle. I braced myself, but the impact was small, puffing a cloud of dirt high above the walls. The block and tackle shook and craned backwards, dropping within the walls, cannon and all. The defenders only had one gun again, but the water-party did their work, and the smoke died down.

Below us, the rowers yelled defiance, pushing their dead and wounded comrades into the water. They pulled hard for the *Blessed James*. Ordene's men fired again from the rocking ship, raggedly, and more of de Groot's soldiers fell. I watched Ty's face, unmoved by so many deaths. Most of the grenadiers died before the boats came within throwing distance; but they were close now, and I saw the corporals holding the slow-matches away from the sacks of grenades, ready to light them.

Again the cannon fired from the ramparts, and again it overshot. Ordene's men catcalled as their powder-men finished packing the second load. As soon as the ship finished rocking, they would fire. The engineer made new measurements and gave an order to adjust the cradle of the Coehoorn.

The soldiers stopped rowing and took a grenade each from their corporals. Matches were passed around care-fully, and I could see the sparks flying from the top of each grenade. Too quickly, still sitting, they flung them, but all fell short or bounced against the ship's hull. Another volley of musketfire, and now there were barely ten men still alive in the boarding-party.

As another ball was hoisted into the Coehoorn's maw, Richard Collingwood stood up in the leading boat, grenade flaring in his hand. He waited so long that I was sure it would explode against his chest. Two muskets fired, and his body jerked, but still he stood. Then he flung the grenade high into the air, too high for any sailor to catch and throw back; and at last he collapsed.

Ty let out a small sound and raised the pistol as if he could still save the Master Secretary. The grenade flashed before it hit the deck, catching the uncovered powder-keg, and the *Blessed James* ripped apart before us. We were half-blinded by the great eruption, which threw us onto our backsides. Spars and timbers flew out in all directions, battering the wounded and dying men in the boats. The broken ship pressed downwards into the sea, sending out a wave that capsized the rowboats. I tried to look for

Collingwood's grey head, but the glare still reddened my sight, and all was chaos in the bay.

De Groot's men cheered from the ramparts and from the muster-ground, not pausing to feel the loss of their comrades on the waters. The commander himself raced to the near side of the walls and yelled orders in Dutch to the two companies on the killing-ground outside. Immediately, they trotted forward, splitting into two columns. One headed for Fort James and the wharves, the other for Church Street and the King's House.

The boy, I thought. I took a step after them, but Ty raised his pistol again, and jabbed me hard in the ribs with the muzzle.

"Stay," he ordered forcefully. "You will live."

The soldiers disappeared behind the buildings. Warning-shouts rang clearly in the still air, and then we heard the *crack-clack* of musketfire as de Groot's company engaged Montalbion's militia force.

To our left, a loud clap of noise: the second Coehoorn had fired. The sun behind us flared on the flying shot as it soared, held for a breath, dropped towards Fort James. It struck the sea-facing wall, exploding violently. Bodies spun over the ramparts and into the water.

But that fort had no powder-store like Fort Charles: it withstood the hit, and now that war had been declared, its own cannon were primed and shotted. Ty and I watched breathlessly as the artillerymen sighted their guns at the King's House, and at the columns of men we could now see marching brazenly up Thames Street towards the fortress.

Both cannon fired, making a louder roar that seemed to shake the whole port, a rumbling groan of defiance and disaster. Men began to flee, and flames rose from the buildings next to the King's House.

I could not leave Emilia and my son to die. Ty seemed to feel my intention: he took a half-step away, still pressing the gun's muzzle into my ribs.

As musketfire bloomed around Fort James, de Groot's second company made for the church, and the cover of the gravestones. It was too far to see, but Ty whispered, "Grenades."

Dozens of muskets suddenly bristled from the walls and windows of the King's House, and two swift volleys drove de Groot's redcoats back into the High Street. Scores of Port Royallers and militiamen poured after them until the roadway was packed with fighting-men. It was not over yet.

Fort James had more cannon aimed at the harbour. With another great burst of sound, they fired at the ship that bore the second Coehoorn. From our vantage on the headland, we saw its side crumple; it listed, and sank quickly. Cheering, the defenders of Fort James sallied out, joined de Groot's second column and drove the militia-men down Thames Street.

I felt the Maroon's presence before I saw him, his blade at Ty's throat.

"No, Prussia!" I snapped quickly.

Ty, tilting his head away from the sharp *afana* at his neck, let me take his gun.

"Let him go, Prussia – you must hide yourself," I ordered; and then I was away, racing down Church Street.

I reached the graveyard, where de Groot had already pinned down Montalbion's forces. The street roiled with men fighting hand to hand. De Groot himself was at the heart of it, leading a small band of grenadiers who were struggling to get close enough to the King's House to throw their ordnance. There was no way to reach Emilia without entering the fray; and I had but one hand to fight with.

I plunged through the battle, and a bluecoat instantly tried to bayonet me. I dodged his lunge and shot him in the throat, left-handed. *Damn you*, I thought, *I've killed enough men already* – but right behind him was a swordsman, who would have taken my head off if de Groot had not stabbed him through the heart.

The Dutchman stared at me for a breath, and then was set upon by two men. I ducked away towards the King's House.

Cannon roared. An instant later, the shot whistled shrilly overhead, smashing into the servants' quarters. The second ball hit the front gate, out of my sight, and plaster-dust filled the air. In the confusion, some of de Groot's grenadiers had time to let fly: the air was riven with smaller explosions.

"Quarter!" cried a powerful voice. "Men, surrender and ask quarter!"

It was the commander of Montalbion's bluecoats. The planter Flowers, who had been hiding in the graveyard, got to his feet and took up the cry; in less than a minute, quarter had been asked and given, and the fighting was over.

"Cease firing!" bellowed de Groot, and the cry was carried all the way to Fort James.

I ran for the breached sidewall of the King's House. The servants' quarters were in smithereens. The muddy ground was stained with blood, gunpowder and food from the stores. The arch to the main courtyard still stood, though the main gate beyond had been smashed to pieces. Ten bluecoated soldiers lay on the ground, only two of them still alive.

Sitting in the middle of it all, his leg smashed and the foot bent out of joint, was Lord Montalbion. His uncovered silver hair was slick with sweat, and his right hand clutched the stiletto uselessly: that arm was broken, a bone shard parting his bloody flesh for six inches. The other hand rested calmly on the earth. His eyes seemed drained of colour, and I wondered if he had taken a splinter to the head.

"Hold fast, Your Grace!" called one of the bluecoats, but his master did not reply. There was a noise behind me: Ty had followed me, and was now clambering over the wreckage of the servants' quarters.

I stood and stared. I knew I should kill Montalbion and his officer before going into the house; knew that Ty, who'd arrived panting beside me, thought the same; but I had shed too much blood already.

The door to the main house opened. Emilia came out, wearing the bleached old travelling-dress she'd been wearing when Montalbion first took her, the day he hanged her father. She dragged the boy along with her, his body shaking with silent sobs.

I did not call out. Jesus, but I should have called.

Emilia saw what lay before her. Let go of her son's hand, descended the steps slowly, eyes on Montalbion. He watched her come, the old cruel smile on his face, and I could see that he was alert.

"Vincent!" he called lightly.

"His name is Benjamin," said Emilia, picking her way through the fallen men. "After his grandfather."

Montalbion's broken arm jerked. Unable to hold the knife, he tried to brush it round towards his left side, wincing with the pain, but she knelt on his wounded forearm before he could manage it. He did not even have time to draw breath before she seized the stiletto and drove it into the roof of his mouth. Still he struggled, his left arm beating on the wet earth. Cradling his head, Emilia pushed the hilt far to one side until the point of the blade came out of his right eye.

Blood dripped from her elbow. He fell still.

The boy Vincent shrieked and darted towards his mother. I ran and picked him up before he could get too close, letting him sob against my chest.

The bluecoated officer drew his sword and crawled towards Emilia. She still held Montalbion's head like a lover, her lips moving silently.

"Be still, and you will live," I said to the soldier, blocking his path.

"I have power of pardon," said Ty, stepping forward. He opened up his waistcoat and freed a chain with a silver pendant: a two-headed eagle with a shield across its breast. He had the manner of command about him, a calm that made the bluecoat drop his arms, nod to the others, surrender.

"*Je l'ai acheté d'un Suédois bourré*," he whispered.

I bought it from a drunken Swede.

I did not laugh.

CHAPTER SEVENTEEN

Scatterwood

Twenty-eighth day of May to first day of June

"The slate should be wiped clean," said Colonel de Groot. "I do not think it serves any man here present to have this *action* recorded. It certainly does not serve His Majesty."

He looked around the room. It was mid-morning, hours after the rebels had surrendered, and we were gathered in his private chamber in Fort Charles. Michael Hicks and the surviving Port Royal captains nodded. Grimly, the militia colonels assented, too; and Ty made a note in his minute-book.

"Then let us speak of the Crown's compensation," de Groot went on. "Sequestration of all goods and land-titles belonging to the known rebels, including the former earl. The plantation known as Alexandria to be allocated to the current commander here—"

"Which is you, is it not?" asked Hicks, mildly.

"Sir, my family was building sugar-mills in Pernambuco when England was still Catholic," replied the Dutchman sharply. "Jamaica has need of such knowledge; His Majesty will need the duties that I shall pay."

Hicks smiled mirthlessly.

"God-damned Jew," whispered Flowers, a little too loud.

"If His Majesty believed it worth sending a *Jewish* commander to save Jamaica, you can be sure he will believe it worth rewarding one," said de Groot loudly. "Now, I believe there has been some dispute over salvage rights off the island. Master Pettit here, of the College Secular, has already a signed paper at fifty per centum, which as commander I deem to be valid ..."

It did not take the Dutchman long to lay out his terms of settlement. The surviving rebels were allowed to keep their property provided they made an annual tithe, to be used for the upkeep of de Groot's garrison. The record-book would absolve the militias and state that only Montalbion and his company had attacked the Crown's forces; therefore, the remaining bluecoats must be hanged in Fort Charles the next morning.

"Furthermore," finished de Groot, "the Crown will take possession of the traitor's vessels and warehouses."

Michael Hicks cleared his throat. De Groot glanced at him, and the Liverpudlian shrugged. Every man in the room knew that Montalbion had brought a king's ransom in gold and silver from his raids on New Spain; but if any of them suspected that the Crown had deliberately planned to seize that treasure, he was too wise to speak of it.

De Groot returned to his desk, dismissing the privateers and planters with a wave of his hand. He motioned for Ty and me to stay. When the others had left, he drew out two papers and signed the first, clattering his quill into the inkpot when he'd finished.

"Here, Spinks: a pardon for the Irishwoman and her child."

Ty took the second paper and signed it. *MANUMISSION*, it said. He offered me both, but I did not take them.

"You will leave Port Royal by tomorrow," said de Groot.

"Emilia de Corvis," I said.

"A murderess. She will hang."

"Can a traitor be murdered?" I mused aloud. "How would such news be greeted in London?"

Ty offered me the papers again. "What do you want, Cal?"

This time I took them. "*Primo*: release Emilia and the boy. *Secondo:* a boat to take across the bay. *Tertio*: I want fifty acres of my choosing, as consideration for serving my indenture."

"The bond was for ten!" snapped de Groot.

I waited.

"Fifty, and in a place of Mister Spinks' choosing," said Ty softly. After a gritty silence, the Dutch colonel consented.

The sun was high overhead by the time I quit Fort Charles. I wanted to find Prussia quickly: it would go ill for a solitary blackamoor if he were caught. Arriving at Lime Street, I called his name. It was eerily quiet; apart from a company of marines, who were throwing dead militiamen onto a wagon, every other man had gone indoors.

Birdsong. I looked up: Prussia had stuck his head out over a parapet. I pointed at the roof of Hoopy's lodgings, four houses along, and he ducked back out of sight.

Something pressed against my leg: the yellow hound who'd followed me round the port, two months before.

I knocked and asked for Hoopy; as soon as the door was opened by another doxy, the dog ran inside. It followed me all the way to the topmost room.

Hoopy looked weary and heartsick: she must have watched the fighting from her high window. The dog, which had been leaning against my knee, darted under the bed and curled up, tail between its legs.

"Francis?" she asked, ignoring it.

I shook my head.

She turned her back and stood still for a moment, then went to draw the locked box out from under her cot. There was little else in the garret room: a basin of scummed water where she'd washed out the last man's spunk, a candle-stub stuck down with its own wax, a dirty dress crumpled in the corner like a crying child.

She had kept it all safe for me. A smattering of coins. A paper, ochre with age, that had been folded small enough to be hidden in my palm. A thimble of whalebone, fashioned into a tiny castle.

Hoopy cupped the treasures in her hands. Was this what a man's life came to? Enough coins to bury him, papers to name him, a second-hand keepsake.

I put the thimble on my smallest finger, then took the coins. Two shillings for me, and the rest of it I gave to Hoopy, thanking her deeply. When she first took my treasures, a dozen weeks and a thousand deaths ago, I'd had little hope she would keep her word.

I opened her garret window and called for Prussia. He was squatting on the roof a stone's throw away.

Before he reached us, the building rose under our feet, flinging me into the air. As soon as I could get up, I scrambled to the window. Prussia was splayed on the roof: some of the tiles had fallen in, leaving him a roof-timber to clutch. Then the entire port shook, as though God himself had stamped. Houses crumbled and huge gashes appeared in the dusty streets, pulling in men, carts and beasts. Fort James tilted and settled again drunkenly as half of Thames Street fell into the sea. I landed heavily on the sill, my upper body sticking out of the window. Behind me, the dog howled. Hoopy grabbed my legs, but I did not want to abandon Prussia. He was crabbing his way across the collapsed roof towards me.

The church tower was spitting out bricks. Its spire was tilting so far that the whole building fell, crushing the marines who had been stacking bodies against the King's House.

And then God struck again.

This time I heard the earth's raging roar. It rose from the depths of the sea, sending the town into a fearful panic. Men who were still standing ran foolishly for the wharves: just beyond them, the waters were dropping rapidly.

As the ground shook again, Prussia yelled and jumped towards me. I caught his hand with my left, and then an invisible force smote Port Royal. If Hoopy had not wrapped her arms around my legs, the Maroon and I would have fallen thirty feet into the riven surface of the street.

Tilting even further, Fort James slid into the spitting waters. The rest of Thames Street, and half the great warehouses, lifted, broke and slipped sideways after the fort, dragging hundreds of men into the depths. On the other side of the port, the church and the seaward half of the King's House were gone, buckling into the ocean.

Grimacing with pain, I seized Prussia's hair with my mutilated hand and pulled him onto the sill. Hoopy reached past me and helped to drag the Maroon fully inside.

"*O Yankipong Asasi, o Krembe Tutu ...*" he choked, praying to his greatest god. In the harbour, a towering wave had gathered and was rushing hard towards the broken wharves. Some of the ships that were moored further out managed to ride the wave, but many others were taken under.

Men who had survived the shaking of the earth began to scream and yell, running up the High Street for shelter. The wave seemed to pull and stretch at the town, dragging the streets apart until the fleeing townspeople fell into the gashes in the roadway. Still the King's House stood, its wooden beams bending like oaks in the storm. Beyond, Fort Carlisle was falling in upon itself.

The great wave drove underneath the *Swan* on its careening ramp, lifted it high up, and smashed it over the first row of houses. As I yanked the windows shut, I saw the ship landing on top of a building, further up the High Street. Foam burst high into the air, hiding the port from view; and then the wall of seawater came at us, spotted with bodies. We turned our backs to the casement. I hunched over, stuffing the painting into my shirt; and then the sea shattered the window and crushed us.

The water battered my senses, pressing the air out of my straining lungs. I held on to awakeness, and then the wave dropped away as fast as it had come, draining through the floorboards.

Hoopy and I stared at each other, sputtering. She had not turned away in time, and her face was spattered with small glass-cuts.

The dog sneezed and came out from under the cot. It shook the water from its coat and nudged Hoopy's ribs.

After I had cleaned the slivers from her cheeks, I joined Prussia at the window to look at the ruins of Port Royal. Where Fort James had stood was now a seething part of the bay; not a single wharf had survived, so that the sea lapped against the ragged edges of the High Street. Out in the bay, some ships had ridden the great wave and were still afloat, among them the *Esperance*.

We sheltered for hours in Hoopy's room. At first we feared another earthquake or great wave. We stood in the shattered windowframe and looked out into the devastation, Hoopy stroking the dog's head.

So many ways to die.

To drown on solid land.

To save yourself with a floating spar, only to have your belly pierced by another.

To hang from the rigging of a beached ship, with your guts trailing for the gulls.

To have your skull smashed against a steel door while your chest fills with seawater.

To cling to your pulley-rope, survive the dashing waves, and have your throat slit by the neighbour who's long fancied your silver.

To be buried alive in the soft sandy earth.

As dusk fell, the surviving soldiers retreated to Fort Charles, and the worst kind of Port Royallers took over the streets. Fights began to break out as the looters squabbled over their prizes. We decided to barricade ourselves in Hoopy's room and had a fitful night's sleep on her floor.

We stayed until dawn. Hoopy had decided to remain in Port Royal until she had the savings she needed. She refused to leave the brothel, so I left her Ty's pistol. I still had Kiet's blade.

The graveyard had been torn up, strewing the High Street with tombstones and recently buried cadavers. Half-rotted, their sunken eyeballs were already prey for the gulls. The yellow dog, which had followed us outside, fed on their flesh.

Despite the early hour, the smashed houses still crawled with thieves: cutting throats, prising rings from the dead, breaking open locked chests for property-papers that could be rewritten in the wreckage of the clerk-offices.

We went down the middle of the street, wary of attackers, but who would have wished to trouble a big knife-wielding redhead and a blackamoor bowman at such a time? I stopped to try to help a shrieking woman who was trapped chest-deep in the mud, but Prussia urged me on. The bright blood trickling from her nose told him she'd be dead before long.

We passed the *Swan*, perched on a nest of roof-timbers. Heads poked out through the gunports: many had taken refuge in her hull.

Fort Charles had sunk three feet into a marsh of stinking seawater. Prussia was unwilling to approach, and so I waved to the sentry and asked for Master Pettit.

Ty was gone. I barely had time to worry for him when Colonel de Groot appeared. True to his word, he requisitioned a rowboat for us, and sent for Emilia and the boy. He stared curiously at Prussia, but did not demand an explanation; he was glad to see the back of me.

The little bay was still sprinkled with pieces of the *Blessed James*, with scraps of cloth, and the limbs of both sides' dead. Emilia tried to shield Benjamin – for so she now called him – from the stinking mess, but from time to time he peeped out at the flies that cloaked the water. Perhaps he had seen worse in Montalbion's household. She herself did not even ask me where we travelled. Though her eyes were free of laudanum's tears, they were glassy, staring at the Blue Mountains beyond the bay.

The Maroon and I had an oar each, and every so often one of us hit a floating lump of flesh. Each stroke brought our faces closer to Emilia and the boy Benjamin. Behind them, de Groot's companies marched out of Fort Charles bearing picks and shovels: bodies were rotting fast in the heat.

As we left Chocolata Hole behind and rounded the point, I looked out to the bay.

"Dolphins," whispered Prussia between pulls. He jabbed his head towards the hundreds of sea-beasts that bobbed and twirled on the juddering surf, shiny and dark in the morning sun. They were so many and so large that they almost made an island between us and the surviving ships at anchor. I had never seen the sea-creatures before, but as we drew further east, I knew that he was wrong.

The floating lumps were swollen carcasses, not dolphins: drowned men, crushed men, half-consumed corpses from the graveyard; guts, brains and bones; the innocent faces of the young, and the worn expressions of Port Royal's whores. Carrion-birds wheeled and dived, tearing at the human flesh.

"Cover your faces," I choked, remembering Ty's lessons on the plague. I ripped off what was left of my bloody shirt, tearing it into rough strips. After covering the boy's nose and mouth, I offered to help Emilia, but she refused to put on a mask.

I glanced at the ravaged shore. The bare back walls of Thames Street's warehouses still clung to land, but the main part of the buildings had ripped away and slid into the sea beneath us.

The timber frame of the King's House towered above the devastation, a mute witness to Montalbion's murder. Emilia put her hand around Benjamin's head, shielding him from the sight of his home. She coughed, closed her own eyes and turned away.

We rowed more slowly now, seeking those choppy patches of sea that were bare of corpses, but they were few and far between. Mostly our oar-blades had to squeeze and thump between the limbs and trunks of the dead. Bugs buzzed and crawled on us, so gorged with flesh that they could barely rise from our flinching skin. Benjamin lifted his mask and was sick on his own feet, unwilling to lean out above the carnage. I tied the cloth back over his face.

Shouts came from the bay. Carrying little sail, the awkward-masted *Esperance* bore down slowly on the floating island of decay. We watched as sailors on the nearside rigged up the scaffold for the Device. From time to time one of them would rush astern and vomit into the crowded waters, jeered by his shipmates.

Prussia and I were barely moving now, watching as the *Esperance* barged the pitiful dead aside. The angel on her bow stared blindly as she furled sails and dropped anchors.

Loud thumps came from the *Esperance*'s hold. Sailors heaved on pulleyed ropes, and the Device appeared between the struts of the scaffold, its cast-iron skin sucking in the Caribbean light. It struck the timbers dully, then swung slowly out over the side of the ship. Its underside was open, crossed with iron bars, and a short rope-ladder was slung from there to the ship's side.

Ty Pettit appeared at the railing. He pointed down at the teeming carcasses, ordering the sailors to clear a space with marlin-spikes. One corpse's belly burst open, spraying the bottom of a spike. Prussia and I pulled harder at the oars.

A bare-chested man with a grappling-hook, a diver by the looks of him, stood next to Ty at the base of the scaffold. They spoke to each other, the diver growing flushed as he pointed at the dead below, until Ty shook his head angrily, seized the grappling-hook, and scrambled clumsily along the rope-ladder to the diving bell.

"Send me those God-damned air barrels, you hear me?" he shouted at the diver, and disappeared into the bell's innards. The pulleys squealed as the Device was lowered through the bobbing corpses. The man who'd been my friend sank to the depths, scavenging gold and silver for his Republic Secular.

For all my misdeeds, I'd never have had the will to rob the dead for an Idea, for a College of gentlemen five thousand miles away. When he struck me aboard the *Esperance*, I had feared that Ty was lost to me; and now I knew it for sure. I watched the shivering of the hawser that held the diving bell; then bent my back to the oars again.

The other two Maroons were waiting for us in the forest: they'd seen the wave coming and had made for higher ground. In the two days they'd been waiting, they had caught and smoked a hog, filled their waterskins and laid in a store of fruit: we would not starve on the long journey to the Mandingo cave.

We men took it in turns to carry the boy Benjamin. He was mute the whole way. Emilia did not protest the hard travelling. Dull-eyed and tight-lipped though she was, she must have known that Montalbion's wife might have an enemy or two once word of his death got out. I wondered if she knew where I was taking her.

It took three days to reach Quamin: days of blustery weather and quiet trudging. Emilia was sweaty, and had begun to cough persistently. By the second morning, the boy had begun to chatter to the Maroons. They replied in their own tongue, which was a game he did not tire of.

Quamin showed little surprise that I'd returned. He ran his eyes over Emilia, who was shivering and withdrawn, then looked from the boy to me and back again, nodding. Perhaps that was the moment he trusted me: a man with a young child makes a better ally than a hunter with nothing to lose.

I knew that I risked more than my own life by taking the Maroons to the plantation. But there was little choice: I took out the painting and spread it open in a shaft of damp light.

"Thief," said Emilia hoarsely. It was the only word she'd spoken since Montalbion's death. It was true, I had taken it from her as a youth. I'd been bewitched by the likeness of her father's house, nestling in the lee of Turkey Head, rising on the spur of Mouth Bone. Bruised skies pierced by the peaks. Neat rows of coffee bushes, heavy with their sanguine fruits.

She knelt and touched the painting. A bead of sweat fell from her face.

I was taking her home.

The de Corvis coffee plantation was ringed by forests on a mist-wet ridge, far above the devastation wrought by the great wave. The air in this place was warm and welcoming, and a stream carried sweet water through the rows of coffee-bushes, which had grown huge and straggly in the years since its owner had died. Weeds sprouted wildly across the plantation.

Everything about the house seemed shrunken next to Emilia's painting, which I'd stared at a thousand times: the whitewashed walls were green with mould, the leaf-thatch yellow and curling.

I was carrying Benjamin, keeping him away from his mother, who'd caught her sickness in the corpse-strewn bay. She stumbled past us towards the house. The door was so weather-warped that she could not open it. She sat down, too tired to weep.

Quamin took a handful of berries from a bush and rubbed them between his hands.

"Coffee," I said. "Income. Powder and shot."

"Red Man," he said, putting an arm around my shoulders, "I give you ten per centum."

I laughed out loud, lifted my son off his feet, and kissed his forehead.

Coleburgh, Carolina

Fourth day of July, Sixteen Hundred and Ninety-Three

Violet came and stood in the doorway behind me. She'd brought the aroma of roasted pheasant with her: this land was bursting with game.

I was watching the carpenter's boy hoisting the sign up across the street: *Benjamin's Coffeehouse.* The paint was not yet dry. It was true that I itched to go back there while it was still daylight: there were benches to make, and our own Jamaican coffee to roast. Quamin's Maroons had pruned and dug, nursing the plantation back to its former fertility.

Our home was at the edge of Coleburgh, though the foundations of a Catholic church were already being laid next door. A Puritan couple was watching the work; Violet gave them good evening, and the husband raised a hand in acknowledgement.

Beyond the tobacco field, men were clearing a road through the woods towards Athens, the new county-town. Snatches of African song reached us, broken by the sound of distant musket-volleys. The Guard Secular, under the command of Landgrave Ty Pettit, holding its weekly drill.

"You'll have work to do, I suppose," said Violet.

"I do," I muttered; though I was thinking of Ty, whose last letter to me I had not opened, even though he lived but five miles away. She held back a retort, and turned back inside. I followed her to the table and made a claw of my half-hand for Simona. Pretending to be frightened, she slid along the bench, knocking Benjamin off the end. He got back up, laughing; he barely asked for Emilia anymore.

Instead of going to the coffeehouse, I scooped up the children, covered their faces with kisses, and wrapped Violet into the wriggling embrace.

She pulled away and gave me a curious look.

"Work can wait," I said.

Calumny's Tongues

Abeng	War-horn (Twi)
Afana	Machete (Twi)
A prandes	Back home (Creole)
Blood-gnats	Mosquitoes
Bloody flux	Dysentery
Bongo	Disparaging term for non-Twi Africans (Creole)
Brat	Fine [fellow] (Cornish)
Brik	Break (Cornish)
Brock-browed	With bushy, badger-like eyebrows
Buckra	White man (disparaging term)
Coverture	Legal doctrine whereby a married woman's rights and obligations were subsumed by her husband
Crakka Juba	Crazy somebody (Creole)
Daabi	No (Twi)
Denchured	Indentured

Emmet	Ant (Cornish) [by extension, Englishman / foreigner]
Exclusivity	Monopoly charter
Fist	Silent flatulence [as opposed to *fart*, meaning to break wind loudly]
Eho fitaa	White skin (Twi)
Gogged	Wide-eyed, staring [literally, "in haste"]
Hobbin	Lump of dough (Cornish)
Hunderprice	Underpriced, damaged goods [slave or servant]
Jack	Low-bred fellow, or knave
Kalken	Father-lasher, whip (Cornish)
Katawud	Scatterwood, runaway slaves who have escaped capture (Creole)
Kerel	Lad, fellow (Dutch)
Landgrave	Carolinian nobleman and great landowner
Manchineel	Tropical tree producing highly poisonous, apple-like fruit
Matchet	Machete
Mincher	Truant (Cornish)
Moiety	50 per cent tax
Molly	Female mule; also slang for homosexual, as in "molly-house"

Mussulmen	Muslims, Turks
Obi	Sorcerer, wise man (Twi); *Obeah men* in today's Jamaica
Obroni	White foreigner (Twi)
Old Stander	Follower of Cromwell; helped to capture Jamaica from Spain
Omadhaun	Fool, simpleton (Irish)
Opete	The vulture dance, a Coromantee custom
Outremer	Overseas (from the French)
Owo ti hwi kokoo	He has red hair (Twi)
Pickaninny	Slave-boy, African child
Piskies	Cornish fairies
Plumeria	Frangipani
Polinck	Allotment for slaves to grow their own food
Saker	Cannon used for naval and siege purposes, firing a 5lb shot
Scadgan	Cornish: tramp, rascal
Scudding	Shovelling dung
Shasiv	Stand up (Irish)
Smokehouse lock	A simple wrought-iron padlock, relatively easy to break open

Sowznac	Englishman (Cornish)
Tisick	Asthma

Note on West African languages and tribes

Many slaves in Jamaica were from the Akan language group, which was then called "Coromantee": tribes included the Ashanti (Asante) and the Fanti, who speak the Twi dialect.

Calumny's Jamaica

The Old Style Calendar and the Julian Calendar

The events in *Scatterwood* take place during a time when two different calendars were in operation. Britain still used the Julian calendar, which by 1692 was ten days behind the Gregorian calendar we now use. To confuse matters more, the year was considered to start on Lady Day – 25 March. Thus, 3 January 1691 for Cal is 13 January 1692 by our reckoning.

White Gold

By the early eighteenth century, sugar had become the most important commodity in the world, and so Jamaica was increasingly important to Britain and her imperial rivals. The huge fortunes made in the Caribbean attracted thousands of entrepreneurs, but also the jetsam of English society.

Sugar cultivation was brutal work. Slaves worked sixty hours a week, and in the cropping and manufacturing season would sometimes work all night.

The Dutch were financiers and technical advisers to the Caribbean sugar industry. Colonel de Groot's story suggests that he was a descendant of the Sephardic Jews who became "New Christians" to escape the Inquisition and ended up in Pernambuco, then a Dutch refining centre. Six hundred Sephardim fled to Amsterdam when the Portuguese reconquered the colony.

Sugarcane requires a lot of fertilizer. There was such a shortage of dung in Jamaica by the end of the seventeenth century that an entire dung-producing industry sprang up. Over two hundred animals were required to service a hundred acres of cane; Kiet appears to have found an elegant if unhygienic solution to this problem.

Slaves and Indentured Servants

At least twenty million African slaves were taken from Africa to the Americas during the centuries of slavery, of whom 13 per cent are estimated to have died on the crossing; staggeringly, a further 4.5 per cent died by jumping into the harbour on arrival in the colonies.

The treatment of slaves in the Caribbean is among the vilest of crimes against humanity recorded. Disobedient slaves would be buried alive; the sick and dying were abandoned in gullies for the crows to pick at; runaways and rebels were castrated, blinded, racked, their wounds rubbed with salt and pepper and lime. Some slaves were forced to eat their own amputated ears, or to defecate in each other's mouths. Beheading, impaling and hanging were commonplace.

The Barbados Slave Code of 1661 called Africans "an heathenish, brutish and an uncertaine, dangerous kinde of people", and specified that a man could be quartered for stealing a pig, or burned at the stake for trying to escape. Many new slaves were suicidal, fearing that they would be lost to their ancestral spirits. One Caribbean slave-owner cut off a slave's head and marched around with it on a twelve-foot pole, telling his chattels that "if your head is still here, your soul ain't going back to Africa".

Female slaves would be lent out or rented to white men, and were regularly prostituted to the army or militia. On slave plantations, the infant mortality rate reached 50 per cent, leading to the notorious phrase "it is better to buy than to breed".

George Washington himself had "shocking" housing for his slaves at Mount Vernon, although he did free 123 of them at his death.

Indentured servitude was the closest a white person could come to slavery. Indenture was originally a way for the enterprising poor to make a life for themselves: servants of the 1630s were entitled to fifty acres after four to seven years. By the 1690s, enfranchisement typically only brought ten acres, which were worth less since commodity prices had fallen, and smallholdings were being rapidly consolidated by the larger planters.

Indentured servants had a harsh existence. On arrival, they would have to build their own shelters out of sticks, vines and leaves. After a twelve-hour day, they would sleep in their clothes, soaked with rain or sweat. By the 1670s, owners were very often treating their white servants worse than their slaves, since they had the latter for life rather than a limited term.

Runaway servants were branded with an "R" on their forehead, shoulder or cheek. They could be given forty lashes and sentenced to a further seven years' servitude. Kiet's cruelty towards Moses Severill is not unusual: many owners would treat their servants viciously in the sixth year of a seven-year indenture, until the latter would plead to be sold for another term of up to seven years.

Colonists in the Caribbean were constantly on their guard against slave uprisings, and were most concerned about the potential for slaves to combine forces with (mainly Irish) indentured servants. A slave uprising in Barbados in 1675 was brutally put down; in 1685, a plot was discovered in which it was believed that white servants were colluding with other slaves. Runaways were feared as sources of unrest.

The Fighting Maroons of Jamaica

The Maroons are among the most successful resisters of European colonisation, remaining independent for a century and a half. They developed many guerrilla warfare techniques including *ambush* (covering a warrior from head to toe in cacoon vines), leaping and rolling to throw off gunmen, and using fire arrows. They would walk backwards to confuse enemy trackers, and sometimes lured English soldiers over precipices. They held regular weapons practice, and led organised raids on plantations – originally for livestock, and later to capture female slaves.

Eating plenty of hog meat, Maroons were known to be physically strong, fit and muscular, with sharp senses. They were originally herders and hunters. Like Quamin, they found it hard to obtain powder and shot, and had to rely on backdoor trading, or stripping fallen enemies. From time to time, they would recapture escaped slaves and sell them back to settlers.

Colonists found it impossible to dislodge the Maroons from their territories. Indians with tracker mastiffs were brought in several times, and sometimes the English soldiers managed to burn a Maroon village, but it was only through devious treaty-making that the Maroons at last lost their independence.

Maroon history infuses the Jamaican national identity. Stories differentiate the Twi-speaking Maroons from other African slaves – "Bongos" – and build up the idea of Maroons as warlike, invulnerable, resourceful. As the great Maroon leader and Jamaican national hero Nanny said, "We fight until the battle is rotten."

Cal refers to Akan-speakers as "Ashanti" – in fact, there were many other tribes that came from the Coromantee coast of Ghana. Most plantations acquired slaves from several tribes within each language group.

"As Hot as Hell, and as Wicked as the Devil": The Decline and Fall of Port Royal

Life in the Caribbean colonies was dangerous and often short. A third of all whites died within three years of arrival. Dysentery – "the bloody flux" – was a major killer. The great majority of the population was young and male, and only a third of marriages produced surviving children, so Jamaica relied heavily on immigration, indenture and slavery.

This produced a rather fatalistic, callous and fast-living culture. Arriving in Port Royal in 1697, the Grub Street writer Ned Ward famously called Jamaica a "Sweating Chaos", with a climate "as Sickly as a Hospital, as Dangerous as the Plague"; the men looked "as if they had just knock'd off their Fetters", and the women had been "either Transported by the State, or led by their Vicious Inclinations; where they may be Wicked Without Shame, and Whore on without Punishment".

The port's roads were poor, made of unconsolidated sand. There was no room for larger ships to moor permanently, so the harbour was busy with rowboats, sloops and shallops bustling back and forth from the wharves. The King's House, originally a Court of Chancery, was in poor repair by the 1690s, unused by a series of Governors; it is more than possible that the Governor of a merchant company such as Lord Montalbion would have been offered its use.

Maps of Port Royal do not show a designated slave market, which explains why Cal sees Africans being taken straight off the side of arriving ships. Foulkes' market for indentured servants would have likely been a temporary setup, hence the wooden scaffolds.

Francis Hanson wrote in 1682 that "almost every House hath a rich cupboard of Plate which they carelessly expose, scarce shutting their doors at night, being in no Apprehension of Thieves for want of receivers".

Port Royal was devastated by an earthquake and subsequent tidal wave just before noon on 7 June 1692, and Cal's description of the effects largely matches the historical record. The tremor was so powerful that every brick-built church, house and sugar works on the island was thrown down. However, there are no official records of a Company of the Caribbean, nor of a battle on the streets of the port. In June 1692, there was arguably a power vacuum in Jamaica that a man like Montalbion might seek to exploit: the only naval ship in Port Royal was being careened, there was no permanent Lieutenant Governor in place, and William III was still consolidating his rule in England.

Many brick-built structures in Jamaica collapsed during the 1692 earthquake, but the King's House survived.

Mortars such as Baron von Coehoorn's devices were still unreliable in the late 1600s. Artillery commanders struggled to predict their range and were heavily dependent on trial and error, and on individual officers' skill.

Governors, privateers and planters
Jamaica was first captured in 1655 as an accidental by-product of Cromwell's Western Design, a plan to disrupt the Spanish in the Caribbean. Emilia's behaviour as Montalbion's wife is reminiscent of Elizabeth Venables, wife of the general who first invaded Jamaica. Mrs Venables

was described as a "virago whose ability to set everyone at loggerheads amounted to perverted genius".

After the Restoration, Jamaica remained a refuge for "regicides": Cromwellians, and the supporters of the 1685 Monmouth Rebellion. Many interregnum land-grants were cancelled, leaving a class of disgruntled men.

The Jamaican House of Assembly was established in 1664, with voting limited to freeholders. It was responsible for renaming Cagway as Port Royal, to show loyalty to the new King Charles II. Two factions emerged: privateers and merchants trading out of Port Royal, opposed to the larger planters. The merchant faction resisted several Governors' attempts to gain tax-raising powers, and generally hampered decision-making (De Jong).

Command of militias was tied to the degree of landowning and political power. Men in Jamaica were given titles based on the ranks they held in the (very poorly organised) militia, which in turn were generally proportionate to their landholdings.

Colonial Governors were appointed by the Crown, and then appointed their own Councils. Assemblies were elected by freeholders, and formally paid and held their Governors to account. Assemblymen's and councilmen's families tended to intermarry. As Governor of a private merchant company, Montalbion would have been outside this power structure.

Thomas Modyford (Governor from 1664 to 1671) treated Jamaica as his private fiefdom, controlling the island's revenue and twice declaring a private war on Spain to justify his raids on their shipping. Modyford also oversaw the concentration of land in the hands of the super-rich.

Jamaican politics was disrupted by the arrival of the Duke of Albemarle, James II's appointee as Lieutenant Governor, in the late 1680s. Like many others, he sought to enrich himself by salvaging wrecks. He sided with Henry Morgan and the privateer faction, and elevated several Catholics to public positions before dying in 1688, on the eve of the Glorious Revolution.

Cal arrives in Port Royal four years after the death of Sir Henry Morgan, the great privateer who became Lieutenant Governor of Jamaica. Morgan led hugely successful raiding expeditions, sacking Panama and Maracaibo, and was the figurehead of the privateer faction in Port Royal. He was buried in the Palisadoes cemetery, which the 1692 earthquake sank into the Caribbean: a symbolic wiping-out of the old way of life.

The golden age of privateering was over by the 1690s. Even Morgan, as Governor, clamped down on piracy in 1680, and James II offered an amnesty to pirates who ceased activities in 1687. Montalbion appears to have stepped into Morgan's boots to appeal to disaffected privateers.

The fall of Port Royal marked a turning point in the governance of Jamaica. Previously reliant on the combined forces of privateers to keep a French invasion at bay, the arrival of Governor William Beeston in March 1693 was part of a consolidation of state power in the Caribbean, and represented a victory for the plantation owners over Port

Royal's privateers and merchants. A new city, Kingston, was built across the bay, and Port Royal was never to exert the same influence again.

A French invasion force landed in the north of Jamaica by 20 June, only two weeks after the earthquake, which lends credence to Cal's story that Montalbion had actively conspired with France against the island's garrison.

The year 1692 also saw the demise of indentured servitude and smallholdings on Jamaica. The indentured population had fallen from 7,800 in 1673 to 1,400 in the 1690s, as recruitment from the metropolis became harder, hence the fierce bidding at Port Royal market – and smallholders had been selling out their plots to larger planters. Diseases spread rapidly after the disaster, and many poorer white Jamaicans left the island for North America.

Jamaican land prices rose eightfold between 1681 and 1701. An asset bubble; rising income inequality; and a corrupt politician taking advantage of both to launch a putsch – Montalbion would have been a thoroughly modern leader.

The Elfin Woodland

Kiet told Cal that the Blue Mountains were haunted by *piskies*, but it seems likely that the sound they heard was of the rufous-throated solitaire, a ventriloquial thrush whose song is very much like a mournful human whistle. It is a spine-chilling sound if you are alone in the "elfin woodland" as dusk falls.

*

Modern visitors to Jamaica will not find any monkeys in the forests. The native species, *Xenothrix mcgregori*, was hunted to extinction by the 1750s. The remarkable buccaneer Alexander Exquemelin had a scatological encounter with monkeys in Costa Rica which bears some resemblance to Cal's own experiences.

Mastery of the seas

The Navy had a mixed relationship with merchants and privateers. Its captains would escort merchant ships; but it also had a policy of taking surgeons from private vessels, and would sometimes press-gang men on the streets and wharves of Port Royal. Navy frigates were also responsible for catching interlopers – slave ships attempting to circumvent the Royal African Company's monopoly.

In 1700, Parliament passed a law to prosecute colonial merchants and governors who harboured pirates. Many hangings followed.

The largest merchant trading companies had their own police forces, standing armies, laws and governments, and their leaders sometimes held absolute authority.

Navy sailors were more than capable of manoeuvring large cannons in the middle of battle. "Rowling great guns upon skeeds" (Pawson and Buisseret) and using tackles to manhandle ordnance were part of the job: when the Navy ship *Mordaunt* reached Port Royal after the earthquake, its crew helped to salvage guns and "weigh" the wreckage of the *Swan*.

*

The earliest recorded use of the diving bell was in the fourth century BCE, described by Aristotle. Attempts to use these devices intensified in the seventeenth century, and in 1691 Edmond Halley completed his design for a bell which had an internal bench for divers to sit in, and which used barrels of air to replenish the atmosphere. In the Royal Society's *Philosophical Transactions* of 1714, Halley says that "the only inconvenience that attends it, is found in the Ears ... a Pressure begins to be felt on each Ear, which by degrees grows painful, like as if a Quill were forcibly thrust into the Hole of the Ear ..."

There was a great deal of public interest in diving bells and apparatus. In the 1680s, a man walked the width of the Thames in a diving-suit. However, Cal's narrative is the only evidence of a "Nereid Device".

Richard Collingwood causes a stir when he announces that the College Secular will pay over half of its treasure trove (a "moiety") in tax. In 1686, Captain William Phips raised over £200,000 from a sunken Spanish treasure ship off Hispaniola, and only paid 10 per cent over to the Crown. James II and his successor/usurper William then got wise to the value of salvage, and increased the rate to 50 per cent.

A "wild gambler" named Thomas Neale, who applied for all kinds of patents in his time, paid William III £450 for a monopoly on all Caribbean wrecks. His venture failed.

It is notable that de Groot grants the College a patent to the same salvage opportunities. Hardly a sign of good faith.

*

Many attempts have been made to discover the riches that sank into Port Royal harbour during the 1692 earthquake, but very little of value has been discovered. Clearly, Ty Pettit's use of the diving bell was very profitable indeed during those mournful, chaotic days.

Further reading

Non-fiction
Niall Ferguson's *Empire* is huge, comprehensive and beautifully illustrated, and first gave me the idea for a story about the Maroons of Jamaica.

The London Mob by Robert Shoemaker

James Robertson's *Gone is the Ancient Glory* is a very useful history of Spanish Town and Jamaica

The Sugar Barons by Matthew Parker: truth is both stranger and more horrible than fiction. This is a compulsive read.

Alan Taylor's *American Colonies* is elegantly-written, full of original details, and an excellent starting point for understanding the colonial era.

Merchant Kings by Stephen R. Bown is packed with men like Montalbion: did you know that California was nearly a Russian colony?

If you love pirates and you haven't read *The Buccaneers of America* by Alexander Exquemelin, you really must: he lived it, he told the story, and we have no idea how much truth he's telling. Wonderful.

Fiction

If you enjoy visiting the "long eighteenth century", I recommend:

The Devil in the Marshalsea by Antonia Hodgson: nasty plots in debtors' prison

Robert J. Lloyd's *The Bloodless Boy*, a crime thriller featuring Robert Hooke of the Royal Society

Anna Belfrage's *A Rip in the Veil*, a timeslip adventure of Scottish Covenanters and kickboxing feminists

Thank you

To the people who made my research trip to Jamaica so easy, funny and quirky: Colonel Wallace Sterling, Elder Mongogo and drummer Dave of the Moore Town Maroons; farmer Ivan, who let me through his land to scout the unnamed place I call Naggle Bay; Lloyd and Katie Edwards at Pimento Lodge, who looked after me like a relative; and Jonai, whose unofficial tour of Reach Falls involved a terrifying swim through an underground tunnel into a secret cave: the man is a legend.

To the generous and insightful readers and editors who helped shape the manuscript: my agent Lucy Luck, Sally O-J, Stuart Emmerton, the historical author Anna Belfrage, Anna-Jean Moriarty at The Pigeonhole and Gemma Wain; and to my mum Anne for old-school proof-reading wizardry.

For historical advice and anecdotes: to Professor James Robertson of the University of West Indies, author of *Gone is the Ancient Glory*, and with whom I spent a memorable afternoon in Kingston; and to Rebecca Simon PhD (C17 pirates, executions and the press), Karst de Jong (Irishmen and indentured servants in Port Royal), and Philippa Hellawell (maritime history, particularly diving bells).

To The Pigeonhole, whose funky serialisations continue to take the publishing world by storm.

To Matthew Bates, Wayne Barnes and the team at WHSmith Travel, for championing *The Bitter Trade* and *Scatterwood* with kindness and flair.

To Rebecca Swift, whose Literary Consultancy has done so much to help writers, especially from disadvantaged groups.

To David Eldridge (cover design), Jessica Bell (Pigeonhole page design), Henry Hyde, Jonathan Baker (typesetting), Heather O'Connell (production), David Flindall (website), Ben Cameron (press) and Conor Masterson (alchemist-photographer).

To my strange, wonderful and supportive – and rapidly expanding – family.

To Rebecca, perceptive story editor, songbird, warrior goddess, love of my life.

Travel to the Seventeenth Century

If you want to experience the seventeenth century for yourself, try a Sealed Knot event.

They're a friendly bunch…

www.sealedknot.org.uk
www.coloneljohnpickering.co.uk
www.tilliers.co.uk
www.newcastlesfoote.co.uk

Also by Piers Alexander

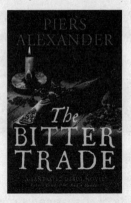

PEN FACTOR WINNER

GLOBAL EBOOK AWARD WINNER

HISTORICAL NOVEL SOCIETY INDIE EDITOR'S CHOICE

In 1688, torn by rebellions, England lives under the threat of a Dutch invasion. Redheaded Calumny Spinks is the lowliest man in an Essex backwater: half-French and still unapprenticed at seventeen, yet he dreams of wealth and title.

When his father's violent past resurfaces, Calumny's desperation leads him to flee to London and become a coffee racketeer. He has just three months to pay off a blackmailer and save his father's life - but his ambition and talent for mimicry pull him into a conspiracy against the King himself.

"A fantastic debut novel"

Robert Elms, BBC Radio London

"The ambitious, cheeky Calumny Spinks is a great guide through the sensory overload of 17th century London, in an adventure that combines unexpected insights with just the right amount of rollicking ribaldry. I hope it's the opener to a series"

Christopher Fowler, author of the Bryant and May novels